Praise for *Allegation*

'This searing debut from a retired social worker of thirty years could not be more timely – nor more true . . . Harrowing, moving and written with a fearsome authenticity, the story forces the reader to question where the truth lies'

Daily Mail

'*Allegation*'s subject of historical abuse could not be more timely or alarming in this smashing debut from R G Adams. Social worker Kit Goddard is an utterly convincing character negotiating an obstacle course of prejudice, gossip and false truths. I hope we see more of her'

Christopher Fowler, author of, *The Book of Forgotten Authors*

'Thought provoking and page turning at the same time. Kit Goddard is a fantastically drawn character and I look forward to reading more in the series'

Jenny Blackhurst, author of, *Someone is Lying*

R. G. Adams is a former social worker with thirty years of experience across all areas of social services. She lives in Wales with her family, and *Allegation* is her first novel.

ALLEGATION

R. G. ADAMS

riverrun

First published in Great Britain in 2021

This paperback edition published in 2021 by

riverrun

an imprint of

Quercus Editions Ltd
Carmelite House
50 Victoria Embankment
London EC4Y 0DZ

An Hachette UK company

A CIP catalogue record for this book is available
from the British Library.

PB ISBN 978 1 52940 467 8
EBOOK ISBN 978 1 52940 465 4

10 9 8 7 6 5 4 3 2

Typeset by CC Book Production
Printed and bound in Great Britain by Clays Ltd, Elcograf S.p.A.

Papers used by Quercus are from well-managed forests and other responsible sources.

For my husband and children
and in memory of my mum and dad.

CHAPTER 1

Sandbeach Council Child Services Office, South Wales

Kit sat looking at the referral a while longer. Then she reached under her desk, slipped her feet into her white Converse, stood up and made for Vernon's office.

'Vern, can I have a word?' Vernon was midway through a bacon bap. He motioned towards the chair in front of his desk with an oily finger.

'Vern, this referral . . .'

'Which one is that? You know what Mondays are like. I've had a shed-load across my desk this morning. What did I give you? The toddler with the suspected bite mark, was it?'

'Ah, did you mean to give me that one? That would be fine.' She'd seen plenty of bitten children, knew the drill with those. 'No, it's the Cooper family. It must have been a mistake. I don't think I'm quite ready for that one yet, do you? Maybe Nazia could take it.'

Vernon held out his hand and Kit passed the referral to him

1

with a sense of relief. Nazia was the most experienced social worker in the team and she handled all the high-risk cases. Vernon had absolute trust in her. Kit watched as he scanned the referral, popping the last chunk of bread into his mouth. When he handed the form back, it had grease marks on the edge. Kit took it from him gingerly. Vernon shoved a ball of bread and bacon over into his cheek so that he could speak.

'Ah yes, I remember. Look, Kit, I know it's a lot to ask. But Nazia's just rung in sick, not expected back for at least three weeks. She's dropped me right in it. I can't send any of the others, they just wouldn't handle something like this. It'll be good experience for you, look at it that way. Those clowns in the Intake Team have done the screening right for once; they've already discussed it with the police and it's definitely one for us. It needs an investigation and a full assessment. You've had enough time to get the hang of things. You need to start picking up some of the tricky stuff now.'

'Tricky's a bit of an understatement, isn't it?' Kit stayed in her chair while Vernon stood up and started towards the door. He glanced back at her and, catching her expression, stopped in the doorway.

'All right,' he sighed. 'If you're really that worried, you could take someone with you, I suppose. Who have we got out there doing nothing today?' He crossed to the door and leant out to look across the main office. 'What about Maisie?'

'No thank you very much. I'd sooner not.'

'Yeah, all right, point taken. Might be safer without her.

Useless bunch, aren't they? Well, looks like you're on your own then, kid. Now, I must love you and leave you. I've a hot date with Judge Peters.' Vernon took his court jacket and tie from their permanent position on the back of his office door. The jacket had been hanging there for years and wouldn't do up across his stomach. Kit wondered why he didn't just buy a new one and why Nell, a smart woman judging by the photo on Vernon's desk, would allow her husband out in public looking like that. She watched as he tied his scraggy tie, then drew a battered plastic comb from his pocket and dragged it through his wiry grey hair, making no impression on it at all. Then he turned to leave.

'But, Vern—' Kit started again.

'Look, Kit, I have not got time for this. I'm already in for a hammering from Judge P. over that cock-up of Ricky's, I can't be late to court on top of that. I know this one's looking like trouble. But try to treat them like any other family. They may be better off than we're used to, nice house, et cetera, but all the usual applies to them, just like it does to everyone else. So, go and ring Dai Davies and find out what the police are planning for the dad. Then get on to Legal and get a letter drawn up. Get the parents in this week with their lawyer. Go from there. No, don't bother with a gateway meeting,' he said firmly, seeing Kit open her mouth and knowing that she was about to suggest just that. 'I'm not having some agency manager who's been here five minutes making the decisions on my cases. I've said that all along, so it'll come as no surprise to anyone. Anyway, Mr and Mrs Cooper are obviously intelligent people so hopefully they will cooperate, in which case it will be straightforward enough. Make sure the kids are protected, get your assessment going, decide whether to take it to conference. That's that.'

Vernon was trying to convince her, or maybe himself. Either way, he was trying too hard, and Kit wasn't fooled. She couldn't even begin to think about the bomb she was about to detonate into the heart of this family.

Vernon turned in the doorway again. 'Actually, now I'm thinking about it, before you do all that, they've come up as known on the system, haven't they? Seems one of the kiddies is disabled – Lucy, I think it is – so you'd better get downstairs and have a chat with that Jean Collins in Child Disability, see what she makes of the family. I wouldn't expect much from her, judging by past experience, but it's protocol and all that, OK?'

'OK.'

'And don't be put off by the Coopers, Kit. Don't be intimidated.'

Only Vernon knew about her background. She hadn't wanted it spread around the team, and he had promised to keep it to himself. But he had a knack of knowing when it was bothering her.

'No. I won't.'

'Good, so get going then. See what she's got to say downstairs, pretend you care, then disregard every word of it and

see for yourself, that's my advice. Now I really have got to run.'
He headed across the team room and out of the door, shouting
instructions to the duty social worker about a medical on an
injured baby as he went.

After he'd gone, Kit gathered up her notebook and the
referral for the Cooper children and went downstairs to find
the Child Disability Team. She hoped she'd get a clue about
how to handle things. Perhaps Jean Collins would even come
out on a joint visit to the Coopers. Maybe Kit could drop
quietly into the background and let her handle it. Vernon had
been disparaging about Jean, but then Vernon viewed every
team in the building as a soft option compared to his own. He
thought the rest of the staff were simply people who couldn't
hack working on the front line. He wasn't necessarily right
about Jean Collins.

Kit arrived at the Child Disability Team and asked for Jean.
The receptionist pointed towards a desk in the far corner. The
woman sitting behind it gave a tight smile as Kit approached.
Jean was in her late forties and quite glamorous. Her hair was
glossy and toffee-streaked, and her make-up immaculate. Kit
was willing to bet that the luminous Jean didn't feel out of
place in the Coopers' kitchen in Meadow View Crescent.

'Hi, Jean. I'm Kit from the First Response Team. The Intake
Team have had a referral from the police about one of your
families. They've had a strategy discussion and agreed it needs
to be investigated so it's come through to us.'

Jean held out her hand for the referral. As she did so, Kit

5

could see that Jean was looking downwards, taking in Kit's Converse and her beaded anklets. In turn, Kit stared at Jean's patent black high heels and her long fingernails, each one of which had a tiny white bow set dead centre in its pale pink lacquer. Kit wondered how anyone could be arsed to get bows put on their nails.

'Oh, I am sorry, but this is just total rubbish!' Jean jumped up, shoving her chair backwards. Her tone was furious. She waved the referral under Kit's nose.

'Which bit?' Kit asked. Jean couldn't have had time to read more than the first page.

'All of it. It's bloody nonsense. You are not seriously telling me you are going to go over there and ruin this . . . this lovely family on the basis of this . . . this . . . crap? They have a very seriously disabled daughter, you know, plus the two little ones.' She sat back down and threw the referral onto the desk in front of Kit.

'Yes, I do know, Jean, that's why I'm here,' Kit started. She felt that she was doing quite well so far, keeping her patience. 'Vernon asked me to—'

'Oh, yes, I might have known he had a hand in it. Well, you can tell Vernon Griffiths from me that there's no need to bother going in there all gung-ho. I'm the case manager for this family and this can be NFA'd right now. Mr Cooper is marvellous with the oldest girl. He is a fantastic father and a very nice man. As if he would need to . . .'

Jean's nose wrinkled slightly. She couldn't bear to say it out loud, Kit realised.

'I can tell you what this is,' Jean continued. 'It's jumping on the bandwagon. End of.'

Kit could feel a burn forming in her stomach. She thought back to anger-management group and how she had learnt to breathe in and count to ten, and she tried to keep the heat down and not let it up into her throat. She seemed to remember something about becoming aware of the real reason behind your anger, but she found that the only reason that she could come up with was that Jean Collins was such an idiot.

'No one's saying he isn't marvellous with his daughter, Jean. That's not really the point, though, is it? It's a historical sexual abuse allegation, it's been referred to us and we need to make sure the children are safe and make a decision about conference and—'

'Conference?' Jean's tone was rising. People at nearby desks were looking around to see what the commotion was. 'You do know he's a very successful accountant? The only reason they're known to us at all is because they were unfortunate enough to have a child with severe cerebral palsy, and a very good job they do looking after her, Mr Cooper especially. He is totally committed to Lisa—'

'Lucy,' Kit interjected.

'Yes. Whatever.' Jean was not deterred. 'Conference? No. You are joking. He'd make mincemeat of you. This is not a family off a council estate, taking drugs and giving the baby Coca-Cola in its bottle. These people are well connected. They

7

are capable of ending your career, and believe me, they won't think twice about it.'

At this, Kit breathed again and told herself three times in a row to keep her temper. Then she lost it.

'No, Jean, I am not joking. This is a serious child-protection matter and we cannot treat it differently to any other referral just because they're a little bit up-and-coming and you fancy the dad.'

Jean was speechless, which Kit enjoyed no end. She picked up the referral and left, taking the stairs two at a time, buoyed by the horrified expression on Jean's face. She re-entered the open-plan office and headed towards her team's section. The noise level was rising as dozens of phones rang and social workers rushed out on urgent visits, or in to make phone calls and get advice from their seniors. Impromptu meetings were going on all over the place: at desks, in corridors, in the coffee area and outside the toilets. Snippets of conversations reached Kit above the hubbub as she passed each team. One social worker was anxious about a teenager, a regular self-harmer who had gone missing from care over the weekend and had not yet turned up. In another team, the manager was trying to allocate the usual batch of domestic-violence referrals resulting from the weekend's rugby-related drinking, her staff trying not to meet her eye. Wales had lost, Kit remembered, so no wonder they were reluctant to volunteer.

As Kit passed the Youth Justice Team, she spotted a young social worker sitting in silence with the phone to her ear, tears rolling down her face. Even from a few feet away, Kit could hear the furious shouting at the other end. She diverted slightly to the team manager's desk and tapped him on the shoulder to turn his attention from his computer.

'Caitlin's crying,' Kit pointed out.

'Oh Christ, not this again. She just can't cope. What the hell am I supposed to do with her?' He looked at Kit as if she might have the answer. Kit shrugged and moved on. She liked Caitlin, a lively young woman who was about her own age and also newly qualified, but she didn't have the time to get involved. She needed to get her head round the Cooper case. It was a new one for her. Burns, bruises and broken limbs she was already used to. But not this.

Kit arrived at her own desk and sat down, doing her best to ignore the noise and focus on what she needed to do. The altercation with Jean had made her even more determined to treat the Coopers exactly like any other family. She looked Lucy Cooper up on the system. She checked the details against the referral and saw that Lucy was fourteen and that she had two siblings, Cameron and Chloe, who were nine and six. She moved to Lucy's care plan, where she saw that Lucy had cerebral palsy affecting four limbs, but with three more severely affected than the other one. Jean hadn't bothered to specify which limb was the least affected, of course. Lucy was PEG-fed, which Kit had to google in order to find out it meant she was fed by tube through a hole in her stomach. Lucy attended Green Trees School during the day. It was seven miles away from her home, and she was transported there by minibus. Kit found that the Coopers had a large direct-payments package to pay for Lucy's care, and that they topped it up themselves, so that she had cover from carers most of the time, including through the night. This was necessary, Kit saw, because Lucy was very unsettled, sleeping little. Unusually, there was no respite provision in place to give Mr and Mrs Cooper a break from caring for Lucy.

Moving on to Jean's case notes, Kit saw a lot of breathless praise of Mr Cooper and his care of Lucy but noticed that less was made of Mrs Cooper's contribution. Jean mentioned in passing that Mrs Cooper was an active member of the local support group for parents with severely disabled children, but then seemed to lose interest in her altogether.

Lucy herself was almost invisible in the file, except as a problem to be solved. It looked as if Jean had turned up once a year to review the care package and drink coffee with the Coopers, and she had certainly made sure that they had everything they were entitled to, plus a bit more than Kit reckoned most families would get. But it seemed Jean had never thought it her business to spend any time with Lucy. Kit remembered what that felt like, and her determination to do a good job of this one hardened still further. The file showed that Lucy had no speech, and Kit saw with irritation that the section of Jean's assessment form which should have told her about Lucy's communication needs had been left blank.

Kit read the referral one more time, then picked up the phone and dialled the number for the Public Protection Unit.

'D.S. Davies.' Kit was glad to hear Dai Davies' voice. Like his drinking buddy Vernon, Dai was middle-aged and definitely old school, operating with the bare minimum of political correctness and somehow getting away with it. But he was experienced. Kit felt sure he'd know how to handle the Coopers.

'Dai, it's Kit. About the Cooper referral. I've been looking into the family a bit.'

'The Cooper case?' Dai's tone betrayed his surprise, sending Kit's heart down into her feet.

'Nazia's off sick.' Kit knew this would be sufficient explanation.

'Ah, right. Well, it's not going to be easy, but I'm sure you're up to it.'

'Yeah, and you're lying, but there's no one else to do it so I guess you're stuck with me.'

Dai laughed. 'Well, we can look after each other then.'

'Is it going to be that bad?'

'Yeah, I think so. Better brace yourself, my lovely. Now, what do we know about them?'

'They've got a disabled daughter, so they're already known to us. Dad's a bit of a superhero, according to the social worker. Gorgeous, fantastic with the children, that kind of thing.'

'He sounds dodgy to me already,' Dai snorted. 'Personally, I'd arrest him on the spot, just on that description. Right, what are we going to do on this one then? I'm thinking we go out there with CID a bit later, so maybe we catch dad home from work. I'm hoping he will cooperate and go to the station, save having a scene at the house, then they'll arrest him at the station. I'm guessing from what we know so far you won't want him home just yet?'

Kit hesitated. 'What do you think?' she hedged.

'This one's pretty credible, I reckon. I've seen the statements and it's not nice at all. I guess they'll want to bail him somewhere else and I would have thought that would suit you right now?'

'Yes, it would. We can see how the assessment goes and I'll sort out contact with the kids for him once we know whether mum's reliable. I might need to put in some extra support as well – this girl's quite severely disabled, plus they've got the two younger ones.'

'All right then. I'll meet you there about six thirty, OK?'

'Yep, sure,' Kit replied, trying to sound more confident than she felt.

'And try not to throw up in their garden, eh? They don't like that kind of thing in Meadow View Crescent.'

'Hilarious.' But Kit was smiling as she put the phone down. Dai had been kind to her when she'd got queasy after helping him to remove a tiny baby from a house full of rotten food and ancient dog crap. But of course, he was never going to let her forget it.

Kit's irritation with Jean Collins had bolstered her for half an hour, but now the panic had set back in. She searched for a distraction. In the end, she picked up her bag and found her mirror. She checked her face, because she knew that was what other women did, but she wore no make-up at all and wasn't really sure what she was supposed to be checking for. Her long fair hair didn't need a lot of maintenance either, just a wash and a straighten every morning and that was that. She liked shoes and jewellery, but she couldn't be bothered with the rest of it. As far as the girls in the children's home had been concerned, Kit's lack of interest in her appearance had marked her out as different. Though that wasn't the only thing that had, of course.

Kit searched deeper amongst the mess in her bag, looking for her cigarettes. She'd go outside for a quiet fag and maybe she'd feel calmer. Downstairs, she nipped through the boiler room and squeezed past a wedding party as they emerged from the registry office. After finding a spot in amongst the trees where she wouldn't get in the way of their photos, she positioned herself so that the May sunshine warmed her back while she smoked and tried to relax. Across the car park, she took in the full view of the Sandbeach council offices. They were housed in a seventies building which had supposedly had a life span of just twenty years. As a result, the two ends of the six-storey building were dropping towards the ground and had been propped up by scaffolding ever since Kit had worked there. Inside, notices instructed staff as to where it was and was not safe to place filing cabinets. A heavy load in the wrong place could bring another portion of the floor down.

Beyond the building, she could see the neat rows of terraced houses, all running in straight lines towards the sea. The huge estates, the Coed and the Hafod, lay halfway up the hill behind the town, giving the residents an outlook so superb that it almost made up for the grim realities of their day-to-day lives. Sandbeach had been an affluent town once, and some areas were flourishing again now. But the hammering caused by the closure of the pits and the steelworks in the outlying areas had left an ugly mark on Sandbeach. Poverty, crime and ill health characterised the little town, all going on in a dark tangle against the backdrop of a coastline so stunning that it featured regularly in broadsheet travel supplements and drew the middle classes from all over Britain and beyond. Kit loved Sandbeach, though. As much as she'd liked living at Cliffside with her foster carers, she'd been glad to come home.

She finished her fag and threw the end on the ground. Over in the car park, she spotted Vernon locking his ancient car. As he got closer to her, his stony face and the handful of greasy paper bags from the baker's over the road told her that things had not gone well in court. She felt sorry for Ricky, because if Vernon had had a bad time with Judge Peters, he was bound to pass it on. She lit another cigarette in order to give time for the dust to settle before she followed him into the building.

When she got to the office, she could see straight away that this wasn't a good time to update Vernon about the Cooper case. His door was shut, but Ricky and Maisie sat rigid at their desks. Their faces told her she'd just missed an explosion. Kit gave Ricky a sympathetic glance.

'Is he pissed off?'

'You could say that.' Ricky gave a slight smile, but he looked like he might cry.

'You can't really blame him, though, can you?' Maisie started up. 'How did you miss it, Ricky?'

Kit hesitated, wanting to defend Ricky, but knowing she did not have the time just now. Ricky was an overseas social worker, drafted in from Harare along with twenty or so others, in an attempt to plug the gaps in Child Services. The Zimbabwean staff were highly qualified, but they'd been placed in the teams that no one wanted to work in. The First Response Team had been the main contender. On top of that, they had had to find their way around an entirely unfamiliar legal and care system and a new culture within a matter of weeks. Ricky had somehow managed all this with very few slip-ups, but Vernon made no allowances whatsoever, and just the sight of Ricky's pleasant, calm face seemed to send him into orbit. He completely overlooked how clever Ricky was, and Ricky was far too gentle a personality to stand up to him, which was exactly what Vernon needed from time to time. Privately, Kit wondered whether Vernon was a little envious of the attention Ricky got. His arrival had caused quite a stir in the department. He was tall and slender, with perfect dark brown skin and a closely cropped Afro that showed off his pretty face. His general air of fragility, as it turned out, had a lot of appeal to a building full of women who got a kick out of assisting the vulnerable.

'I mean,' Maisie continued, 'you can't just accept the

explanation you're given for an injury, you know, not when the kids are on the register. You have to check it out every time.'

As much as Kit would have enjoyed a ruck with Maisie, she could not afford to get sidetracked, even if Ricky was the first friend she had made since she'd left care. Ricky would have to fight his own battles. She braced herself, crossed to Vernon's office and tapped on the door.

'What now?'

Kit opened the door slightly. Vernon was at his desk, signing off closure records, which were sprinkled with the remnants of his pasties.

'Can I have another word about this visit, Vern?'

He puffed out his cheeks but resigned himself. 'The historical allegations? The two girls?'

'Women.'

'Look, it's a colloquialism, I'm Welsh. I'm still one of the boys and I'm sixty-two.'

'I'm Welsh, too. I can still say the word "women".'

'You're Welsh-Italian. That's different.'

'Doesn't affect my speech much.'

'Makes you a stroppy bugger twice over, though. Now stop overreacting and get to the point. What's with the Coopers? What did what's-her-chops downstairs have to say about it?'

'Jean Collins said dad's fantastic. She told me to tell you to keep out of it. She wants it NFA'd.'

'Well, she can sod off for starters.' Vernon's expression was brightening at the possibility of a row. 'I'll go down and have a word with her manager right now. I'm in just the right frame of mind to tell her where she can get off. Bleeding cheek. So, have you looked at the file? Have you spoken to Dai Davies?'

'Yes. Two younger kids, nine and six, nothing of any significance. Older child Lucy's fourteen and severely disabled. Minimal communication, or possibly none.'

Vernon tipped his chair back and raised his eyebrows at Kit. 'Same age as the alleged victims and no communication? Better be extra careful there then,' he said.

Kit nodded. 'Yeah, I know. Dad's going to be arrested and bailed to another address anyway, so contact depends on mum.'

'What's bothering you about it most?'

'All of it. I mean, what do I say to mum? How the hell are we going to tell her and how am I supposed to work out whether we can trust her?'

'Maybe you'd better let Dai tell them. He's done all this any number of times. You can talk to her after they've gone about the allegations, but just roughly. Don't give her any details – the police won't like it; it might screw up their investigation. Just be clear that it's historical sexual offences we are talking about, and that it involves kids. We can see what else she needs to know further down the line, when you've got a relationship going with her. At this stage, you just want to know –' he counted it out on his big fingers – 'whether she understands the offences and whether she is willing to cooperate with us. You need to get an idea what their relationship is like, that's the important bit. Is he in charge at home? Can she stand up

17

to him if need be? If he gets convicted, is she determined to stand by her man and all that crap? If so, she's in trouble with us, isn't she? And make sure you get Dai to run PNC checks on them both, soon as, see if there's been any domestic abuse, anything like that. Right? Now go and speak to Legal, for God's sake. I know you're nervous and I can see why. But the best thing you can do is to make sure you've got all your ducks in a row, because if it kicks off when you break it to the mother, you need to be ready, OK?'

'Yes. OK.' Kit got up to go. Vernon was sifting through a bag in a desperate search for a last pasty. He found one and looked up, pausing to speak before he threw it into his mouth.

'Make sure you talk to the kids, won't you? Especially Lucy.'

'Of course,' she told him. That was the one thing she knew she could get right.

CHAPTER 2

By the time Kit reached the Coopers' street, the heat still hadn't died out of the day. Looking about, she couldn't spot Dai anywhere. She turned her car round at the end of the cul-de-sac and then drove back and pulled in diagonally opposite the Coopers' house.

She opened the car window. Just time for a quick fag. The day's heat had stuck her shirt to her back. A thunderstorm was overdue, and she longed for it to freshen the air. Kit felt closed in by the rows of houses she could see spreading in every direction. The sea wasn't visible from this part of Sandbeach; the estate could have been anywhere, you wouldn't even know it was near the coast. She couldn't understand the point of living there. She started to feel the pull to be at the beach, to get air into her lungs and cold water onto her sticky skin. She promised herself that she'd pick up her stuff and go down for a swim after this visit, holding the idea in her mind as an incentive to get her through what was coming.

Kit's nerves had settled a little now. Would they ever go away altogether, in this job? Every single child-protection inquiry she'd been out on so far had been an absolute nightmare: furious, aggressive parents, sobbing kids and all hell let loose the second the social worker got a foot in the door and waved an ID badge. Kit remembered the whole thing only too well from her own childhood. Except that, when the social workers finally came for her, Tyler and Danny that last time, she hadn't been sobbing. She'd been relieved. Christine had put all of them in and out of care so many times by then, using it like a free B & B. Every time she was fed up with the kids, she'd simply chuck some of their stuff in binbags and leave them outside a police station or the council offices. One Christmas Eve, she couldn't even be bothered to do that, and had just put the five of them out on the street, where they'd sat on the kerb shivering in the dark, until one of the neighbours had phoned the out-of-hours social worker to come and pick them up. Once they were out of the house, Christine would always switch her phone off, lock the door and retire to bed with a bottle of vodka.

And there had been the other times, when someone would report her for one thing or another – leaving the kids alone or being drunk or whatever. Those times were worse. A social worker would arrive to remove them, and Christine would jump at the chance to take the moral high ground, reacting with outrage, screaming and shouting about her rights and refusing to have her precious children taken from her. A fair bit of furniture would usually get thrown before the social worker managed to get them out of the house.

In the end, a social worker had come along who had actually stayed for a couple of years. Carmel had had the sense to see that the plan of 'rehab to home' was nonsense for the Goddard kids. Realising that Kit couldn't possibly study in Redbridge House, unless she wanted to get beaten up on a daily basis, Carmel had talked Menna and Huw into taking her, their last foster placement before retirement. Kit's near-perfect grades had been achieved at least as much for Carmel as for herself.

Kit brought herself up short. She couldn't think about this now, she needed to focus. She glanced around the close. The overheated tarmac was giving rise to a rich smell that wafted in through her car window, sticky and delicious. Children's voices rang out around the close, coming from gardens where little ones could be seen splashing in paddling pools and tottering on the steps of water slides. Some older boys were playing on bikes in the road, yelling at each other, but not swearing, Kit noticed. The houses were neat and modern, all placed at peculiar angles, because of the need to squeeze as many as possible onto the plot, she supposed. There were deliberate differences in their shape and layout, but this did nothing to overcome the feeling of them all being pretty much the same. Kit took in the Welsh-slate house numbers, the decorative lamp posts, the hanging baskets, the wooden blinds at the windows. From the vantage point of an outsider, she recognised it as a scene of affluent suburban normality. She was suddenly overwhelmed by the sheer impossibility of the idea that a sexual predator might live like this, might come home from the office to a list of dad jobs – power-washing the decking, reinflating the sinking paddling pool, tending to the Moroccan chicken on the gas barbecue, bottle of beer in hand. As soon as she thought it, she felt a pulse of irritation with herself. She knew full well that this was exactly what a determined paedophile might do – taking years, perhaps a whole lifetime, to carve out that perfect niche of respectability, which in turn encouraged trust and therefore easy access.

Her attention turned to the Coopers' house. She examined it carefully, but it told her nothing much. It was mostly similar to the others on the estate. The house was one of the larger, detached ones, with a big ground-floor extension to the side that had taken a lot of what would have been the garden, but otherwise it fitted the mould. The only other visible difference was the red Fiat Doblo parked on the drive. It was adapted to take a wheelchair and it stood out a mile, a lump of a thing compared to the sleek Audis and Mercs sitting outside the other houses.

At that moment, a black BMW swept past her and drew up on the Coopers' drive next to the Fiat. Kit put the car window up and slid down a bit in her seat. She watched, curious to get a look at Matt Cooper, the details of the referral running through her mind once more. She caught a glimpse of a tall, well-dressed man as he got out of the car and went to the front door. She didn't know what she had expected. But he looked ordinary enough. No, more than that, he looked pleasant, maybe even attractive. Kit was cross with herself as soon as she thought that, because it was the type of thing that Jean Collins would say, and she would have despised Jean for it. But somehow, with sexual offences, it *was* quite hard to resist the thought. Though she would sooner have died than admit it to Jean.

The door opened before Matt Cooper got to it. A slim woman with blonde hair stood there waiting for him, smiling. They hugged on the doorstep and went in together, his arm around her shoulder. Kit saw herself from outside now, sitting in her car, watching the daily routine of the family, her mind full of suspicion. How could she just walk in there and smash it all to pieces? Whatever happened afterwards, they would never recover from what was going to take place in the next hour or so. And did she even have the right, based on something that two women claimed had happened all those years ago? Jean Collins' warning rang in her ears; she started to feel afraid. Was what she was about to do going to end her career before it had even started? She tried to imagine how Mr Cooper was going to react. At least he wasn't likely to turn violent. He had too much to lose for that.

Another car pulled in behind Kit's and Dai Davies emerged, along with a woman, probably in her forties, of average height and build. The woman had cropped hair and acne-scarred skin. Dai came across and leant down to Kit's car window, giving her a reassuring smile. He was perspiring heavily, whether from the heat or his nerves she could not tell. Her own heart was racing now, and she would have done anything, anything at all, to avoid going into that house. But Dai raised his eyebrows to indicate that they needed to get on with it. Kit gathered her courage and got out of the car to join the others on the pavement.

'This is Kit Goddard,' Dai said. 'Kit, this is D.S. Beth Mackay from CID. I suggest we let her handle the first part, get Mr Cooper out of the way, and then we can go through things with Mrs Cooper. OK with you, Beth?'

'Sure.' Beth Mackay smiled at Kit. 'Don't look so worried, love. I won't stand for any nonsense from him, and I don't care who his father is either. I've had every senior officer from the Chief Constable downwards bending my ear about this Len Cooper today. I'm sick of the sound of his name already.'

Kit was extremely relieved to hear Beth's bullish tone. She'd had a couple of bad visits with officers who were so young and inexperienced that they'd had even less of a clue about what to do than she had. This had resulted in some nasty incidents, especially when Maisie was in the lead. But Beth clearly wasn't that type. Someone must have decided to send the big guns this time. Though, come to think of it, she didn't know whether that made her feel better or worse.

As the three of them made their way up the Coopers' drive, Kit saw a movement at one of the downstairs windows and a face appeared. Kit met Matthew Cooper's eyes and she registered his expression. It was fleeting but she saw no hint of surprise. Was it nonchalance, or a touch of arrogance?

Beth rang the bell. Kit hung back, still hoping to stay in

the background. The door was opened by a small girl with a pretty face and a wild tangle of blonde curls. This must be Chloe, Kit thought.

'Yes, can I help you?' Chloe said. She seemed totally unfazed by the appearance of three strangers at the door. Kit suppressed a smile. She liked the child immediately.

'Can we come in, sweetheart?' Beth asked. 'We need to speak to Mam or Dad.'

'Who shall I say is asking? Because you are strangers, aren't you?' Beth was caught off guard by this, Kit could see. She didn't want to have to tell Chloe that it was the police and social services at the door.

'You must be Chloe,' Kit said, reluctantly taking the lead. 'My name's Kit. You are quite right not to let strangers into the house, Chloe. Would you tell your mum or dad that there are three people here to talk to them, please? We'll wait out here while you do.'

Chloe stood, swinging the front door back and forth, weighing things up.

'Who is it, Chlo?' Mr Cooper interrupted Chloe's deliberations, appearing behind her in the hallway. His face wore a questioning expression now. He came to the door and Chloe darted back into the house and left them to it.

'Are you Matthew Cooper?' Beth asked.

'Yes. What can I do for you?'

'Can we come in?' Beth flashed her badge at him. 'D.S. Beth Mackay, CID.'

Matt Cooper hesitated. 'Nothing wrong, I hope?'

'Might be best if we come in, sir. It's not really something to discuss on the doorstep.'

'Yes, of course.' Matt Cooper stood back to let them into the house. The hallway was cool and dim, and the sudden change in temperature made Kit shiver as the sweat chilled on her damp back. The house was full of the smell of dinner cooking, something spicy. Matt Cooper led them into a living room, where his wife sat on the end of a brown leather sofa watching the news, a glass of red wine in her hand. On the floor, a little boy was playing on an iPad.

Mrs Cooper looked up as they trooped in. She looked at the three of them in turn, her gaze finally resting upon Kit, taking in her skinny jeans and her Superdry coat. Mrs Cooper herself was turned out like a catalogue model, in a lilac tunic top and cream palazzo pants. Her silver earrings matched her necklace and her long blonde hair was tied back in a neat ponytail. She wore high-heeled lilac sandals with straps around the ankle, the sort that Kit knew bit into your flesh at every step. Annie Cooper didn't want to spoil her look with a pair of slippers, Kit realised. She could certainly see where the common ground lay between Mrs Cooper and Jean Collins.

'Cameron, go and do that in your room, please,' Matt Cooper said. Cameron tutted but he got up and left without further argument, showing a nine-year-old boy's complete lack of curiosity about adult affairs. Matt Cooper waved his hand at the sofa and two armchairs. They sat down, Dai and Beth taking the sofa next to Mrs Cooper, while Kit ended up in the chair directly opposite her. All three perched uncomfortably on the edge of their seats. Sitting back would seem relaxed, and therefore too friendly. Kit's skin prickled as she waited for someone to speak. She suppressed another shiver. Matt Cooper stood by the bay window, one hand on the windowsill and the other in his trouser pocket, either very calm or very determined to appear it.

'Annie, these are police officers, CID—' Matt Cooper started.

'What's wrong? Has something happened?' his wife interrupted him. 'Is it my mum?'

'Actually, this is D.S. Davies from the Public Protection Unit, and Miss Goddard here is a social worker,' Beth said. The Coopers both looked at Kit, and again, Kit felt Mrs Cooper appraising her. Returning the stare, she took the opportunity to study Annie Cooper's expression. She could see that Annie had no idea what was coming next. Her brow was furrowed, and her hand still held the glass of wine in mid-air.

Beth kept her eyes on Matt Cooper's face. 'Mr Cooper, I'm going to have to ask you to come with me to the station—'

'What on earth are you talking about?' Annie Cooper broke in. She stood up and placed her glass of wine on the mantelpiece. Then she turned towards Beth, her face furious.

'I am sorry to have to tell you this, Mrs Cooper, but we need to speak to your husband in relation to an investigation that we are conducting.'

'What investigation?'

'Annie, sit down,' Matt Cooper said quietly. His wife looked at him with surprise, but she did as she was told, sinking back onto the sofa where she fixed Beth with a simmering stare.

'Could you explain what this is all about, D.S. Mackay?' Matt Cooper asked. He smiled warmly at Beth. 'I'm sure you must be able to give me some idea. Is your superior officer fully aware of what's going on here, I wonder? D.I. Kirk, isn't it? I've known her for some years, of course.'

So, Mr Suave he might be, Kit thought, but he wasn't above delivering a veiled threat. He was definitely someone who was used to getting his own way, and especially with women. It wasn't going to wash with Beth, though; she was unmoved by him, and what's more, she was already running out of patience.

'I'm afraid I can't tell you any more than that right now, sir,' she said firmly, treating the remark about her D.I. as if it had never been said, which Kit thought was a great tactic and one that was certain to infuriate Matt Cooper. 'But if you would follow me to the station, we can discuss the matter there. D.S. Davies and Miss Goddard will stay here and speak to your wife separately and they will tell her what they can. I am sure you will understand the need for that, Mr Cooper. I hope you aren't going to cause us any difficulties. Not the best thing for the children, I am sure you would agree.'

Beth held his gaze. The moment lengthened as everyone waited to see which way Matt Cooper would fall.

'All right then.' His voice was taut with anger, but he clearly knew better than to turn it on Beth. 'Let's get this nonsense sorted out, whatever it is. I need to make a phone call first, just to make sure this really is necessary. I don't know what all this is about, but I will be taking legal advice.'

'Yes, of course, sir, that's no problem at all and you will certainly be needing legal advice. Why don't you make the call and then we can leave; you can follow me to the station and perhaps you can ask your lawyer to meet us there.'

Kit continued to watch Annie, whose incomprehension was deepening as she registered her husband's acceptance of the situation. Matt Cooper walked to the door, where he stopped and turned to his wife. 'Don't worry, darling,' he said. 'I'm sure this is something that can be sorted out in no time. It will be some kind of a mix-up, that's all. Pure incompetence, no doubt. I'll go and give Geoff a ring now. He'll sort it.'

Matt Cooper left the room. Annie Cooper remained frozen in her seat, not speaking, looking from Kit to Dai and back again. Matt Cooper's voice could be heard on the phone in the hall, but Kit couldn't make out his words. Minutes ticked by. Kit had no idea what to say. She desperately wanted to smile at Annie Cooper, to try to make her feel better, but she knew that would look like reassurance, and that was hardly fair given what they were about to tell her. Dai sat in silence, regarding the floor, apparently unaware of the tense atmosphere. He had the ability to do this, Kit had noticed, disappearing into some alternative state when it suited him, no matter what was going on around him. She found it frustrating, but she envied it too, and she didn't imagine that she would ever achieve it. Beth fiddled impatiently with her bunch of keys, smacking them into her palm repeatedly, a gesture which Kit thought had unfortunate connotations in the circumstances. It was one of the most awkward situations that she had ever been in. She started to wish that someone would throw a couple of chairs.

'Right, Geoff Lane will meet us there. He's a very experienced criminal lawyer, as I am sure you know.' Matt Cooper was addressing Beth as he came back into the room.

'Criminal lawyer? What the hell . . . and what is she doing here anyway?' Annie Cooper's anger had settled on Kit now. 'Jean Collins is our social worker, she knows us very well – we have a disabled daughter. So you get Jean on the phone right now, she'll tell you there's no problem with our children. We don't need you here, so you can get out of our home.'

Matt Cooper crossed the room and crouched down in front of his wife, taking her hand in his and speaking gently. 'Annie, listen. It's obviously a mistake, isn't it? We haven't got anything to worry about. So just stay here and talk to them and I'll go and get it all sorted out at the police station. You have to stay calm, Annie, because otherwise the kids will hear you and they'll be frightened. We need to cooperate for now, and we will be making our complaints known first thing tomorrow morning.' He touched the side of his wife's face. The gesture was tender and reassuring, and Kit warmed to him a little, in spite of herself.

'OK, I will,' Annie Cooper replied, calmer now.

'Wise words, Mr Cooper. Right, let's make a move then, shall we?' said Beth.

'Sure.' Mr Cooper followed her to the door. He turned and spoke to his wife again. 'I'll see you in a bit, Annie. God knows what this is about, but it's a hundred per cent sortable, I promise. Now, just make sure the kids are OK.'

She nodded and watched him go. When the door shut behind them, Kit was glad to have something to say that was relatively easy. 'Mrs Cooper, could I ask you first whether you need to see to the children?' she asked. 'We will want to speak to you for quite some time, I'm afraid, and it's not something that you will want them to overhear. I know that Lucy has special needs, will you need to make any arrangements for her while we are speaking to you?'

Annie Cooper got up. 'My daughter's carer is still here. I'll see if she can stay a bit longer and give them their tea.' She left the room. She was gone for a few minutes, during which time Dai absented himself again. The sound of female voices carried from the kitchen and Kit thought she detected a muffled argument involving Chloe. It stopped after a few seconds and Annie Cooper returned to the room.

'Right, now please tell me what is going on here.' She didn't sit down but took up her husband's previous position by the window.

The room fell silent as Kit and Dai both waited for the other one to start. Kit wanted to grasp the right words, but they kept slipping away. She knew that these were the last few seconds of Annie's 'before' – the biggest 'before' of her life. No matter how much she might front it out, Annie was about to lose her certainty. In this second, she still felt sure about what she knew. That was about to go up in the air. By the time Kit and Dai left her home that evening Annie would have lost any firm boundaries between what she knew and what she thought or felt or suspected about her husband. She might push it all down inside her, eventually, but she would always have a shred of doubt. She would never reset the clock back to this moment.

Dai spoke, his voice gentle. 'Mrs Cooper, my name is David Davies. As my colleague said, I am a detective sergeant in the Public Protection Unit. Miss Goddard here is from the First Response Team. We need to talk to you about what is happening with your husband.'

Annie Cooper looked at him, but she didn't speak. She looked pale and her breathing was coming quickly. She was terrified, Kit could see that. She wished she could comfort her, take her hand or just make a move towards her, but she knew it wouldn't be well received.

'Mrs Cooper,' Dai continued, 'this is going to be very upsetting for you. Miss Goddard and I will do our best to help you, but there isn't going to be any easy way to say this.'

'Please just tell me what you mean,' Annie Cooper said.

'I'm afraid an allegation has been made.'

'What do you mean?' Annie Cooper was getting impatient now, and Kit didn't blame her. She knew Dai was trying to be kind, but it was time to get to the point.

'It's an allegation of a sexual nature,' Dai said. Annie Cooper stared at him for a few seconds, then she shook her head.

'Who on earth would say something like that about Matt? It's disgusting.'

Dai started to clear his throat carefully and Kit could see that another detour round the houses was in the offing. She decided to take charge. 'Mrs Cooper – or can I call you Annie? And please call me Kit. The thing is this. Two women have accused your husband of sexual assault.'

Annie Cooper gasped and put her hand to her mouth.

'I'm afraid it is just as serious as it sounds, Annie. These women have alleged that your husband sexually abused them about seventeen years ago. They were aged thirteen and fourteen at the time.' Kit stopped to let the information sink in. She waited, but Annie was silent, her face blank. 'We need to talk to you about the implications of this for your family. Do you have any questions first?'

'Who the hell are they? Who has said that about my husband?' Annie asked.

'Their names are Nicolette Baxter and Stephanie Harman.'

'I've never heard of either of them. Matt doesn't even know them. It's a pack of lies.' Annie was spitting her words out now, her panic making her livid.

'Could I ask how long you've been married?' Dai asked her.

'Fifteen years,' she replied.

'Well, you see, Annie, as Kit said, the allegations go back a bit further than that. Seventeen years, in fact. So perhaps you hadn't met your husband then?'

'No, I hadn't,' Annie snapped. She had taken it in now and was starting to process it, and her anger was rising even further. 'But he has never so much as mentioned those names to me and I can assure you right now that Matt would never do anything like that. This is absolutely outrageous. I don't know who these two sick individuals are, but this is slander. Are they after money? I think you will end up regretting it very much if you pursue this any further.'

Kit knew that the news was only going to get worse for Annie. Here goes, she thought. 'Annie, I need to be clear with you about why I am here.'

'Yes, why don't you do that? Why don't you explain yourself? Because I can assure you, I will be making a formal complaint about you, and I will take it all the way. I will be on the phone to Jean first thing tomorrow morning. Heads will roll over this, Miss Goddard, and yours will be the first.'

Kit ignored this, trying out Beth's strategy. 'As we have said, the alleged offences relate to two women who were under the age of consent at the time,' she went on. 'Your husband would have been about twenty-three, and they were thirteen and fourteen when the offences are reported to have started. So, these are child-sexual-assault allegations and that does have implications for your own children.'

'Implications? Meaning?'

Kit felt in her coat pocket and drew out the envelope containing the letter she had collected from Legal before she left the office. She held it out to Annie, who snatched it from her and stood with it in her hand, refusing to look at it and staring at Kit belligerently.

'Annie, that is an invitation for you and your husband to attend a meeting with myself and a lawyer from our Legal Department this Wednesday. You are asked to come along with your own lawyer to discuss the arrangements for your husband's contact with the children.'

'I really haven't got the faintest idea what you are talking about,' Annie said.

Kit realised that she was now the one skirting round the difficult bit. She braced herself. 'Annie . . .' she started, but she then she hesitated, unable to find the words.

'Your husband is going to be arrested at the station tonight,' Dai broke in, rescuing her. 'If he is released after his interview, he will be subject to bail conditions. I'm afraid he won't be able to live here in the family home, at least until Kit has conducted an assessment and put in place whatever arrangements are necessary to protect the children. The only alternative would be for the children to be cared for elsewhere – with family members or in foster care.'

At this, Annie Cooper crossed to the sofa and sank down opposite Kit. 'I don't understand,' she said quietly. 'Where will he go?' Her head was bent, and her face was partly hidden, but Kit could sense that, for a moment at least, her rage had swung back to fear.

'What we are saying is that your husband is accused of serious sexual offences against children. We can't allow him to have unsupervised contact with your children until we are sure that it is safe. I will need to make an assessment and I will work with you to see whether we can agree arrangements for him to see the children until the outcome of the whole thing is known.'

'He isn't coming home?' Annie asked, her head still bent.

'Not for the time being, no,' said Kit. 'He will need to come up with an alternative bail address. Family members or a friend, perhaps. If you will come along to the meeting on Wednesday, we will talk to you then about how we are all going to work together to manage contact.'

'Work together?' At that, Annie's head came up and the anger was back in her eyes. She was enunciating every word with exaggerated care. 'You really haven't taken in a word I've said, have you? What are you – twenty, twenty-one? You're just some scruffy kid. And you think you can barge in here with your ridiculous accusations and start throwing your weight around, do you? What happened to innocent until proven guilty? Well, let me tell you, you have picked the wrong family here. You are not going to break us up. You don't tell me what to do, and you certainly don't tell my husband. You are going to be so very sorry that you ever tried, I can promise you that. Now, both of you, get out of my house.'

'Annie, I really think it would be better if—' Dai started.

But there was no stopping her. She stood up and faced them, her arms crossed in front of her body and her face defiant. 'I believe I asked you to leave my home. I don't think you can stay without my consent. Am I right?'

She was absolutely right. They both stood up and made their way into the hall, Annie Cooper following closely behind them. No one spoke. Kit opened the front door with relief and Dai followed her out. Then Kit realised that he had turned on the doorstep behind her and was about to have another try. It was a lost cause, Kit knew.

'Annie, can I just say—'

'No, you can't.' She slammed the door in his face with an almighty bang.

They set off down the drive together, not speaking until they were well out of earshot.

'Debrief?' Dai asked her when they reached her car. 'You can leave your car at mine, pick it up in the morning?'

Kit was tempted, but she was too tired, and still shaky. She couldn't even face the beach, she just wanted to go home. 'Sorry, Dai, I can't tonight.' She unlocked her car and reached into her pocket for her cigarettes.

'OK then. Perhaps it's best, I think Martin's planning a casserole.' Dai's partner had recently retired from a very demanding job in the tax office. He had taken up cooking to fill his time. Dai gave the impression he rather dreaded Martin's efforts; Kit suspected he secretly yearned for the days of takeaways and microwave meals. 'Give me a bell in the morning, though. Looks like you'll have your work cut out with this one, eh?'

Kit nodded in agreement. She lit a fag and opened the car

door, then got in, immediately lowering the window as the heat of the car enveloped her.

'What's up?' Dai had seen her expression.

'It's just . . . we've wrecked their lives, haven't we?'

'You're wondering whether we did the right thing? Whether he could really be guilty?'

'Yeah. I guess that's it.'

'We didn't have a choice, Kit. I know it's hard, they seem like a lovely family. But if the allegations are true, those kids are at risk. That's the long and the short of it. Plus, if he is abusing them, and we leave him there, he's got time to work on them and make certain they don't tell. If he can't be alone with them, then he can't be accused of that later down the line, so it protects him, too.'

'I suppose so.' But Kit wasn't reassured. As she started the car engine and drove away, she glanced at the Coopers' house in the rear-view mirror, feeling horrified by her own power. She knew that if Matt Cooper was guilty, his family would suffer the consequences alongside him. But if he was innocent, the allegations themselves might well be enough to ruin him, especially in the claustrophobic atmosphere of Sandbeach. Either way, she had just altered the direction of the Cooper family's lives forever.

CHAPTER 3

On the way home, Kit heard her phone buzzing over and over again. Her throat tightened slightly, which she told herself was ridiculous. It could be anyone. She pulled over and rummaged in her handbag, finally picking the phone out from underneath a wodge of tissues and chewing-gum packets. She flipped it over. And, of course, it was Tyler. Three missed calls.

'What the hell is wrong with you?' she muttered to herself. Then she thought about the date. Tyler's benefits weren't due for another three days, and by now he would have run out of money. She sighed and then tapped out a text.

I'm on way home now

She sent the message and put the phone in her pocket. Then she drove on, wondering how much he needed this time. Out of the five Goddard kids, Tyler had always been her biggest worry. At least Jazz and Josie had families and homes, although in Josie's case it was dubious whether she was going to avoid the booze for long enough to hang on to either. But she was giving it a go, and Jazz was doing fine, she had even got a job in a call centre. But Tyler had struggled to get it together when he first got out of secure, and although he was doing better, there had been plenty of slip-ups along the way. Two doing OK, two dodgy and one dead. Not a great record, she thought. Bloody Christine, what a waste of space she'd been as a mother.

Kit drove the long way home so that she could pass the beach. It made her feel better, reminding her of the summer holidays when she still lived at home, when she'd go to the beach every day with Tyler and Danny. They'd set up camp in the same spot, lie on towels and bake in the sun until they couldn't stand it, then run into the cold water and swim out as far as they could, past the life buoys that were meant to keep them safe. She missed swimming with Tyler and she wondered whether they'd ever get that back now.

Arriving home, she parked in her designated space outside the flats. She could see Tyler waiting for her at the main door. He was standing up straight, and, once she got out of the car and got nearer, she could see that he definitely looked sober. This was good news. Tyler was unable to resist temptation and totally oblivious to risk. He loved a good time and never thought twice about where it might lead. But she knew how hard he'd been trying to sort himself out recently, and she was starting to think he might actually manage it.

'All right, Krystal?' He was grinning as she came up the path.

She stuck her middle finger up at him. 'No one calls me

that anymore.' But she was smiling. He wound her up like no one else could. But he could make her laugh, too, especially at herself. She didn't tolerate that from many people. She hadn't seen much of the fun side of Tyler in the past few years and she was starting to enjoy being around him again, now that she didn't have to be looking after him and sorting him out. It was early days, though, and she was still wary about the reason for this unexpected visit.

She opened the main door to the block and they made their way up the stairs to the first floor. Inside, she passed by the flashing answering machine, deciding to leave it for later. It would be Menna, checking in to see if Kit was OK, as she did every couple of days. Kit went straight into the kitchen and put the kettle on. Really, she wanted a drink, but she didn't want Tyler to have one. 'Coffee?' she asked him.

'Got any vodka?'

'No,' she lied. She made him a coffee with three sugars and took it through to the living room, where they sat down on the sofa. Tyler was looking around the room.

'It looks like no one lives here. You ought to get some stuff.'

'What stuff?'

'I dunno. Ornaments and that.'

He was right, of course. She looked around the room. The flat was a modern, neat little box. The rooms had all been painted magnolia and white when she'd moved in six months ago and she'd left them that way. She thought it looked fresh and light, and she was glad of it after the chaos of Huw and

Menna's rambling, cluttered house. But she realised now that it looked bare, and she had no idea how to make it feel like her home. She didn't even know what her taste was, what she liked or didn't like.

'I don't know what to put in it really.'

'Yeah, I know what you mean. Get some pictures or something. Remember that girl, what was her name?'

'Maddie.' Kit remembered the story well. Maddie had been a mate of Tyler's for a while, a right mess. She'd left care at sixteen and gone into a flat, just like Kit's. Tyler had been to see her, and he'd come back to tell Kit that Maddie had a pinboard on her living-room wall, covered with photos of the staff from Redbridge House. Including one of a support worker who had just come back to work after three weeks of sick leave caused by Maddie losing it one night and chucking a kettle full of boiling water over his arm.

'Sad cow. Like they were her family or something,' Tyler said, rolling his eyes.

'Yeah,' Kit agreed, but she thought that he was being both mean and stupid. He knew as well as she did that the staff were the closest thing that Maddie had to a family. But she didn't want to start a row, and let it pass. She rubbed her eyes and stretched her neck, trying to ease the tension in it.

'Bad day?' Tyler asked her.

'Yeah, shocking.'

'Serves you right, though, really.'

'Thanks very much.'

'Welcome.' He meant the job. No one in her family had been able to understand why she wanted to do it. They all held social workers responsible for what had happened to them, more than they blamed Christine. This had never seemed logical at all to Kit, though, when it was the social workers who had finally managed to get them all away from her. But then, none of the rest of them had ended up being fostered by Menna and Huw in their big house at Cliffside. Kit knew that if she had had to stay in Redbridge House, she probably wouldn't have felt particularly grateful either. Still, his remark irritated her.

'What are you here for anyway? Money?'

'Don't need it.' Tyler gulped his coffee. 'Got any biscuits?'

'In the tin. What do you mean, you don't need it?' But Tyler had gone into the kitchen. He came back with the biscuit tin and started searching through it for a chocolate one.

'Ty, what do you mean, you don't need it? Have you been dealing again? Because if you have, I am not going to be able to help you this—'

'No, I bloody haven't, as a matter of fact. I've got some money left this week, that's all.'

Kit was instantly suspicious. 'Where did you get the money from, Tyler?'

'I told you. I kept it. I don't only come over here for money, you know,' he said.

'Bollocks.'

'Well, all right. But not this time. I made my money last the whole week and I've come to visit my little sister.' He grinned at her again. She was the younger by just six minutes. 'Might even have enough for a takeaway if you're too lazy to cook me anything.'

Kit stared at him. What the hell was he up to?

'Don't look so worried,' he told her. 'I'm sorting myself out, that's all. That's what you're always telling me, so you should be happy, I reckon. You can stop nagging my face off now.'

'Yes, but—'

'Look, I've got a new probation officer.'

'So?' This was hardly an explanation for anything. Tyler had been through any number of probation officers. Not to mention social workers, support workers, advocates, lawyers and psychologists. He'd played every single one of them, as far as she could see.

'This one's different. She gets me.'

'"Gets you" in what way?' Kit was trying to stay calm, but she needed this like she needed a hole in the head. Tyler's ability to play the game was in no small part due to his astonishing good looks. She'd always suffered a bit in comparison. Like all the girls in the family, she'd inherited Christine's tendency to mousiness, whereas the boys had landed Gino's striking colouring. Every girl on the estate had known and admired the Goddard boys. Kit had had several worries about taking her first social-work job in her old hometown – the main one being that she might end up taking kids into care who would later turn out to be her own nephews and nieces. Tyler loved female attention, and females loved him. So far, this had enabled him to evade all the questions he didn't like and to avoid facing up to anything much. Worse, there had been a few incidents of outright unprofessional behaviour from women who Kit could only assume had been drawn to the caring field by a worrying penchant for the heartthrob/crim combo. She stared at him now, his muscular frame stretched out on her couch, an infuriating grin on his cocky face.

'What's up with you, arsey? Girls find me irresistible, I can't help that.'

'Women. And it's inappropriate when it's their job to help you. I've told you that loads of times. It's not a joke.'

'I don't see why, but all right, don't start. I'm being a good boy, doing what you said. Even if it is a load of crap.'

'Don't smile at me like that, you're not funny, you're annoying as fuck. You don't take anything seriously. That last woman lost her job because of you.'

'Yeah, well, it could have been love.' He grinned again. 'Anyway,' he continued, getting in before she boiled over, 'I won't be doing that again. I don't want to be giving witness statements and getting dragged up in front of those knobheads again – what d'you call 'em?'

'The Professional Misconduct Committee.' Kit cringed at the memory.

'Yeah, them. I'm not saying anything is going on with her, it's not. She's not like that at all actually. I'm just saying I think she can help me, you know. I've told her some stuff and she seems to know what I'm on about.'

Tyler looked at Kit then, and she sensed that he wanted her to ask what he meant. That this was why he'd come, in fact. But she didn't want to do it. She stood up and headed for the kitchen.

'Well, all right, stay out of bother then. What about this takeaway?' She felt a throb of regret as she saw on his face that he felt let down by her. But she couldn't face it, and she saw him accepting that, too.

'I'll get the menu up then.' He picked up his phone and started studying the Just Eat app.

After he'd ordered a Chinese for both of them, Tyler got up and began wandering around the room. He picked up a letter from the windowsill and studied the handwriting on it.

'You're still in touch with him then?'

'Let's not have a ruck about Jem.'

'I don't see why not. Jem's never gonna sort himself out, you know he isn't. He's gone down for a long one this time, so forget about him. He was a good mate to Danny, but I'm sick of seeing you waste your time on him. I reckon you could do better.'

'Christ. That told me.'

'Yeah. You needed telling.'

'As a matter of fact, I've ended it with Jem. Months ago.'

'Really? Thanks for mentioning it. I've heard that story a few times before, though.'

'Really, this time. He keeps writing, I haven't written back. That's that.'

Kit couldn't blame Tyler for his cynicism. The pull to keep Jem in her life had been strong, going right back to when they'd met in Redbridge House. It was the only thing that she had ever lied to Menna and Huw about, hiding that she was still seeing him all the way through her years with them out at Cliffside. But Jem was in hospital now, being treated for a psychotic episode which had been triggered by the drugs he had promised her he wasn't taking anymore. There was no knowing when he would be back in Sandbeach, if he ever made it at all. She had Tyler to look after and her job to do, and she couldn't deal with Jem's problems as well. She couldn't hang on to him just because he was kind and warm, and understood what her past meant, what it felt like to not have the birth family that most people took for granted. Favourite holidays, Christmas traditions, family arguments that got resolved in a flurry of apologies and hugs, or even those that went on and on for years – chilly and bitter, maybe, but with no one actually getting charged with assault or carted off to a children's home in the process. She had to get past feeling hurt about all that. She was an adult now, with a proper job and flat and a car and a life. It might not feel right yet, like wearing clothes that still smelt new, so you couldn't forget that you had them on. She would grow into it eventually. But not with Jem around, to keep reminding her about how her own weird shape had been formed.

Eventually, desperate for a drink, Kit relented and volunteered the presence of a half-bottle of vodka in her kitchen cupboard. Tyler moaned about it being Aldi rather than Absolut, but he drank it. After their meal, they settled on the sofa with a glass and an ashtray each and put a movie on, a mindless comedy that Kit chose so as to deter Tyler from starting any serious conversations. It was easy and comfortable, and she realised that it was nice to have someone else in the flat for once.

When the movie ended, Kit made up a bed for Tyler on the sofa and left him to settle down. She went to sort out her clothes ready for work the next day and to put her pyjamas on. Coming back into the kitchen for a glass of water a while later, she glimpsed him through the open door, stretched out on the sofa, sleeping peacefully. It was unfamiliar, and she realised that she hadn't seen him asleep for years. Kit and Tyler hadn't stayed in the same place overnight since she'd left Redbridge House, and not all that often even before that – Tyler and Danny had been AWOL most of the time. She'd felt jealous of their closeness at times, she realised that now. It wasn't that they were alike in personality. Tyler could blow up, but he cooled down more quickly than Danny did and always regretted it afterwards. He was kind underneath the swagger and didn't want to hurt anyone, whereas Dan was tough and untrusting, with a very short fuse. But they'd been joined together, the two boys, bonded by their liking for trouble – the drinking and the girls and the petty crime. Danny had wanted Kit to be a good girl and he wouldn't have accepted that sort of behaviour from her. She knew he'd loved her deeply, but it was Tyler he'd spent his time with, and they'd had their secrets, she'd sensed that. Things that Danny insisted she was too good for, things that he thought would soil her somehow. When he'd died, she'd known his death must be connected to all that, and she had a sense of what it was about, and her feeling of being excluded vied with her reluctance to find out the details.

In the morning, Kit woke Tyler early and got him breakfast, ignoring his complaints.

'I'll drop you home on my way to work,' she told him.

'Don't trust me in your flat, eh?' he said, shovelling Coco Pops into his mouth.

'That's right. Do you blame me, after last time?'

'OK, fair,' he said, not wanting to discuss the last time, involving as it had both a police raid and her front door being broken down. 'Drop me in town instead? I see my probation officer Tuesday mornings.'

'Yes, OK.'

'Miss Morrison, her name is. Emily.' He was looking at her again, willing her to ask him more.

'Shift your butt then, Ty, some of us have got jobs to get to.' She turned away to pick up her coat and bag. He said nothing but got his leather jacket and they headed out to the car. They were silent for the whole journey until Kit pulled up in front of the complex that contained the Magistrate's Court and the Probation Office, where she paused with the engine running and waited for Tyler to get out. He didn't move.

'Seriously, Tyler, I'll be late, and Miss Morrison will be waiting for you,' she told him.

'Do you know why I like her?' he asked as he got out of the car.

'Because she's dead fit, knowing you?'

'Well, she is, as it happens; I'd definitely give her one, like, but I already told you she's not up for it.' Every word of this made Kit flinch, but she reminded herself not to expect too much of him. One step at a time.

'Too professional she is, or something,' he continued, making Kit worry that he might already have given it a shot. 'No, it's all right, don't look so worried. It's not like that. I like her because she doesn't make out like stuff never happened. A lot of them do, social workers and that. But she doesn't play with my head that way, you know? I reckon she'd listen to anything.'

Kit recognised the rebuke. 'Well, that's good then,' she said. It was the only thing she could think of, and she knew it was inadequate.

'See you then.' He gave her another grin, because he knew his point had gone home, then slammed the car door. Kit drove off towards the council building, glancing at Tyler's retreating back in the rear-view mirror. She'd screwed that up completely. A memory came to her of the last time she'd seen Danny, and a similar conversation, which she had avoided in the same way. She promised herself that she'd text Tyler later, try to sort it out. Right now, she needed to deal with the Coopers.

When she arrived at work, she found Vernon sitting in the

main office, his feet up on Ricky's desk. No one else was there. For once, Vernon wasn't eating. He was drawing in the margins of the *Guardian*. Glancing over his shoulder, Kit could see it was a cartoon of Maisie, dressed head to toe in a vast patterned kimono and carrying the tatty wicker shopping basket that she insisted on using instead of a briefcase.

'It didn't go great last night then?' Vernon said as soon as he spotted her.

'You've heard about it already?' Kit dropped her rucksack by her desk and headed for the coffee maker.

'Yeah. Saw Dai in the pub after.'

'I thought Martin had a casserole in.'

'Well, if he did, it will have been burnt to hell by the time Dai showed his face.' Vernon grimaced. 'Let's hope that's not going to lead to another domestic, I don't think I can go through all that again. Anyway, Dai told me about it, yeah. How was it? Did he handle it OK?'

'He was all right, when he was with it,' Kit said, pouring a big mug of coffee for each of them. No need to ask Vernon if he wanted one.

'Zoned out on you, did he?'

'For a bit. Like no one else was in the room.'

Vernon tutted. 'Yeah, he does that. Bloody hippy.'

Kit thought it would be difficult to imagine anyone less like a hippy than Dai, with his M&S outfits, his chalet holidays in Tenby and his love of the soaps.

'Lucky you had Beth with you. What did you think of her?'

'Oh my God, I thought she was fantastic.' This came out before Kit could think about it, and she was immediately embarrassed, but Vernon just nodded.

'Yep, she is. She's tough and she's clever. You can always rely on Beth.'

'Anyway, I gave Mrs Cooper the letter, but she chucked us out then.'

'What did you make of Mr Cooper?'

Kit thought a minute. 'He cooperated. Quite charming really. But then he's arrogant, too. Very keen to let you know how important he is, who he knows.'

'Goes back a long way with the Lord God Almighty and all that?' Vernon said. 'I know the type.'

'Yeah, that's him. But then it was him who talked his wife down when she started to get worked up. He was very warm with her, but totally focussed on the kids and what was best for them. I was quite impressed with that.'

Vernon raised his eyebrows. 'Well, that's as clear as mud then. Sounds like you don't know whether you want to shag him or punch him in the face.'

Kit laughed. 'Yeah. That's about it.'

'What about her?'

'She was wearing high heels. In the house. Sat on the sofa, drinking wine, reading the paper, wearing strappy high-heeled sandals.'

Vernon was nonplussed. 'What's the significance of that then, Miss Marple?'

'Does Nell allow shoes in the lounge?'

'God, no. Nell wouldn't stand for that type of nonsense,' Vernon said, as if the wearing of shoes in the lounge was the very height of depravity. 'She's got mules. M&S. Fluffy ones. I get her a pair at Christmas. A different colour every year, to keep it interesting.'

'She's a lucky woman, Vern.'

'You don't know the half. Anyway, go on, what's the deal with the shoes?'

'Annie Cooper's uptight, that's the point. Very tense. She's got a severely disabled child, plus two younger kids, but the house is immaculate and so is she. She wasn't really relaxing, but she wanted to appear as if she was. Or maybe she wanted to feel as if she was. But she still had to look exactly right, and slippers would have ruined the outfit.'

'Very insightful. So how did she take the news? Did she have any inkling, do you reckon?'

'Badly. Wouldn't you? They weren't married at the time, and no, it didn't seem to me like she had a clue. She'd never heard of Nicolette or Stephanie.'

'Right, well, we can't blame her for being shocked then, so that explains her throwing you out. We'll have to give her the benefit of the doubt for now or we'll be in trouble if this lands in court. Let's have another go at persuading them to cooperate before we start getting heavy. I don't want these kids in care, Kit, especially not Lucy, it would be a bloody disaster for her. I can just imagine what Judge Peters would have to say about it. You'd better get on the phone to Dai and see what the news is. I'm assuming they arrested Mr Cooper. Beth doesn't usually mess around. Once you've got that sorted, give Annie Cooper a ring and let's see if they're planning to come along to the meeting. Make sure she understands he's not to have any contact with the kids in the meantime, OK?'

'Yeah, sure.'

At this point, Maisie arrived, her flip-flops smacking against her grubby heels. She hauled her shopping basket onto her desk. She was panting heavily.

'Morning.' She proceeded to glare at them both.

'Coffee?' Kit asked.

'Herbal tea, if you don't mind. You two shouldn't drink so much coffee, it rots your insides.' Maisie drew an evil-smelling pack of herbs out of her shopping bag. Kit took it gingerly and crossed to the kettle, glancing over Vernon's shoulder on the way. He was carefully adding a detail to the paisley kimono. Kit made a mental note to speak to him about that. It was the kind of behaviour that she'd heard had landed him in griev- ance hearings in the past.

Kit made Maisie her tea. By the time she put it down on her desk, Maisie was already busy on the phone, berating a client at high volume. Kit made herself and Vernon another coffee and then made a cup of tea for Ricky, who was utterly predictable in his time-keeping and was due to arrive in ten minutes. She covered the cup with a coaster to keep it hot until he got there. She debated whether to make him some toast but thought about how that might look and decided against it. She made herself and Vernon three slices each, adding jam to his, and then finally sat down at her desk. She rang Dai first.

'Morning,' she said when he answered, sounding tired. 'Got time for a post-mortem?'

'A short one. Just to warn you, we've got a toddler with a broken arm in A & E. Who's duty social worker with you today?'

Kit consulted the rota on the wall. 'Maisie,' she replied.

Kit registered a pause at Dai's end and she thought she heard him sigh. Maisie's approach to joint-working with other professionals tended towards the outright confrontational. Even gentle, kindly Dai had reached the end of his tether with her. 'Great, thanks,' he said. 'Right, what about last night then?'

'Vernon thinks we need to give them another chance. But we can't push it very much further now. I didn't even get to see the kids properly, and I didn't see Lucy at all. What's happening with dad?'

'Arrested and bailed to reside at his parents' address. Very nice address indeed, by the way. No conditions. Beth thought we'd leave that side of it to you to tie up with a written agreement. The grandfather's Len Cooper, he's friendly with some of the town councillors. So, you might want to watch your back a bit.'

'I bet Matt Cooper made damn sure everyone knew about it, too,' Kit said, revising her opinion of him yet again.

'Yes, according to Beth, he was very keen to point it out.'

'What was he like in interview?'

'Denied the whole thing. Admits he knew the two of them, remembers them vaguely as two annoying kids who hung around with his younger sister Katie, more or less like they said, but that's it. Totally denies anything ever happened. He reckons his wife has seen some woman hanging around outside their house recently; he thinks it might be Stephanie Harman, taking a look at what they've got, hoping to get some cash out of them maybe. He's a very cool customer indeed, Beth says. And if she couldn't scare him, no one can. She bloody scares me.'

'OK, thanks. I'm going to ring Annie Cooper now, see if I can get her to work with me. We've got the meeting tomorrow and we should start getting the checks made after that because his lawyer's bound to be pushing us hard for contact. Then we need to decide about conference. What do you reckon?'

'I don't know about conference. It might be good to have everyone around the table to discuss it, but even if we did put the kids on the register, what do we gain from that? We either trust them or we don't. I wouldn't trust him one inch. But the six-million-dollar question is, can we trust her?'

'I really don't know. I'll see how it goes. Perhaps she will have calmed down a bit or maybe they'll get a decent lawyer who'll warn them about not cooperating.'

'OK. Well, speak later then. Good luck.' Dai was suddenly sounding hurried.

'Didn't you want a word with Maisie?' Kit asked him.

'Er, no. Not yet anyway. There's still just a slim chance the doctors will decide it was accidental. I'll call her if I need her.'

'OK.' Kit put the phone down, noticing as she did so that Ricky had arrived. He was leaning against the wall, drinking the tea she'd left him. She noticed that he was wearing shorts. She guessed he must be planning to go to the gym after work, but she decided she'd better have a word with him about it later. It would be yet another opportunity for Vernon to tell him off; better coming from a friend, she decided.

Kit went into the records and got the Coopers' phone number. She picked up the phone and started to dial it, then she put it down again. What Dai had said about the Cooper family was playing on her mind.

'You all right? You look like someone's smacked you in the face with a cricket bat.' Vernon had emerged from his office. Picking up his words, Ricky and Maisie both stopped what they were doing and turned in her direction. Ricky wore a concerned expression. She knew it was genuine. Now that they'd got past a brief awkward stage caused by Ricky getting totally the wrong idea, they had started to settle into an easy friendship.

'Yeah. It's just . . . Dai says the grandfather's got some connections with some of our members.'

'Is that right? Who's grandad then?'

'Guy called Len Cooper, according to Dai.'

Vernon's face took on a new expression, one that Kit hadn't seen it wearing before.

'Should I be worried?' she asked him.

'Well, no, not really,' Vernon said. 'He knows some councillors, that doesn't make any odds to us. Just do your job, as usual.' But his words hadn't extinguished that look. He was wary. Vernon, the most unafraid person Kit had ever met, had the wind up him.

'So, forget what Dai said, and just get on and get it done, eh?'

After Vernon had gone back into his office, Maisie sidled over to Kit's desk. 'Watch your back on this one, kiddo.' She was whispering, even though everyone else in the room was too busy to be interested and the morning racket was at its height.

'That's what Dai said. What am I watching it for exactly?'

'Kit, getting involved with an elected member's family or friends – well, it's the short route to career suicide in this authority, if not the sack.'

'Don't the members have a code of conduct or something?'

'This is Sandbeach we're talking about.'

'So?'

Maisie wasn't making any sound at all now. 'Rotten to the core, trust me,' she mouthed. Then she flip-flopped away to her own desk and went back to her phone calls.

Kit pondered for a few minutes, but she still wasn't getting why Len Cooper knowing a few local councillors mattered. They might be in charge of the council in theory, but surely they couldn't actually interfere in child-protection work? She didn't believe a word of what Maisie said, and while she trusted

Vernon implicitly, she thought she could only have misinterpreted his face. Vernon would never let anyone get in his way if he knew the right thing to do. She had to get the phone call with Mrs Cooper over with. She picked the phone up again and dialled the whole number this time.

'Hello,' Annie Cooper answered, her voice wary.

'Annie, it's Kit Goddard. From social services.'

'Mrs Cooper, if you don't mind. I'm not your friend, Miss Goddard, so don't behave as if I am. What is it you want?'

It seemed that Annie hadn't calmed down and probably hadn't got legal advice either. Or if she had, she hadn't listened to it. Right then, missus, Kit thought. Time for a reality check.

'I'm ringing because I understand that your husband has been interviewed by the police and bailed to another address. I need to make clear to you and to him that we would not be happy for him to have any contact whatsoever with your children in person or by phone over the next couple of days. Any contact that takes place after that will need to be agreed with us, which is one of the things that we can discuss when—'

'You are seriously telling me that you think you can dictate whether or not my husband sees our children? What is it that gives you that authority exactly?' Kit felt sorry for Annie Cooper, but her air of talking down was beginning to grate.

'I realise that this must be very difficult for you. But the fact is that your husband has been interviewed in relation to serious sexual offences against minors. Now what that means is that I have a statutory duty to ensure that your children are protected. We either need to arrange for his contact to be supervised by our contact team, or we might consider running checks on a family member if you can suggest someone suitable. I am giving you an opportunity to cooperate with that.'

'Are you really? How very kind of you. And what will happen if I don't?'

'That is entirely up to you.' Kit kept her voice firm. 'I can't make you work with us. But you remember that I handed you a letter yesterday? It's called a letter before proceedings. And if you will refer to that, you will see that it tells you quite clearly that if you are not prepared to cooperate with us in order to protect your children, we may consider taking action via the court. We may issue care proceedings in respect of Cameron, Chloe and Lucy.'

Looking up, Kit realised that the team room had fallen silent. Everyone had picked up on the situation and they were waiting to see what would happen next. Kit knew she had to think on her feet. She wanted Annie Cooper to agree. She didn't want to have to go to court and she certainly didn't want the children in care. But the confrontation had backed Annie right into a corner, Kit realised, and she was definitely someone who did not like to climb down. Kit understood that, because she didn't like climbing down either. She knew that Annie Cooper needed a way to retreat.

'What I suggest is that you give your husband a ring. It's a decision for the two of you to make, of course, and he may feel differently to you. Speak to a lawyer, if you want to. Then come back to me by midday. If you are going to work with me, we'll make all the arrangements at the meeting tomorrow. But if you won't, then you must understand that I will get legal advice myself today about what action we can take. So, have a word with your husband, then let me know what the two of you decide.'

'Fine,' Annie said, and put the phone down. Kit looked up and saw Vernon standing in his office doorway.

'You do realise that if she comes back and tells you where to shove it, you'll have to go home and put a tidy skirt on for once, don't you?' he said. 'I'm not explaining to Judge Peters when you turn up in her courtroom in jeans.' He glanced at Ricky. 'And as for you, lad, I don't know what you've come as today, but let's hope to God you don't get called to court.'

Ricky looked hurt, but Vernon had already turned back to Kit. 'Plus, where do you reckon we'll get an emergency foster placement for three sibs together, including one with a severe disability? And what foster carer is going to be able to stand up to the Coopers, eh?'

'What did you expect me to do exactly?' Kit asked him, needled.

'I didn't say I thought you were wrong. I'm just pointing out the downside. Now you'd better give Legal a ring and check out where we go with this next, OK?' He winked at her. Kit was relieved. He wasn't annoyed with her at all, she realised, he was just covering up that he thought she'd done well.

Kit spoke to the duty lawyer in the Legal Department, who

assured her that she had grounds for an application if the Coopers didn't cooperate, but warned her that, even so, she could expect a hard time if the case came before Judge Peters. He enjoyed himself by reinforcing this with an anecdote that Kit had already heard numerous times in the past few months, about the time when the judge had spent forty-five minutes bringing one of the department's most experienced managers to the brink of tears in the witness box after she became hopelessly confused in her evidence.

'Would we be better off just leaving it alone until we know the results of the criminal investigation, then go for a care order if he's convicted?' Kit asked hopefully.

'Christ, no,' the lawyer told her. 'Turn up asking for an order after leaving the kids unprotected for months? She really would tear you to pieces for that.'

'So, I can't win then?'

'You've got it,' he said. 'Just make sure you get them to cooperate is my advice. It will be easier on everyone, including you and me.'

'Great.' Kit put the phone down and tried to focus on paperwork. She typed up her recording of everything that had happened so far. Then she answered a few emails. Finally, at eleven thirty, her phone rang. At the sound of it, all the staff who were left in the office resumed their listening positions and Vernon reappeared in his doorway as she answered the call.

'I've spoken to my husband,' Annie said, without preamble,

'and we have decided that we will go along with your ridiculous games for now. My husband won't contact the children today. But I want you to know that we are keeping a full record of all your actions and, as I have said, we will make complaints at the highest level afterwards. We will be at the meeting tomorrow. We will be represented by Miss Bruce of Bruce Ladd. We'll see what you think after you've had a full discussion with her.' Bruce Ladd was the biggest and most successful law practice in the town, and Mandy Bruce was widely known as the most persistent and aggressive childcare lawyer in south Wales. Kit had heard that she was fresh from a bitter case that had seen two children returned to their family from the brink of adoption and the social workers concerned referred on to their professional body over concerns about their evidence in court.

'Our position won't change,' Kit said. 'You're going to have to work with me. I know you don't like it and I can see why, but that's the way it is.'

'We'll see about that,' Annie replied. She hung up.

Vernon let out a huge sigh of relief. 'You played a blinder, kid,' he told her.

'Hmm,' Maisie said. 'I think you could have been a bit more assertive with her.'

Kit didn't bother to answer that. She felt in her rucksack for her fags and, once she found the packet, she waved it at Vernon.

'Yes, go on then,' he said. 'Don't bother clocking out this

63

time, but don't be long.' Kit smiled at him gratefully. As she made her way across the room, she could hear Ricky speaking.

'Maisie,' he was saying, 'I sometimes think your attitude to clients could be a little more conciliatory. And you could be more supportive towards your colleagues, too.'

Kit closed the office door on the ensuing scene and set off for her fag break. She spent the afternoon catching up on her visits and then she drove home, collected her towel and her swimming costume and drove out to the west of the town. After parking in the council car park at the end of the road, she crossed over and followed the footpath that went out onto the headland. She could see across to the town beach, where throngs of people lay on the sand and bobbed in the water. Her path was deserted; the holidaymakers wouldn't go anywhere that involved a long walk. Most of them didn't even know that Rockpool Bay existed.

When she reached the tiny bay, she slipped into a cave to change and hide her car keys and clothes, then emerged onto the scalding-hot rocks, picking her way across them until she found a point from which she could make a clean dive into the icy water. She swam out until the cold sting subsided on her skin. Then she turned onto her back and used her arms and legs to keep herself afloat. The tightness that always seemed to lie in her chest these days had loosened. She felt so good that she found herself grinning idiotically. It always worked; the sheer physical pleasure of being in the water was the only thing that could stop her fretting in its tracks. No one was around to see her, so she continued to float and swim in turns, laughing and singing quietly, until she had driven her job out of her mind and she felt like herself again. She padded back across the rocks just before darkness fell, and when she got home, she fell into bed without bothering to eat and slept until morning between damp, sandy sheets.

CHAPTER 4

'Court, funeral, or giving it all up to become a silver-service waitress?' Vernon asked as Kit walked into the office on the day of the legal meeting.

'The last one, if she's got any sense. It'd be a treat compared to working for you,' Maisie muttered, making her way to the coffee area.

'Feel free to give it a try yourself any time you want,' Vernon snapped back at her. 'Right, so, come on then, Kit-Kat, what's the outfit in aid of?'

'It's for the Coopers' legal meeting.' She had stopped short of putting on her one and only skirt; she wasn't going to court, after all. But she had wanted to look more professional and confident than she felt. So, she had found a pair of black trousers and a plain black shirt in the back of her wardrobe; she had ironed them both carefully before putting them on, and after looking through her entire shoe collection, she had added a pair of flat-heeled leather boots. She had even found her most sensible earrings, a pair of silver studs, and had put them in the lowest hole in her lobes, leaving all her other piercings out for once.

Vernon nodded. 'Ah right, I'm with you. Well, I won't be dressing up for it myself, if it's all the same to you. They can take me as they find me.' He was looking particularly untidy today, dressed in baggy grey trousers and a mustard shirt that had worn so thin across his stomach that it looked as if it might disintegrate at any minute. Kit wondered what the Coopers would make of him. She wasn't worried, though. It was common for people to underestimate Vernon, based on his appearance. It always turned out to be a mistake.

'Watch your backs, everyone,' Vernon said, looking over Kit's shoulder. 'Looks like we're up for a visit from the senior clerk.'

This was Vernon's name for Cole Jackson, the head of Child Services. Mr Jackson's background was in administration, and his rise into senior management had irritated Vernon beyond belief. He disliked every single thing about Cole Jackson, from his lack of a social-work qualification, to his Porsche, his loud ties and his overenthusiastic use of aftershave. On his pinboard, Vernon kept a memo that Cole Jackson had sent out, asking that staff should refrain from greeting him in the corridors, because responding to them was taking up too much of his time. If anyone suggested in Vernon's presence that Cole Jackson had any redeeming qualities whatsoever, he would unpin the memo and wave it at them, as irrefutable evidence to the contrary.

Kit turned to watch Cole Jackson making his way across the office towards them. Following closely behind him was a tall woman in her early sixties, dressed in dark blue from head to toe. She was wearing a square cloth hat, which sat very high up on her forehead, increasing the imposing effect of her height and drawing attention to the severe bone structure of her handsome face.

'Who's that?' Kit whispered to Maisie.

'Councillor Desiree Palmer. Vice Chair of the Social Services Committee. Looks like we're in for it. Wonder what Ricky's done now?'

Kit's heart sank. She knew this wasn't about Ricky. It had to be about the Coopers. There wasn't another case going on at the moment high profile enough to draw Cole Jackson onto Vernon's territory.

'Vern, good morning.' Cole Jackson arrived in their team area, bringing with him a waft of something with quite a lot of citrus in it, which caught in Kit's throat and set Maisie rummaging in her wicker basket for her asthma pump. Kit saw that Vernon didn't make eye contact with Cole Jackson, but that he gave Councillor Palmer a warm smile, which she returned.

'Vern, could Councillor Palmer and myself have a quick word with you and Ms Goddard?'

'Certainly. Fire away, Cole.' Vernon crossed his arms, on the defensive at once. Cole Jackson gave Maisie a disdainful look, lingering for a few seconds on her leopard-print leggings. 'In private, Vern, if I can ask that of you? It's a highly sensitive matter.' He nodded towards the door of Vernon's office.

Vernon led the way. Cole Jackson and Councillor Palmer

followed him, Kit last. She found Vernon already seated behind his desk, while Cole Jackson and Councillor Palmer had taken the other two chairs. Kit had no choice but to stand in the corner next to Vernon's desk. She took the opportunity to open the window on her way through, hoping to lessen the citrus tang, which was now dominating the confined space.

'Thanks for this, Vern,' Cole Jackson started, leaning forward and interlocking his fingers in front of him. 'We've got a bit of a thorny issue, quite frankly, and I'm hoping we can engage you in a resolution.' This was the kind of jargon that got on Vernon's nerves in a big way. Not a good start, Kit thought.

'Go on.'

'I gather you've had some involvement with the Cooper family.'

'That's right. We've got the legal meeting this morning as it happens.'

'Can I ask where you're going with the case, Vern?'

'Father out of the house and then straight into care proceedings if it's up to me. And come to think of it, it is up to me actually. Why do you ask?'

Kit knew that they were nowhere near care proceedings as yet. Vernon was overstating his case, to emphasise from the start that he was in charge.

'I'm not sure if you're aware that the Coopers intend to make a formal complaint about your involvement.'

Vernon snorted with derision. He had been complained about so many times over the years that the process held no fears for him. 'They can do what they like. There's three kids in that house, one severely disabled and a similar age to the alleged victims at the time of the offences. If those children need safeguarding, that's what we're going to do. Any problem with that, Cole?'

Cole Jackson shook his head. 'I'm with you on that, Vern. You know my track record on safeguarding issues.' Kit cringed, but luckily Vernon let the point pass without comment. 'Obviously the children's safety is the priority,' Cole Jackson continued. 'But how reliable are these allegations against Mr Cooper? My understanding is that they've been cooked up by a couple of rather damaged women who are hoping to wring some money out of the Coopers? Isn't one of them from the Coed estate?'

'We've got no proof of that whatsoever and where they live is irrelevant. The fact is, the allegations have been made, the police are investigating, and we have a responsibility to ensure that the children are safe in the meantime.'

'Vern, the situation is quite delicate. I wouldn't want to interfere with your decision-making in any way. Your integrity is well known within this department and I hope you know how much I respect that. But I need you to help me out here. The Coopers are a well-respected family and Len Cooper is very upset indeed about what's happening to his son. Would it not be more balanced, under the circumstances, to await the outcome of the criminal process before taking action?'

Vernon, predictably, was having none of it. 'No. Absolutely not. We don't do that with any other family, so why should we do it for the Coopers? If this case gets into care proceedings later, the judge will have my guts for garters if I've sat on my backside doing nothing while I've waited for the police and the CPS to get their act together. You can go into court and explain it to her if you like, but if it's up to me, no, sorry, it's just not happening.'

Cole's face dropped slightly at the thought of having to explain himself in court. It was a position Vernon had put him in before, and the rumour was that Mr Jackson hadn't come out of it well. But after a few seconds, Cole rallied and went in for another go. 'You clearly feel very strongly about it. I don't want to insist, Vern, but you're placing me in a difficult position here.'

Cole's gleaming white smile had disappeared now, and his tone was becoming fractious. It had no effect on Vernon, though.

'You can insist all you like,' he said. 'Over my dead body do we close that case. If you are implying that you will make me do it, I'm telling you right now, I refuse. Discipline me if you want. In fact, sack me. Get an agency manager in, see how long they last in this job, even at three times my hourly rate.'

Councillor Palmer cleared her throat. 'I don't think it needs to come to that, Vernon,' she said. 'I'm not sure the department would manage without you.'

Cole Jackson's dental work was back on display, his mouth hanging open in surprise as he recognised the existence of a past acquaintance between Councillor Palmer and Vernon.

'But I know Mr Cooper's father has been speaking to the police and the CPS,' Desiree Palmer continued. 'And he's expecting to get the decision about prosecution expedited. So surely you can just hold off until then? If the decision goes the other way, you will have my full backing to take whatever action you need to, of course.'

'Nope, sorry, no can do.' Vernon sat back in his chair, folded his arms and stared at the two of them. Kit could see that Cole Jackson was furious. He exchanged glances with Councillor Palmer.

'This really is puzzling me,' she said. 'From where I'm standing, it looks as if you have made up your mind on these allegations before due process has taken place. I've known Len Cooper a long time, and my Griff was at school with Matthew; he was a lovely boy and there is no way—'

'Desiree, forgive me, but you cannot possibly know that. From what I understand, this is nasty stuff, and the police seem to think it's credible. We're talking about a young man of twenty-three and two vulnerable teenage girls. Lots of grooming, really careful, long-term planning. The way they tell it, they were manipulated by an expert. Now we don't know which way the whole thing is going to go, but I'm wary about this one. I'm not taking any chances, just because of who the Coopers are and who they know. It could blow up in our faces, and none of us want that, do we?'

'For God's sake, Vernon, it's blowing up now!' Cole Jackson leant forward and smacked his hand down on the edge of

Vernon's desk. 'Len Cooper's climbing the bloody walls. He's been on the phone to everyone this morning, all our councillors, the Children's Commissioner, assembly members, the lot. I'm under siege in my own office.'

Vernon shrugged. 'Well, I expect there's something in your pay packet for that, Cole. Now, I don't know how many other ways I can say it to you two but let me be crystal-clear this time. I don't give a rat's arsehole what Len Cooper does, who he phones, or what he says about any of it. I am not closing this case.'

Councillor Palmer closed her eyes for a moment and stroked her forehead with an elegant navy-nailed forefinger. After a few seconds she looked at Vernon. 'I'd thought better of you, I have to say. You are overreacting and treating this poor man like a criminal when there's nothing to say he has ever put a foot wrong. Surely we could at least avoid putting the Cooper children's names on the register?'

'Christ almighty, Desiree, let it rest. You know I can't agree to that. It will depend on Kit's assessment.'

They all looked at Kit, having seemingly forgotten that she was in the room.

'Could we at least get the case allocated to someone more experienced?' Cole Jackson asked, looking Kit up and down. 'I understand the Coopers are very upset that they appear to have been given the most junior member of the team as their social worker. They feel it says something about the low priority you are giving to the case.'

'I know your background isn't in social work, Cole, so perhaps that's why you're making a mistake there,' Vernon said. 'What you need to grasp is that Kit is not Mr and Mrs Cooper's social worker at all. She's the children's social worker. So, no, I won't be reallocating the case. Kit's a very able member of my team. She can work with those kids and that's what is needed here. I don't care whether Matt Cooper likes her or not.'

Cole Jackson opened his mouth to object, but Desiree Palmer cut across him. 'All right. I can see we are getting nowhere here. Let's leave it at that for now. Cole, you and I had better have a chat.' They all stood up and Cole Jackson held the door open for Desiree Palmer. She turned in the doorway.

'I just hope you know what you are doing. I've never doubted it before, but I'm not so sure this time.'

'You don't need to worry on that score, Desiree. Good to see you, as always.' Vernon smiled at her, and Councillor Palmer returned it, but Kit could see it was an effort. She left, Cole Jackson following her without a word.

Vernon was chortling. 'He's got his tail between his legs now. Right, time to get to this legal meeting then.'

'Good to see you as always? Desiree? What's that all about?'

'Len Cooper's not the only one who goes back a long way with some important people.'

'Really? And what does Nell make of you having history with the glamorous councillor?'

'Nell's got nothing to worry about. Doesn't hurt to have a

couple of friends in high places, though, especially where Len Cooper's concerned.'

'Who the hell is he anyway?'

'Coopers' Ltd. You must have seen the lorries? They're a haulage firm, plus they've got all that warehousing on the business estate. They've got a few other interests now, of course. A couple of restaurants, and the last I heard, Len had built a residential home. God help any older people who land up in that. Haulage is what he knows and that's where he made his money.'

This explained nothing, as far as Kit was concerned, but Vernon was on the move, so she gathered her papers and followed him out of the office, still pondering on why it was that Len Cooper had so much power. She did vaguely recall seeing the lorries now, with a garish red and black livery and orange flames painted around the wheel arches. She wondered whether the dismissive remark about one of the women being from the Coed estate had originated from Len Cooper, and she felt a hatred of him forming rapidly.

Kit could see that winning the fight had put Vernon in a good mood, but by the time they reached the bottom of the stairs his expression was already shifting to one of anxiety. As they crossed the reception, Kit spotted Matt and Annie Cooper standing on the far side of the car park, talking to Mandy Bruce. Her stomach lurched. All the legal meetings she had sat in on so far had been horrendous, with aggressive lawyers challenging every detail, not letting any of the proposed agreements pass without head-spinning levels of scrutiny. She fully expected this one to be the same. Or worse.

Vernon unlocked the meeting room and they arranged the chairs quickly. When their own lawyer arrived, Kit was glad to see that it was Sue Sullivan, the deputy head of Sandbeach Council's Legal Services. Big guns once again, Kit observed, with mounting unease. Sue Sullivan was such an experienced lawyer that she came to every case with an air of boredom. Smart, silver-haired, easily in her mid-sixties, she had no discernible sense of humour. Vernon had worked with Sue Sullivan for years and thought she was fantastic. Kit usually found her terrifying, but she was glad to have her on their side. It left no room to doubt the Coopers' ability to put the wind up absolutely everyone.

Vernon briefed Sue Sullivan while they waited for the Coopers to arrive. Kit handed her a copy of the proposed supervised contract agreement and she scanned it.

'They're going to want mother supervising contact. That's going to be a major sticking point. Why don't you trust her to do it?'

'She's arsey,' Vernon replied.

'Right. Or as we will perhaps put it, we don't feel we can rely on her cooperation as yet.'

'That's it.'

'All right, so we're saying he can continue to live at his parents' and have some scheduled contact with the children every day, supervised by appropriate family members. We'll ask them for some names and Kit can set up the police checks and the visits. If mother's attitude changes and she's workable-with, we can review things. Better be ready for a long one. Ms Bruce had me in here for four and a half hours on one of these last week.'

'I haven't got four and a half hours to spare,' Vernon said firmly. 'I'd miss my lunch.'

After a loud knock on the door, Mandy Bruce entered without waiting to be asked. A small woman in a perfectly cut black dress, she wore a stern expression as a matter of habit. The sharp lines of her outfit emphasised the gauntness of her face, and her hair was pulled up into a tight bun from which no strand would dare to escape. It made Kit's head ache just to look at it. She watched Mandy Bruce acknowledging Sue Sullivan with a neutral nod and no deference. With a twinge of fear, Kit saw that the Coopers had chosen their lawyer well. They were following her into the room now, both dressed for a formal meeting: Matt Cooper in a beige suit, white shirt and a striking rust-coloured tie, Annie in high heels and a fitted grey dress with matching cropped jacket. They sat down on either side of Mandy Bruce, who drew a pile of papers out of her briefcase and placed them on the table in ominous silence. Annie looked just as furious as she had when Kit had seen her last, just before she slammed the door in Dai's face. Matt Cooper kept his gaze downwards and Kit couldn't read his expression at all.

Sue Sullivan got the introductions over with and passed three copies of the supervised-contact agreement across the table. As Annie Cooper read through it, angry lines cut into the skin on either side of her mouth. Mandy Bruce scanned her copy and put it down on the table.

'Right, let's get started, shall we? We're prepared to accept most of these arrangements.'

Vernon, Kit and Sue Sullivan all looked up in unison, such was their surprise. Mandy Bruce's strained expression told Kit that her words were practically choking her.

'Sorry?' Sue Sullivan said, caught on the hop for the first time that Kit was aware of. 'Could you just repeat that?'

'My instructions are that my clients accept most of this document. We are confident that Mr Cooper will be cleared. In fact, we don't even expect the prosecution to proceed, so that will be the end of the matter.'

'Not necessarily,' Vernon interjected. Kit knew that he was disappointed at missing out on a fight. 'Whatever happens in the criminal case, we still have the option of care proceedings. We could go into court for a finding of fact. Our assessment will be ongoing, too. This case won't close until we are completely satisfied that the children are safe.'

'We are confident on that score, too, Mr Griffiths. My client has nothing to worry about here. The fact is that these allegations are quite ludicrous. That will soon become obvious. In the meantime, and for the short term, we will go along with this. But we have one caveat. Mr Cooper very much wants contact to be as normal for the children as is possible under the circumstances. I am sure we would all agree that is best for the children, particularly Lucy, who is finding her father's absence very confusing. We would like Mrs Cooper to supervise the contact. Mr and Mrs Cooper will tell the children that Mr Cooper is having to live with his parents for a while because his mother has been unwell.'

Kit and Vernon exchanged glances. Sue Sullivan interjected. 'Can I have a few minutes with my clients, please?'

Mandy Bruce nodded. She got up and left the room, the Coopers following after her.

'Well, what do you make of that?' Vernon asked Sue Sullivan, as soon as the door closed behind them.

'Very strange. And Mandy Bruce doesn't like it at all. Did you hear her? "My instructions are . . ." That's a message between us lawyers. She's doing as they've told her to, but she is making it clear she doesn't agree. They're going against their own legal advice. Why would they do that?'

'Beats me,' Vernon said. 'Kit, what do you reckon? Do we let her supervise the contact?'

Kit thought for a few seconds. 'They've got a fair point about the kids and they are doing their best to cooperate, I guess.'

'Maybe that's the whole point, though. Maybe that's exactly what he wants us to think, that he's willing to accept it, but the price we pay is that he still gets access to the children. Maybe he's just being very clever.'

'Maybe he is or maybe he's genuine. How can we know? But perhaps it would help me to get somewhere with Annie if she felt that I was willing to give some ground, trust her a bit.'

Sue Sullivan frowned. 'I wouldn't advise it, Kit. It's natural enough for you to be quite trusting at this point. This is your first serious-abuse case, isn't it? With experience, I think you'll become a little less naive about some of these people.'

Kit felt both patronised herself and offended on behalf of her clients, but she didn't want to argue with Sue Sullivan; the very idea of it frightened the life out of her. She knew that it would be up to Vernon to decide which way to go, and Sue Sullivan was looking at him now, too, waiting for him to decide, clearly thinking that she had dispensed with Kit's role in the whole business.

'We could specify that he mustn't be involved in any personal care and we could ask for his contacts to be in the daytime only. Then we could get a schedule of his contacts with the kids and we could spot-check them to make sure they were complying?' Kit said quickly, appealing to Vernon.

Sue Sullivan looked exasperated now, but Kit could see that Vernon was listening. 'I don't know, Kit,' he said. 'It looks like we are contradicting ourselves a bit if the police won't have him living at home but we're letting her supervise him with the kids in the day. Even with spot checks we'd be trusting her with an awful lot. We know what her attitude to the offence is. She's adamant he didn't do it. She won't have it at all. How can we trust her?'

'But what do you expect, Vern?' Kit asked him. 'He's her husband. Of course she doesn't think he did it, not right now anyway. What would Nell say if it was you? Just the same, I reckon.'

Vernon raised his eyebrows at her, an acknowledgement that she had a point.

'But that's not the issue anyway,' Kit went on quickly, while she was winning. 'What we need to know is, what will she do if he's convicted, or if there's a finding of fact that goes against him? That's what I have to ask her, but I haven't had a chance yet. It's going to take time for me to have that kind of conversation with Annie, she's so spiky. In the meantime, I think we need to give her a chance. Let's be clear, Annie Cooper hasn't done anything wrong at all here, as far as we know.' She knew that appealing to Vernon's sense of fairness was her best hope.

He was nodding now. 'All right then. If that's Kit's gut feeling about it, I'm prepared to give it a go. But we have to tie the agreement up tight, Sue. I don't want him alone with those kids for so much as two seconds.'

Sue Sullivan appeared to take the defeat with good grace. 'No problem, Vern. Leave that to me.' She got up and opened the door and ushered Mandy Bruce and the Coopers back into the room. This time the Coopers sat next to each other, to the right of their lawyer. Everyone waited for Sue Sullivan to start.

'We've had a discussion, Ms Bruce. My instructions are that the local authority is prepared to find some middle ground. Ms Goddard feels that it would be beneficial for the children if we went along with your suggestion.'

Annie Cooper shot Kit a look. It fell short of gratitude by quite a long way. In fact, it looked rather more like triumph.

'However,' Sue Sullivan continued, 'we are placing Mrs Cooper in a position of trust and we expect her to work with us and facilitate our role in working with the children and keeping them safe.'

'Of course.' Mandy Bruce had her eyes fixed on Sue Sullivan's face, no doubt hoping for a sticking point so that she could create an argument.

'We will need your clients' agreement to some stringent conditions, Ms Bruce. Firstly, Mr Cooper is to provide no personal or intimate care to the children. This is especially relevant for Lucy, of course. But we would want it applied to all three children. Secondly, he is to visit the home at agreed times during the day only and is not to be left alone with them at any point, for any length of time. Thirdly, Ms Goddard is to be given access to the children to undertake some direct work. She will replace Mrs Collins as the children's social worker for the time being. And finally, we will be spot-checking your clients' adherence to the agreement. We will expect access whenever we make an unannounced visit, day or night, and if we find any instances of non-compliance, we will review the situation and that may well mean our taking further action.'

'Oh, for God's sake,' Annie Cooper burst out. 'You mean that I have to put up with someone turning up at all hours to check whether I've left my husband alone with our children? That's a gross invasion of my privacy. Surely I have some rights in all this?'

Vernon cleared his throat in preparation for a speech, but

Kit got there before him. 'Look, Annie, the reality is that we're already cutting you some slack here. We need to safeguard the children, you need to have a family life. This is the best compromise we can come up with between those two things. The alternative is that we get a lot heavier and ask you to provide a list of other people to supervise contact. I'd have to interview all of them and they'd have to be checked to make sure they had no convictions. That all takes time, and while it was being done, contact would have to be supervised in a Child Services contact centre. We can go down that path if you like, but I very much doubt it's what you want. We are really trying to help you here.'

Matt Cooper put his hand on his wife's arm, settling her instantly in a way Kit recognised from her last encounter with them. 'We're prepared to agree,' he said. 'It's very disruptive for us, I hope you recognise that. But all we want is to get this experience over with, and if we can move things along, and I can at least see my children, then that's the most important thing and we'll do anything to make that happen. Please just tell us what we need to do next.'

Susan Sullivan had been writing on her papers while all this was going on. 'I've amended the agreement. It sets out all the points we've covered. We'll get a copy out to you later today. If you could get it signed and back to me today, contact can start straight away. Ms Goddard will begin her assessment and her visits and the outcome of all that will determine what action the department takes next. We are putting you on notice that we regard these allegations very seriously, and we will not hesitate to issue care proceedings if we consider it necessary.'

'And we will not hesitate to challenge them if you do.' Mandy Bruce rose to her pin-sharp dimensions, keen to make a swift exit now the business of the meeting was done. Matt Cooper stood up too and motioned for Annie to do the same. The three of them left without another word, Matt Cooper ushering his wife out with a hand on her back.

After they'd gone, Kit ran out for a quick fag, then she followed Vernon up to his office where she found the door standing open for her.

'What do you make of Mr Cooper then?' he asked as she dropped into the armchair opposite his desk.

'I thought he was arrogant when I met him first, all that name dropping about who he knows. But I guess I can't blame him for that – he was panicking, he's got connections, maybe it's human nature to try to use them. And he put his kids first in that legal meeting, he was willing to cooperate. It's all so positive, the Coopers, the family unit. It's hard to imagine, isn't it?'

'That he could be an abuser, you mean? You know it happens, though, Kit. You know it better than anyone, I would think.'

Kit nodded. He was right. But somehow, she still found it hard to get a grip on the possibility when it came to Matt Cooper. Every time she tried to see it, something snapped shut in her mind.

Vernon was watching her face. 'Abuse happens in middle-class families too, you know. We don't see a lot of it, but that's just because they've got more ability to cover it up.'

'Do you think he could have done it?'

'Look, Kit, I can see you're struggling. You're just like the rest of us. You know full well that children get sexually abused, in theory, but when you're faced with an actual situation, you can't quite believe it. There's always that little bit of you thinking it can't be true, because it's so bloody abnormal, it's so far away from how the rest of us think. Plus, we've got an added complication with this one.'

'Have we? What's that?' She sat forward, hoping for help.

'These girls were teenagers.'

'So?' She shrugged, but she knew exactly what he meant.

'Let's be honest here. Are you telling me you haven't wondered why they didn't just walk away the minute he started touching them? Or why they didn't tell someone?'

Kit wanted to deny it, but there was no point. Vernon was looking straight at her face and he would rumble her.

'All right,' she admitted. 'I have wondered. The girls were old enough, it's not like they were tiny kids. They could have stopped it, couldn't they?'

'But you're missing one crucial point there.'

'Am I?' She sat forward, genuinely lost now and hoping Vernon was about to come out with something to show her the way.

'For God's sake, don't they teach anything on those bleeding social-work degrees? Grooming, girl, grooming. That's the thing. Maybe he got close to them, got to know their problems, gave them things they wanted – it might have been attention or maybe it was more obvious than that, maybe he bought them stuff. That's the first bit.'

'OK, go on.'

Vernon got up from his desk and walked over to the window. He stared out into the car park and his voice was quiet. 'He starts testing it out, touching them. Acclimatising them. This is what you have to understand, because most people don't. By the time the actual abuse happens they are in the palm of his hand. They don't know which way is up, they're not even sure it is abuse. They can't tell anyone because they think it's their own fault. It's a perfect trap. People just don't realise the time and attention these guys will put into all this. It's the main thing in their lives, their driving force. They are willing to spend months or even years grooming kids if need be.'

Kit felt shivery and a bit sick. 'Inside the mind of a paedophile, eh?'

Vernon turned to face her, snapping back into the room. 'A hebephile, in this case, on the surface of it.'

'Which is what?'

Vernon tutted. 'It's someone with a sexual interest in children who are around the age of pubescence. With a paedophile it's pre-pubescence.'

'Why only "on the surface of it" then?'

'It's like a Venn diagram if you ask me.'

'You what?'

'Got your GCSE in maths, did you?'

'A* actually. At A level. I know what a Venn diagram is, Vern, but what's it got to do with Matt Cooper?'

He tutted again but she could see that he was dead pleased; Vernon loved a pet theory. He picked up a notebook and his pen and drew two overlapping circles.

'Right, so here you've got the ones who abuse pre-pubescent children. Right?'

She nodded.

'And here,' he said, tapping the other circle, 'you've got the ones who abuse pubescent children. I reckon that in the middle, you've got some who will abuse either. Now, what's the common ground with all of them?'

'Go on.'

'Power and control. It's not just that consent doesn't matter to them. That's what everyone thinks but it's totally missing the point. It's not in spite of the lack of consent, it's because of it. That's exactly what they like. You with me?'

She nodded.

'So, once you understand that, you realise that there may be more in the middle group than you think. Or maybe they move in and out, it's opportunistic – they have a preference but if that isn't available, then they'll take advantage of what is. Take someone like Savile. You could keep adding more circles.' He drew three more circles onto the diagram. 'In this one you've got children with disabilities, this one's adults in secure psychiatric care and here are nurses and so on who can't report him for fear of losing their job. Maybe even another one for dead bodies, we don't know. One of his victims was seventy-five, so you could add another there. It goes on and on. What was important to him was that he knew he could do it and they *had no say*.' He tapped his pen on the notebook in time with his last three words.

'OK, I've got it.'

'So what I'm getting at is this – yes, think about the age and gender of the child, but don't rely on that a hundred per cent. You can't be sure you're not dealing with one of these in the middle. They are unpredictable in who they will target and that makes them even more of a risk. It's only my theory, mind, but I'm definitely right. Now, are you any clearer on all that?'

'Yes, I suppose so.'

'OK, sod off then and let me get some work done.'

After lunch, Kit spent the afternoon getting some of her other work finished and, just before four thirty, she sent her case closures over to Vernon. Then she packed her bag and put her head into his office. He was at his computer, signing off the closures.

'Good work. Clearing the decks, are you?'

'That's it. All right if I go?'

'Yeah, go on. Got plans?'

'Kind of.' She raised her fingers in a half-wave and left. Tyler's comments about her flat had hit home. She had to start behaving like she was going to be staying, she realised, like home could be a permanent scenario, even though the feeling wasn't yet there to match the thought.

She drove to the nearest retail park, where she parked and then made for the home section of Asda. She picked up a few cushions, choosing the colours she liked, and then went down the ornament aisle, where she stood staring at the shelves. She picked up a black and white china cat and then a dog made out of a piece of wood with a metal head and legs. Were they nice or just tacky? She had no experience of ornaments. Christine had never bothered with them, probably because it would be one more thing to clean. And any trinkets that might have entered Huw and Menna's house would have been instantly buried under layers of newspapers, books, dog leads and children's toys. In the end, she chose a couple of tiny silver Buddhas, thinking that she couldn't go far wrong with something spiritual, and added them to her basket. On the way to the checkout, she spotted a silver and purple throw which she thought matched the cushions quite well, and she dropped that in, too, feeling a satisfying glow – she had got the hang of this home-accessorising thing. She thought maybe next time she'd look for some pictures, get something up to brighten the plain walls. If she just kept doing this, surely the flat would feel like hers eventually?

She picked up a ready meal in Tesco and, once home, dumped her shopping on the bed, and went into the kitchen, where she put her food in the microwave and got a beer out of the fridge. Before she sat down to eat, she noticed the light blinking on her answering machine. Menna making her twice-weekly call. She picked up the phone and called her back, using the other hand to fork up her food.

'How are you, lovely?'

'I'm good, thanks.'

'You what?'

Kit cleared her mouth of lasagne. 'I said I'm good. Sorry, eating my tea.'

She listened as Menna chattered on about Huw, and the dogs, and the weather out at Cliffside. It was mindless and comforting and, what with this and the successful shopping trip and the warm food, Kit was starting to feel more relaxed than she had for a couple of days.

'When's your next visit going to be then? Jess is pining. And I called in the café today – Alex was asking how you are.'

Kit was pleased by this news. As soon as she'd decided to end things with Jem, she'd become conscious of Alex in a way she hadn't been for all the years they'd worked together. She had no idea how he felt. Alex led a laid-back existence, in which the universe or the runes or the cards led the way. It left a lot of room for doubt where initiating relationships was concerned. It wasn't much of a business model either, and she worried about how he was managing the café without her there to order the stock and help do the books.

'I'll come soon, Men, I promise. I've got a big case on at work. Tricky one.'

'Well, I hope you do OK. I know you're up to it.'

'Hmm.' Dammit, Kit thought, trying to close her mind to the Cooper case. It had taken so little for the tendrils of doubt to start coiling themselves into her thoughts again.

'Are you worried about it?'

'No, I'm fine. Honestly. A bit confused about what I think about it, that's all.'

'They haven't given you something you're not ready for, have they? You know I warned you about them doing that.'

'No, no, they haven't,' Kit lied.

'Well, you know where we are if you need us.'

'I do. I'm going to get to bed now, I think.'

They said goodnight, and Kit went into the kitchen and burrowed in the back of her cleaning cupboard to find the tin within which she kept her supply of chocolate hidden from Tyler. She felt the occasion demanded a Starbar and she sat at the table awhile, chewing on the heavy toffee and the gritty peanut filling, then smoking a last cigarette. She did her Snapchat streaks, which she kept up without fail as a way of staying in touch with Jazz and Josie's kids. She was trying to clock up enough friends to set up an Insta account. It would make her look totally tragic if she started one with just her nieces and nephews. By the time she had finished the streaks, the light was fading in the room, but she was nowhere near ready for bed and couldn't think what to do with herself next. She teetered on the brink of feeling lonely, but pulled it back by thinking about Menna, whose calls came like clockwork, reminding her there was somewhere for her to go if being an adult turned out to be too hard. She didn't want to do it, but at least she had a fall back position.

She was trying to reassure herself. But she had to face up to the fact that she might lose her career over the Cooper case. The risk was that she might make a judgement about Matt Cooper, based on what she could see at the time, and end up being punished later, when things she couldn't possibly have known emerged and everyone thought they should have been obvious all along. She only had to miss the tiniest of clues, something one of the children said, something in their behaviour, and their father could get away with abusing them. Or she could overreact to the same thing, see a clue where there wasn't one, and set off a chain of events that would drag a loving family through care proceedings for no reason at all. Damned if you do and damned if you don't, she worried. It was the stuff of inquiry reports and tabloid headlines. But at least she only had so far to fall before she hit her safety net – she had Cliffside, Huw and Menna and the dogs, and her old job with Alex at the café. Menna might fuss and Huw would tut and roll his eyes, but they would be play-acting; neither of them would care in the slightest if she gave it all up and went back to them. She could afford to be brave, she realised. As her fear drained away, she felt instead an urge that was so strong it filled her chest and pressed against her ribcage, making her want to get to the truth no matter which way that might lie, and to do her best for the Cooper family.

CHAPTER 5

Kit left it until the next day before she called Mrs Cooper. She hoped that Annie would have simmered down overnight, but she knew this probably wasn't the case. Once at her desk, she found herself reluctant to get on with it. She busied herself with getting other cases up and running, but the Cooper children were on her mind almost constantly, and in the end she knew she couldn't put it off. She decided to make the call without an audience this time. She waited until lunchtime, when the office was more or less deserted, and then she dialled the Coopers' home number. The reception was predictably chilly but Annie agreed to a visit from Kit later that day, after the children got in from school.

Kit spent some time putting together some colouring exercises to do with the children and then packed them in her bag along with her assessment forms. On the way to Annie's, she stopped at a newsagent's and bought two packs of brightly coloured felt-tipped pens and a big pack of Maltesers.

Kit arrived at the Coopers' house just as Lucy was getting home from school. She waited in the car while Lucy was wheeled up to the house, and watched as Annie greeted her on the ramp at the door and gave her a big hug. Once the minibus had driven away, Kit got out of the car and started up the drive. Annie had seen her coming and was waiting for her at the door, her mouth tight.

'Hi, how are you?' Kit said, thinking it was as well to try and start with a friendly tone.

'What a ridiculous question. What response do you expect me to give to that?'

Kit didn't bother to answer. It was going to be as difficult as she had thought. In her new brave frame of mind, though, Kit was not worried. She followed Annie into the living room and sat on the sofa, waiting while Annie went to sort out the children. After a few minutes she came in, closing the living-room door behind her. She sat down opposite Kit, folded her arms and fixed her eyes on Kit's face. Chin up, spoiling for a fight.

'So, what are you here for exactly?'

'I need to complete an assessment for each of the children.'

'And what does that mean?'

'It's a document that gives us a picture of how they are doing. It covers a lot of different areas – their health, education, emotional well-being, and also how they are being parented.'

'The purpose of all that being what?'

'At the end of it, we will have a look at the information I collect, and it will help us to make a decision as to whether we proceed to case conference. Obviously, what is happening with the criminal case against your husband will be a factor as well.'

Annie laughed. 'I wouldn't worry about that too much if I were you. I think you'll soon find that the criminal case won't proceed very far at all.' She spoke quickly and with absolute certainty, but her eyes dipped away from Kit's face and she stared at the carpet. Her words hung there, emphatic but not followed through. It was odd, but Kit couldn't grasp what was going on.

'And what if that doesn't happen?' Kit pushed. Annie's eyes still did not come back to Kit's face.

'What do you mean?'

Annie acting stupid was totally unconvincing to Kit. She knew for sure that sharp, clear-thinking Annie would already have gone through all this a thousand times in her own mind. She'd probably worked out all the twists and turns and implications within minutes of hearing the allegations.

'So, what if it goes ahead and your husband is convicted? What if he goes to prison and then in a few years' time he's released? Or if the criminal case fails but there is a finding of fact against him in the civil court? What if you find you are married to a sex offender, Annie? What then?'

'There is no chance of any of that happening, I can assure you.'

'But what if it did happen? What would your attitude be then? I need to know what you'd do.'

Kit waited for Annie to bite, thinking that if she lost her

composure, she might let something slip. But instead Annie sighed. 'All right, I'll play along if that's what you want. Obviously either of those things would mean the end of our relationship. Is that what you want to hear? You're wasting your time and mine with these games, so let's just get on with your assessment and get it over with. What do you need to know?'

Kit hesitated but there was no way she was going to get past Annie's defences. 'All right then, what would help me most is if we could spend some time now getting the basic information down: the kids' health, school, your wider family and support network, all that. Obviously, we need a lot of information about Lucy and her needs. Then, if I could spend some time alone with the kids?'

'Doing what?' Annie's eyes were back on Kit's face, her usual confrontational stare resumed.

'I have some colouring exercises that we do with children, just to get them talking. Look, I'll show you.' Kit drew the sheets out of her bag. 'This one's a house. We get the kids to colour it in and then they write all the things that make them happy and sad at home. Then there's this – it's a fairy, she has a magic wand and there are three bubbles, and we get them to—'

'Colour it in and then write their three wishes in the bubbles? Yes, I think I can just about figure it out. It's not very sophisticated, is it?'

'It doesn't need to be. It's just a tool to help children relax and start talking. I've brought pens, and some sweets as well.' Kit got the packet of Maltesers out of her bag. 'Is that OK with you?'

'I suppose it will have to be. There's one thing you don't seem to have thought about, though.'

'What's that?'

'This is all very well for Cameron and Chloe. But colouring and bribing with chocolate isn't going to be possible with Lucy.'

'I realise that. Lucy is more complex, of course. What do you suggest is the best way to communicate with her?'

'You're the social worker. You tell me.'

'Does she have any communication at all? That's what I'm asking you. Only, I know Jean Collins has been involved, but she doesn't seem to have recorded any direct work with Lucy.'

'No, she wouldn't have. She never did any. I don't think she saw the need. It was obvious to her all of the children are very well cared for. She called in once a year to see how we were, that was that.'

'Right.' This was just what Kit had suspected. She tried again.

'So, how do you communicate with Lucy? And what about the school, how do they manage?'

'Lucy lets us know what she needs. She can make some sounds and movements and we are good at interpreting them. We don't need speech – we can anticipate nearly everything she needs before she needs it. The school have learnt from us and they're very happy with the way we do things.'

'OK then. Let's get the basic information completed, shall we?' Kit could see that Annie was enjoying herself and would keep the put-downs coming all afternoon if given the chance. Best to get on with it and work out what to do about Lucy later.

They spent half an hour going over the information that Kit needed. It went along easily enough, with Annie giving clipped, efficient answers, and Kit starting to relax a little. Annie told Kit that she had been a trainee accountant herself when she got pregnant with Lucy; she hadn't worked since, but she seemed proud of her involvement in the parents' support group. She became animated and forgot to be hostile when she was telling Kit about the battles she was fighting on behalf of several of the other mothers in the group.

Kit found herself agreeing with Annie as she listened. Annie clearly cared deeply about the families concerned, especially the children. Kit recognised the stories. She knew all about turnover of social workers, none of whom had ever read back in the file before they came to visit, so that the painful stories had to be retold again and again. She knew, too, about the endless communication problems and delays and the struggle to get the right support at the right time. She understood how all of that happened now, but she hadn't forgotten what it was like to be on the receiving end of it. It was clear to Kit that Annie had only tolerated social workers so that Lucy would have the extra support she was entitled to. Kit didn't imagine that Jean had presented much of an obstacle to that. But other parents weren't as tough and articulate as the Coopers, and

Annie's commitment to helping them impressed Kit no end. She could imagine that having Annie in your corner would make you feel pretty powerful.

Kit looked back at the assessment form again and saw the only section left to complete concerned Lucy's medical history and needs. She glanced up at Annie. 'I need to understand about Lucy's day-to-day care. What can you tell me about her routine?'

Annie started to describe Lucy's life, going through the timetable of hoisting, washing, dressing, incontinence care and feeding.

'Tell me about the tube feeding?' Kit asked, feeling her own ignorance keenly.

'She has a hole cut into her stomach, called a stoma. There's a tube in it.'

Kit's own stomach lurched at the thought. She hoped she had hidden her squeamishness but when she glanced up, Annie's eyes moved across her face and Kit knew it had been registered.

'The tube has a cap on the end of it. To stop the stomach contents leaking out. We inject her feed into the tube. It needs an eye keeping on it, you know? Sometimes it can get infected. It has to be kept clean. So, I'll explain that bit, shall I?'

Kit nodded, her head down, perspiration gathering on her brow.

'There's an external fixing disc around the stoma and another one on the inside. I lift the external one up and check the edges of the stoma closely to make sure it isn't red or inflamed. Then I have to wash around it. The tube has measurements on it, so we can make sure it's sitting in the right place. It can slip into the stomach otherwise. So, I check that it's right and then I push the tube into her stomach and rotate it right round so that the fixing plate on the inside won't be stuck in her stomach tissue. Then I pull the tube back up until I feel resistance and clamp it in place.'

'Thank you. That was very detailed. Shall we move on now?'

Annie nodded, letting slip a tiny smile.

'So, tell me about when Lucy was diagnosed?'

'Tell you what?' Kit could hear immediately that something had changed. Looking up, she saw that Annie's expression had taken on a rigidity.

'I need to know about Lucy's exact diagnosis, what caused her disabilities, and what her needs are now.'

'You can get all that from Jean Collins, surely? Lucy's disability and her care package are all fully set out in your records already, I'm sure.'

This was, of course, perfectly true. Kit searched for what she felt was lacking in the material that Jean Collins had put on the system.

'But how have you and your husband been affected? And how do Chloe and Cameron cope? I know it's not easy for kids to have a sibling as disabled as Lucy is.'

'They cope just fine. We make sure they do. You can ask them about that yourself.'

Kit wasn't inclined to let Annie off the hook. 'What about the other part of my question?'

'Which was?'

'How has it affected you and your husband? Tell me about Lucy's early years, when you found out that she was disabled, and what that was like?'

Annie's gaze fell to the floor and stayed there for a while. Kit wondered if she ought to say something else, but she wasn't sure what. Finally, Annie looked up.

'I don't see any need to go into that. This is about the children, as you said at the beginning. It's not about me and Matt, and that is really none of your business. As I said, anything else you need to know about Lucy's needs, you can get from Jean.' Her words were firm, but her voice was less certain than Kit had ever heard it. Kit was sure that she could see the hint of a shine in her eyes.

'I didn't mean to upset you.'

Annie looked away from Kit. 'I'm sorry. But it's just not something that I can talk about.'

Seeing the usually hostile Annie so upset rattled Kit, and she couldn't bring herself to persist. 'OK. Shall I see the kids now then?'

Annie gave Kit a small smile of relief and got up to leave the room, returning a few minutes later with Cameron. Once Annie had gone, Kit started to explain to Cameron why she was there, as best she could without saying anything about Matt. Cameron looked blank at the mention of Jean Collins' name, but he accepted Kit's explanation that she was his new social worker and was there to check how he was and whether he was happy. Then she explained the colouring to him. He settled down to it at once, munching his way through half the bag of chocolates. His three wishes were for more time on his Xbox, a holiday in Spain and a pet tarantula. In his house, Cameron wrote that he was happy with everything except that he wished he had a brother.

'Why's that then, Cam? The girls get on your nerves, do they?' Kit asked him.

'Chloe does. She takes my stuff all the time. She thinks she's special.'

'What about Lucy?'

He shrugged.

'I guess she takes up a lot of Mum and Dad's time, doesn't she?' Kit was remembering everything she had read about kids with disabled siblings, how easy it was for them to feel overlooked and less important.

'She can't help that.' Cameron's tone was fractious, and his face creased into a frown. 'Why are you smiling?' he demanded.

'You reminded me of your mum for a minute.'

'Oh.' He stared at her and took another Malteser.

'You don't mind Lucy then?' Kit tried to get Cameron talking. But he just shrugged again.

'What about Mum and Dad?'

'Yeah, they're fine. I miss my dad. I've got no one to play football with. He's away because Nanna's ill.'

Kit felt uncomfortable. She didn't like lying to the children, but she knew better than to risk Annie's ire by telling him any of the truth.

Cameron finished his drawing and Kit asked him to call Chloe, at which point her head immediately popped round the door. 'Can I do colouring now?'

'Yes, come on then.'

Kit could hear the sound of a small scuffle in the doorway as Cameron went out and Chloe replaced him. 'Ouch!' Cameron said. 'What are you pinching me for?'

'For saying I think I'm special.'

'You do.' Cameron's feet were heard running away up the stairs before Chloe could get hold of him again.

'And you're a liar anyway, you're always fibbing – Dad told me,' he shouted as he went.

Chloe made a move to go after him but Kit intervened. 'Come on then, Chlo,' she said. 'Let's do our drawing, shall we?'

Chloe accepted this surprisingly easily, her eye on the bag of chocolates. Kit went through the explanations about being the new social worker again and then she watched as Chloe carefully coloured the house and the fairy. She coloured the fairy itself in vivid pink and carefully wrote her wishes in the three bubbles. She chatted as she went along, telling Kit that the family were planning to move.

'Where to?'

'Llanfair.'

Kit made a mental note. She knew this was one of the most

desirable suburbs of the town. The Coopers were on the up and up.

'Daddy says we'll have a big garden and me and Cameron will go to a private school.'

'That will be lovely.'

'Yeah. Lucy will have her own wet room then. It's because Grandad's businesses are doing well, you see.'

'Really?'

'Yes. Daddy works for him. But it shouldn't mean that Daddy has to be available to Grandad twenty-four/seven.'

Kit suppressed another smile, hearing Annie's voice once again.

'I'm finished.' Chloe turned the pictures round for Kit to see.

'Those are fantastic, sweetie.' Chloe's three wishes were for a pony, a Disney holiday and high-heeled shoes. The happy things in her house were her mum, her cat and her roller-blades. The sad things were her nanna being ill, her mummy being sad and her hamster being dead.

Glancing at her watch, Kit saw it was nearly five. She'd finish up with Chloe, spend some time with Lucy, and then she'd get off home. Maybe she'd text Tyler and see if he was up for a curry. She thought she could start writing up her assessment on Monday; she'd need to visit again, but so far it was all straightforward stuff, no nasty surprises. She checked herself, wondering if she was a bit disappointed to find everything so happy at the Coopers'.

'Lovely, Chloe, thank you. I'd better see Lucy now.' Kit was starting to feel peckish. She thought about her curry again. Perhaps she'd get a biryani. And maybe she'd pick up some lagers on the way home.

'I'm not done.' Chloe picked up a pen and started adding some detail to her house.

'I really do need to see your sister, too. We can do some more drawing next time I come?'

'Oh, OK.' Chloe's face brightened. 'I didn't know you were coming back. Will you bring me more Maltesers? I can't finish my picture anyway. There's no room for Lucy in this house.'

'Draw one on the back for her.' Chloe was so cute, she couldn't help relenting. 'Look, I'll show you.'

She picked up a pen and drew a box on the side of the house. Chloe looked at it. 'Yes, that will do,' she said. Then she took the pen from Kit and drew two beds in the room.

'Who sleeps there then?' Kit pointed at the beds.

'Me and Lucy.'

'You sleep in Lucy's room?'

'We share. It's our room.'

'Why's that?' It hardly seemed necessary for the girls to share in the Coopers' decent-sized house.

'We like it.'

'Lucy doesn't sleep much, though, does she? Doesn't she keep you awake?'

'I don't mind. I don't like sleeping, it's boring. Sometimes when Lucy's carer falls asleep we put the telly on without any sound. I'm learning to read, so I put the subtitles on.' Chloe's grin told Kit that Annie wouldn't be happy if she knew about this.

'Oh, OK, that must be nice. What are you drawing now then?'

'This is the put-up bed, for someone to sleep on when they see to Lucy in the night.' Chloe started to draw a stick figure sitting on the bed.

'So is that Lucy's carer?' Kit asked, tidying up the pens as she did so.

'No, that's Daddy. It's his night.'

Kit stopped pushing pens into her bag. Her mind jumped back to Lucy's care plan. 'I thought Lucy had a carer with her every night?'

'No, I just told you, she doesn't. Daddy sleeps in with Lucy on Fridays. So he can have some time with her.'

Kit was determined not to read too much into it. But the hairs on her arms rose all the same. She didn't recall seeing anywhere in the care plans that the carers only slept in six nights per week. Did Jean Collins know? But then again, did it mean anything anyway?

'I need to pack up now. Can I have your drawing?'

'One minute. I have a bit to finish.' Chloe carried on scribbling for a few minutes more, while Kit continued to wonder about Matt's night with Lucy, trying to figure out the significance of it. She wondered what her mind would be like after thirty years in this job, if it was this suspicious already.

Chloe folded her drawing up and wrote on the outside, then she handed it to Kit. 'There you are.'

'It's lovely, Chlo, thank you.' Kit put it in her pocket and reached out to touch Chloe's mop of curls. Chloe immediately ducked away from Kit's hand.

'Sorry, Chloe, I didn't mean to make you jump.' Kit dropped her hand back to her side and gave Chloe a reassuring smile. 'Will you show me where to find Lucy now?'

'I'd better get Mum,' Chloe replied. She led the way to the kitchen and Annie came out, her face as grim as usual.

'I need to see Lucy now,' Kit told her. Annie moved past them in the hallway and silently crossed to an open door near the bottom of the stairs. Chloe tagged along behind Kit. As she drew near, Kit could hear a voice speaking quietly. Annie led her into the room, where Lucy was sitting in a chair, watching a music channel. A very overweight middle-aged woman was standing behind the chair, brushing Lucy's thick curly hair with gentle stokes and talking to her as she did so.

'Is that all right for you, darling?'

Lucy seemed to shift forward a little.

'That's good. Let me know if it's uncomfortable.' The woman went on pulling the brush though Lucy's hair, looking up with a start when she noticed Kit and Annie in the doorway.

Glancing around the room, Kit could see that the walls were covered with posters: 1D, Five Seconds of Summer. Annie, probably, doing her research, making sure the room looked just right for a teenage girl. Lucy was dressed in navy leggings and a long blue T-shirt, and a pair of blue Converse lay near her chair. In fact, she was dressed very much like Kit was. This conjured up an immediate picture of Annie in Topshop, not choosing what she liked, but figuring out what Lucy would have chosen if she could.

'This is Fay,' Chloe said, indicating the woman.

'Hello, Fay. I'm Kit. I'm Lucy's social worker.'

'And mine.' Chloe was put out.

'Yes, of course, I'm yours and Cameron's, too. You've helped me a lot, Chlo. I'd better speak to Lucy on her own now, though.'

Chloe sighed but she left the room. Annie and Fay both ignored the hint and stayed just inside the door. Kit let it ride for a minute, not wanting Lucy to be unnerved by being left alone with her too soon. She pulled a chair out of the corner and put it near to Lucy.

'Hi, Lucy. I'm Kit. I'm your new social worker.'

Lucy continued to stare at the TV. Kit searched about for something to say.

'Do you like Taylor Swift?'

Lucy didn't react. Kit stood up and turned to face Annie and Fay, who had stayed at the back of the room. 'Does Lucy use a communication board or an iPad or anything like that?' Kit had pulled her old lecture notes out from under the bed the night before and had read up on anything she thought might help her to communicate with Lucy.

'No, sorry.' Annie's reply came at once, but Fay looked as if she might have answered if she'd had the chance. Kit looked directly at her.

'How do you manage, Fay? It must be hard with all her personal care and so on.'

'Fay knows Lucy very well. She understands her needs.' Annie interjected again. Fay appeared to be incapable of independent speech. Kit decided to give it up and chuck them both out. 'OK, well, thanks. I'd better speak to Lucy alone now. I'll give you a shout when I'm done.'

She moved towards the door and, once they had gone, she shut it firmly behind them, and sat back down. She wasn't going to give up, but Lucy's eyes were still fixed on the TV. Kit looked down at Lucy's hands, wanting to touch her to get her attention. She saw that Lucy's left elbow, which was nearest to her, sat at an odd angle. Kit had read up enough to know that this was due to the contractions caused by the cerebral palsy. She reached out gently, not wanting to hurt Lucy, and touched her fingers lightly on the back of her left hand, which she saw was also clenched into a tight ball. Lucy turned her head then, and her perfect blue eyes scanned Kit's face.

'Hello, honey. I'm here to see if everything is OK with you. Can I talk to you for a while?'

Lucy made a noise, deep in her throat, but Kit couldn't recognise whether it was a yes or a no. 'Does that mean it's OK for me to talk to you, Lucy?' Lucy jerked her body forward a little. It was the same movement that Lucy had made in response to Fay. Kit remembered from her reading the night before that some children found it easier to use their bodies to communicate. Maybe she was making a connection with Lucy now.

'Your room is lovely. Did your mum get the posters for you?'

Lucy continued to look at Kit for a few seconds longer. Then she returned her gaze to the TV. A tiny crease played around the side of her mouth. Having been ignored by countless teenagers, Kit suddenly found herself on home ground.

'Ah, OK, cheeky. You just don't feel like answering stupid questions, is that it?'

The crease popped up again but Lucy's head didn't turn.

'I don't blame you. It was a rubbish question, I'm not doing very well, am I? It's quite hard, though, because I don't know the best way to speak to you, and I need to find a way to do it, because it's my job to make sure that you and Cam and Chloe are OK.'

Lucy didn't move or turn her head, but the near-smile had dropped away. Something in Kit's words had caught her attention, and she was waiting to see what would come next. Kit had to get it right. There was silence from the hallway, no one seemed to be about. She leant forward and touched Lucy's hand again.

'Lucy, it's my job to help you,' she whispered. 'I can see that you can answer me, I just need to ask you the right questions. If anything is worrying you, I can help sort it out. I promise.' Kit paused for a while, trying to read the situation and give Lucy a chance to give her a sign if she could. Then Kit stood up and returned her voice to normal. 'Bye, sweetie. I'll come back and see you again soon, OK?'

From outside Lucy's room came the sound of footsteps. Kit

crossed the room and went out into the hallway. She saw that Chloe and Cameron were in the living room, both intent upon their iPads. Had one of them been listening, and could they have heard what she said to Lucy? In the kitchen, Kit found Annie standing with her back to the sink and her arms crossed in front of her. Fay sat at the table, a coffee mug in her hand.

'I'm finished for today. I'll give you a ring to arrange my next visit.'

'And what did you discover about my children? Anything you feel I should know?'

'Chloe and Cameron seem like great kids. And it's nice that Chloe and Lucy are so close. Chloe told me they share a room.'

'Chloe's got her own room so you needn't start thinking they're not provided for. She's only been sleeping in with Lucy since just before Christmas. Chloe got a little bit nervous about Santa getting into her room and she just stayed with Lucy after that. Just a phase, I expect. How did you get on with Lucy?'

'I didn't really manage to communicate with her, I'm afraid.'

'That doesn't surprise me. You can't really expect to just come along and start chatting to someone as disabled as Lucy. As I said, you'd have to put in the time to get to know her and I doubt you'd get much response even then. Why should she talk to you anyway? She doesn't know you from Adam.'

Annie was back to normal, but it was a fair point, Kit had to admit it. 'I can see that. I do need to keep trying, though. I need her views for the assessment. Have you got any suggestions, Annie?'

'Sorry, no, I haven't,' Annie said. 'That's something you're going to have to work out for yourself. And please call me Mrs Cooper.' She picked up a mug from the worktop and took a sip of coffee, but not in time to hide her smile.

'Right, I'll get going then.'

'Would you mind seeing yourself out?'

Kit nodded and made for the front door, as pleased to be going as Annie clearly was to see the back of her, yet kicking herself for slipping up over Annie's name again. She hadn't meant to annoy her, but the friendly tone wasn't working. She'd have to make an effort to get that right from now on.

Once in the car, Kit got her phone out, ready to text Tyler and arrange for him to come over. But inviting Tyler over was bound to lead to another bout of him trying to tell her something that she didn't want to hear. And actually, she was feeling lost with the Cooper case and it would be good to talk it over with someone. She texted Ricky instead and, finding that he had arranged to meet Maisie for a drink in town later on, she agreed to meet them there. Then she drove home, where she fell into a shallow sleep on the sofa until it was time to leave. In her dreams, she was in that teenage bedroom again, the TV on low. She saw Lucy speaking, but she couldn't hear what she was saying.

CHAPTER 6

Ricky and Maisie were already settled at a table in the corner when Kit arrived. The bar had been a night shelter until the previous year, but it had become an embarrassment: sitting right in the centre of Sandbeach's latest regeneration attempt, spilling the homeless out onto the street whenever there was a fight inside, and generally spoiling the outlook. The shelter had been relocated to the grim ghetto of Welfare Services behind the police station, and the building had been transformed into the kind of place that had unisex toilets and served food covered in half a pound of avocado, smashed. Ricky loved it, otherwise Kit wouldn't have set foot in there.

Ricky had already ordered Kit a bottle of Beck's and she downed half of it immediately.

'It didn't go too well then?' As usual, Maisie was keen to hear the bad news.

'I wouldn't say that. It was difficult but I think I'm getting somewhere with Lucy.' Kit glanced around, conscious that anyone might be listening. The place was deserted.

'Well done. Much good may it do you. It's one of those cases, isn't it?' Maisie took an uncharacteristically delicate sip of her pint, waiting for someone to press her for her expertise.

'What do you mean?' Ricky was completely lost.

'There's not likely to be a successful prosecution, that's the reality. It's not going to be proven beyond reasonable doubt, is it? But the standard of proof we work to is different. It's civil law, so it's lower. So say this fella gets off with no criminal conviction, because the evidence isn't there for beyond reasonable doubt. He thinks he's home free. But could be enough evidence on the balance of probabilities. It's a mess.' Maisie frowned with concentration as she rolled a cigarette, which she then put into her tobacco tin, ready for when she got outside.

'Is that right? Really?' Ricky looked up from ripping open a bag of dry-roast peanuts.

Kit held out her hand for some nuts. 'I guess that's the top and bottom of it, yes. The children seem fine. The truth is that the allegations against Matt Cooper are the only worry. We'd be nowhere near this family otherwise. Somehow, I'm meant to work out whether those allegations might be true, and whether we can justify putting the whole family through a court case. A bit of me thinks we've got a bloody cheek to be interfering at all. Maybe he should be innocent until proved guilty.'

Maisie was unearthing her velvet tie-neck money pouch. 'Same again?'

'Yeah, go on.'

Maisie set off for the bar. Kit threw a few more nuts into her mouth. She realised she hadn't eaten for hours.

'This case is really getting to you, isn't it?'

Kit realised with a shock that Ricky was right. 'Yeah, it is. I'm being asked to guess whether something has happened or might happen. And I have no way of knowing. No way whatsoever.'

'Well, that's true. If something is going on, he's certainly not going to tell you; his wife probably doesn't know herself or she'd have left him; and he knows how to make sure the kids don't tell, otherwise they'd have told and he'd have been caught already.'

'You're not making me feel any better.'

'I suppose what I'm saying is, it's out of your control. You can do your best, but that's it. So why have you been letting it get to you so much?'

Maisie arrived back with the drinks and a plate of bar snacks. 'Bruschetta?'

It looked like chunks of rubble covered in slime. 'No, thanks. The thing is,' Kit continued, focussing on Ricky and hoping that Maisie would be distracted by the food, 'there's all these threats about me losing my job. It seems like Mr Cooper's father is practically royalty in Sandbeach. He's gunning for me, Cole's not standing up to him, everyone's panicking, even Vernon. A lovely family gets wrecked for no reason, or kids could get hurt. That's the choice and it's down to me.'

'That's what the job's all about, isn't it?' Maisie had managed to clear her mouth.

'Guesswork, you mean?'

Ricky laughed. 'Forget about the grandfather and Cole and all the fuss. Spend some time with the kids and see where that leads you. They're not going to come straight out with it, are they? Look at indirect stuff.'

'You mean, like anxiety, bed-wetting, all that?'

'Yes, but more than that – clues and hints maybe. Sometimes kids want you to know, but they can't say it, so they lay a trail and hope you'll follow it. They think they'll get into trouble for telling, I suppose. So they end up a bit ambivalent about it – putting a clue forward then panicking and backing off. They need an adult to pick up on it.'

Kit shook her head. 'That's OK usually, but in this case, it's not going to happen. Lucy can't do any of that. I tried to let her know I'd help if there is anything wrong, and I probably risked getting sacked in the process. But she can't just respond, Ricky. It's so hard for her to tell me anything.'

'Just keep talking to them, Kit. If something's not right, I reckon you'll pick it up, then you'll just keep nagging at it like a total pain in the arse, the same way you do about everything.'

She recognised herself in the description and felt better than she had done for a few days, as if she'd clicked back into being the real Kit, the one who could always get to the bottom of stuff. 'Thanks, Ricky. That does help.'

'No worries. Right, I'm guessing from your face you're not sold on the food. What about some chips?'

The three of them finished their drinks and headed for the chip shop where they bought cheesy chips and gravy and picked up some cans as well. The sun was still warm so they got their chips wrapped to keep them hot and walked up the footpath to the side of the Bryn, passing the estates on the way up and then dipping into the forest, finally emerging into sunlight again at the break in the trees just below the summit of the hill.

They sat on the grass and, after a few minutes of regaining their breath, and a puff of Ventolin for Maisie, unwrapped their chips and opened their cans of lager. The whole of the bay was visible in front of them, sweeping out to both sides of the town as far as the two curving headlands that hugged the sea on either side. In the shimmering gap between the arms of land, a few boats bobbed about, the finishing touches in a scene too picture-book perfect to seem real. In the distance wisps of smoke rose from the beach, as people lit makeshift barbecues and settled in for the evening. Others could be seen pitching tents for all-nighters. Neither were allowed, but nobody cared about that; it was the town's beach. Everyone felt it belonged to them.

'Shame about the crap down there.' Maisie waved her fag in the direction of the estates. 'Shocking. They should tear them down.'

'I grew up on the Coed actually.' Kit bit back her irritation. She should be used to this.

'Didn't mean to offend you, I'm sure. Nothing personal. But you can't deny it's an eyesore.'

Kit didn't reply, because she couldn't be bothered. They sat in silence a while longer and eventually Maisie moved out of the sun and lay back on the grass behind them. She put her head on her folded cardigan. After a few minutes, she started to snore quietly.

'I didn't know you grew up on the Coed,' Ricky said.

This was the downside of friends as far as Kit was concerned. You had to tell them stuff about yourself. She knew all about Ricky's childhood in Harare and his parents' ambition for him to become an architect, a lawyer or an accountant. She admired his resolve to do what he wanted, even if she thought he had been naive to jump at the offer of getting some post-qualifying experience in the UK. She'd got the gist of him. Now he was wanting to know more about her.

'Yeah, well, I was in and out of care. We all were. But I got a foster placement after a bit, two retired teachers, a big house out west at Cliffside. The others weren't so lucky. They stayed in Redbridge House.' She hoped that would be enough for now. She looked about for a means to change the subject but Maisie was still snoozing.

'What was happening with your parents?'

'They'd split up, so it was just my mother. She wasn't great, she drank and that. I didn't see much of my dad – still don't now.'

'Why's that?'

He really was not going to give up. It was time for her usual strategy. If she gave Ricky a good chunk of the misery memoir, that would be enough for him to chew on and he wouldn't see any further than that. He wouldn't have to know about the real tragedy. Not yet.

'My mother didn't have a great start in life. Her dad died when she was quite young, her mum was in and out of psychiatric hospital. She more or less brought herself up. But in the end, she got lucky, with my dad. He was the best-looking boy in the school. She was pregnant at sixteen and had five by the time she was twenty-three.' The five had slipped out. She was usually more careful than that.

'Bloody hell,' Ricky said. 'Five kids in seven years. Is that even physically possible?'

'Just about. And I've got a twin brother.'

'Sounds like a nightmare.'

'I don't think it was, not at the start anyway. I think my mother felt special for a while. My dad's family had the Italian café in town. He ran it for them.'

'Posh Welsh, eh?'

'Not exactly, but they did all right.'

'So how did you end up in care?' Ricky turned to face her, crossing his legs and settling in for the long story.

'I think my dad got a bit fed up with having a milk bottle cracked over his head every time he came in late from the pub. He met someone else. They sold the café, they run a wine bar up the coast a bit now.' She thought of Marilyn, with her bleach-blonde hair and her low-cut tops. She could see why Marilyn had seemed a better prospect than Christine, but it had quickly become obvious she wasn't up for any parenting.

Gino might as well have gone to the other side of the world. He sent money, turned up to see them for Christmases and birthdays. That was about it.

'So, then you ended up living on the estate?'

'Yeah. My grandparents threw us out of the house they'd bought for my parents, so the council put us there. The Coed was new then. It had won awards and everything. It's all right actually, if you look at it properly.' She looked down at the square white houses of the estate, all the same as each other. The houses were a good size, and solid. The streets were wide and there were playgrounds and grassy areas dotted around. It wasn't far from town or the schools and shops. It definitely wasn't the design that was at fault. But the estate was tatty and badly maintained now, and the residents were losing the battle against vandalism and crime. The look of the place didn't fit with Sandbeach's civic ambitions towards smart coastal affluence either, and the fact it could be seen from every single part of the town was a niggling thorn in the side of the council.

'I guess so. So what happened to your mum?'

'She didn't cope. She went downhill pretty quick, we all got taken off her. She still lives down there. So do my two sisters – they ended up moving back after they left care. They've got kids. They're doing OK. That's about it.' She started to stretch her legs out, ready to stand up, indicating that she had drawn a line.

'That's four.' Maisie had sat up on the grass behind them.

'I thought you were asleep.'

'I was meditating. Four. You, your twin, two sisters. You said there were five.'

Now she was screwed, because this was the one thing she couldn't manage to lie about. Bloody Maisie.

'Yeah. I had another brother. He died.'

'Oh Kit, I'm sorry.' Ricky stopped packing their chip papers into his rucksack and looked up at her, his eyes wide with concern. 'How did it happen?'

'Long story. Shall we make a move now? How's it going with Meg, by the way?'

Inviting Ricky to talk about his new girlfriend was a sure-fire way of diverting him. He chatted happily all the way back down the hill. Kit listened with real interest. She liked Meg, a self-assured paramedic Ricky had met on a difficult call involving a suicidal teenager. Kit hoped that Ricky would stick with her, not least because that would extend the membership of her own friendship group by one. Maisie walked beside them in silence; being in the present, Kit assumed. When they got to the bottom of the hill, they stopped to say goodbye, then Maisie and Kit continued towards Maisie's turn-off.

'Was your brother Danny Goddard?' Maisie couldn't contain herself any longer.

'How did you know that?'

'I worked it out. It wasn't hard. It was in the papers when he died, wasn't it? About the right age, grew up on the Coed, care leaver, same surname. All the clues.'

'Yes, that was him.'

'Serious-case review said Child Services weren't at fault, if I remember correctly. No one knew why he'd done it?'

'Spot on.' Kit prayed Maisie wouldn't push for more details. If she remembered the story at all, surely she must recall Danny had hanged himself in the park, that he'd been found alive by a man walking his dog but had died in the ambulance? A few seconds earlier and he might have lived. Kit still couldn't think, let alone talk, about it. She upped her pace. The end of Maisie's street was only yards away.

'I expect you've got your own views about why he did it?' Maisie persisted.

'Not really. Well, here we are. See you tomorrow then.' She didn't wait for Maisie's reply.

Once in her flat, Kit put the TV on and flopped on the sofa but couldn't settle. Familiar feelings were washing over her, and she knew she wouldn't sleep, in spite of the lager. Her mind couldn't keep away from Maisie's question about why Danny had killed himself. Her response, that she didn't really know, was partly true. She certainly hadn't bought into the story constructed by everyone at the time; the one where Danny was doing well, getting his life together, had no reason to do it.

She knew it had been more complicated than that. She'd known things weren't right with him. But the worst thing was that he'd tried to tell her about it. Her thoughts slid out of control and she found herself replaying the scene, as she had done over and over. Danny turning up at the café where she was waitressing, sleepy after the long bus ride out to Cliffside, looking for a free breakfast to kill his hangover. Alex would never charge him for food, or any of Kit's family for that matter. He had sent her on her break as soon as Danny arrived, giving them the chance to sit together. She hadn't seen him in a few weeks and he'd looked rough. Danny had never really bothered with drugs much, but she'd guessed he'd been on one of his long drinking binges. He did that a few times each year, keeping going until he was really ill, getting into fights and spending nights in the cells. If he didn't land up in prison, he'd go on and on until one day he would just decide to stop. Then he'd dump the latest damaged and besotted female, hit the gym hard, and not touch another drink until something or other triggered the next bout. She didn't know what the triggers were, and he'd never volunteered a reason. She kept away from him during those times, preferring not to know what was going on, waiting for him to get back in control of himself again. Sooner or later he'd turn up to see whether whatever she was doing met with his approval.

When she'd seen him in the café that morning, she'd assumed it was one of these check-in visits, and she'd been pleased at the idea he'd got himself sober in time for her GCSE results. She'd watched him devour his double bacon and eggs, white bread and butter and a large glass of Coke. Alex had brought over a brownie, too, placing it in front of Danny with one hand and giving Kit's shoulder a reassuring squeeze with the other. He'd seen both Tyler and Danny in various states enough times to know when something really wasn't right.

'What?' Danny had caught Kit and Alex exchanging concerned glances.

'You OK? You look awful.'

'Thanks very much. No, I'm all right. Just hungry and a bit wrecked, that's all. What's happening with you?'

She'd told him that she was going to get her exam results in a couple of days and that she was excited because she knew she'd done well, rambling on about which A levels she was going to take and what she had finally decided she wanted to do after that.

'A social worker? What the fuck?'

Her heart had sunk. She had been half expecting this, but it had needled her at the same time. 'Why not?'

She couldn't find a way to explain, of course. Not without saying outright that she'd been the lucky one and that, although the social workers had been pretty crap for most of the time, Carmel had been the exception. Even at thirteen, Kit had admired Carmel's attitude. To the others, the only answer was to try to keep the five Goddard kids alive until they were old enough to stop being the department's responsibility, at which point they could all be dispersed into prison or psychiatric care or homelessness, and everyone in Child Services could breathe a sigh of relief. The five of them had marked time, moving aimlessly around the system together, not for their own sakes but because no one had the time or patience to untangle which of them needed what and make a proper plan. Until Carmel arrived, and immediately became determined to get Kit out of residential care and into a foster placement, a battle which she had won in the end, leaving Kit to contend with an uneasy combination of gratitude and survivor guilt.

'I'm sorry.' Danny's apology had brought her back into the room. He'd known that he'd hurt her. 'Look, you go ahead if that's what you want. I can't get my head round it, that's all. Social workers never did us much good, as far as I can see.'

'They couldn't do much about Christine, though, could they?'

'I don't mean that.' He had stopped then, and looked her in the eye, waiting, refusing to speak until she asked the question.

'What do you mean?'

'It wasn't just Christine. That wasn't the only thing that was wrong. That was the easy bit. She's a waster, we all know that. We survived, didn't we? But there was other stuff. No one does anything about that. No fucker does anything. That's why I keep ending up like this. Get straight, then it's going around in my head all the time and I can't stand it and I screw it up again. I'm sick of it.'

His voice had been shaking and Kit still remembered the sight of his hands trembling as he drained the rest of his Coke. He wasn't just hungover, she had realised, he was still drunk. No wonder he wasn't making much sense. She didn't know exactly what he was talking about, but, at the same time, she had known, somehow, that she was about to get out of her depth. And she had wavered inside, wanting to help him but scared to try. The truth was that she had ducked it. And why? Because it didn't work that way round. She didn't help Danny; he was supposed to help her.

'I guess they did their best.'

He'd looked up at her again then, and he'd seen her refusal to go on with it. 'Yeah, well, for you maybe. You're doing good.' He'd got up and picked up his jacket and slung it across his shoulder. 'I've got to go see Tyler, make sure he's OK. Call me when you get your results?'

'Yeah. I will.'

'Big Mac after, if you've done well, all right? See you.'

He'd smiled at her and left. She'd got on with her work, promising herself that she'd text him later, arrange to see him, give him another chance to explain what he'd meant. But that night she'd been tired, and she'd let it go, and the next night the same. And on the Wednesday morning, she'd woken to a call from Tyler who'd heard around the estate that Danny had been taken to hospital in an ambulance.

The brutality of what he'd done shocked Kit to the core. She couldn't understand him leaving her and Tyler alone. He'd known that they both needed him, and he'd never once let them down before.

She got up from the sofa, got herself a can from the fridge, took it to bed with her, knowing that this was going to be one of those nights when she would lie awake until dawn, trying to blot out the smile Danny had given her when he left that day. The smile that said he had tried to disrupt the way things worked and knew she couldn't cope with it, so he was putting it all back the way it had always been.

CHAPTER 7

On Friday afternoon, Kit pulled up outside the huge iron gates of Matt Cooper's parents' house. She wondered what it might have been like for him to be living there for the last ten days. It would have been about nine days too many for her to put up with either of her parents. She saw an entry-phone on the gatepost. She pulled down the car window and pressed the button. After a few seconds, Matt Cooper's voice came through the intercom.

'Hi, Kit, I'll buzz you in,' he said, before she could speak. Kit found this disconcerting, partly because it presumably meant that he could see her somehow, but mainly because of his use of her first name. She wondered whether his strategy was going to be to try and charm her. Or was she being hyper-sensitive? Maybe he was just going to be pleasant and helpful? She steeled herself, just in case. Outright aggression was one thing, she knew where she was with that. But parents being reasonable – how did you know whether to trust it? As she parked the car on the wide sweep of driveway and got out and crunched across the gravel, she thought about an essay she'd written on false compliance during her course. The parent who appeared to be so cooperative with professionals that their actual non-compliance got overlooked. A carefully created facade of pleasantness, politeness and respect. She knew it held a huge danger, and that professionals often got it wrong, but when she tried to remember what she'd been taught to do about it, nothing much came to mind. Her confidence of a few days before had slipped away, and she felt intimidated and uncertain now, too young and too inexperienced to be able to handle this man and his outspoken, confident family.

Matt Cooper opened the door before she put her hand to the brass knocker. 'Kit, hello, please come in.'

His manner was relaxed. She might have been popping in for afternoon tea. He led her through to a large sitting room. The wall opposite the door was made entirely of glass and gave a panoramic view of the bay. Matt Cooper indicated that Kit should cross the room to two armchairs that were placed in front of the window. As she did so, she found herself transfixed, and could not resist stopping for a few seconds before she sat down. The May sunshine was pouring down onto the sea and the reflection was so bright that it hurt her eyes, which started to water slightly. The air in the room was bitingly fresh. Looking up, she could see that a few of the upper windowpanes were open, letting in the sound of the waves as they broke on the sand, together with the fresh scent of seaweed. Kit had a sudden longing to be back at the Cliffside Café, working for Alex. Why hadn't she just stuck to that? No responsibilities except getting the orders right and totting up the figures now and again. Long swims and beers after work every day. Some nights she'd stayed on the beach until the early hours, content just to lie curled up by the fire she'd built in the dunes, listening to the Atlantic as it crashed onto the shore, hypnotised and soothed into a doze by the sound. Instead, here she was, with the job of trying to figure out whether an apparently respectable father was, in fact, a grotesque psychopath who posed a serious risk to children. Kit thought she must need her head read.

'It's superb, isn't it?' Matt Cooper was offering her the armchair again. It was placed so that it faced the window but was slightly angled towards the other armchair, where he was now settling himself. She tore herself away from the view and sat down.

'Can I interest you in a cup of tea or coffee?'

'No, thank you.' Kit was longing for a coffee, and maybe he was just being polite, but she was wary of being manoeuvred into the role of visiting friend.

'Do you mind if I have one?' Matt Cooper asked.

'No, of course, go ahead.'

He jumped up again and left the room, giving Kit an opportunity to have a good look around. The Coopers were obviously loaded. The room was a bit old-fashioned, though. It had a heavily patterned carpet, and a huge sideboard loaded with framed photos. There were numerous knick-knacks on the mantelpiece, which topped an ugly red stone fireplace at the far end of the room. But the sheer size of the house, and its perfect location right above the beach, told Kit that it must have cost a fortune. The Coopers were proud of it, too, Kit thought, looking at the enormous television. She noticed it was located way too high up on the wall, above the fireplace. You would have to strain your neck to look at it, which told her the Coopers were people who loved showing off more than they actually loved TV. One decent series of *I'm a Celebrity* and your neck would be knackered for weeks.

'It's a great TV. My father loves his technology.' Matt Cooper appeared to the side of her and settled himself back in the chair. He put his mug down on a small table. He was wearing grey shorts, a shapeless navy-blue T-shirt and tatty trainers, as if he had just come back from a run or a game of tennis. He leant back, stretching his legs out in front of him and crossing them at the calf. 'So, what can I help you with?' He was smiling at her, and she started to relax. It was clearly going to be nothing like the visit to Annie.

'Would it be helpful if I started by running through the purpose of the investigation and the assessments?'

'Well, as I understand it, the investigation is the first bit. The idea is to see whether the children are at risk and need safeguarding, in light of these allegations against me. Then that feeds into the assessment, which is to identify the children's wider needs and to look at how well Annie and I can meet those needs. Or whether we need any outside help or monitoring. Would that be right?'

Kit searched for something to criticise in this explanation but failed to find it. Surely he'd googled that before she got here? It sounded as if it had come straight out of the procedure manual. But she could hardly blame him for being well prepared; his family was at stake, after all. 'Yes, that's right. And I need to get your perspective as part of that. The focus is very much on the children's needs and how you and Annie meet those needs. Both long-term, and in the context of the current police investigation.'

'So, more or less as I said then.' He was smiling, but there was a hint of banter in his tone.

She smiled back at him. 'Yes, I suppose so. I need to ask you quite a lot of questions, and I will record your answers and then put them together with all the other information that I've gathered. I'll analyse the material at the end and that will help to inform the way forward and how the cases are managed.'

Matt Cooper made a pained noise, just a small suck of air between his lips. Kit looked up from her papers.

'Sorry, Kit. I appreciate you have a job to do. It's just very hard to hear my children referred to as "cases".'

Kit hated hearing that too, it went right through her. She put her pen and her assessment form down on her lap and looked Matt Cooper in the eye. 'Mr Cooper,' she started.

'Call me Matt, please.'

'Matt. I'm sorry for that remark. I don't usually use the term and, actually, I don't like it myself. It was a slip of the tongue. I don't think of Lucy, Cameron and Chloe in that way at all. I realise this is a very painful situation for all of you and I am not here to make it any worse if I can help it. But you are right, I do have a job to do. I hope we can work together on this and cooperate in the interests of the children. But it has to be done, either way. That's the bottom line.'

'Sure, that's all I want as well.' Matt was smiling again, but she noticed the fingers of his left hand were working at a loose thread on the hem of his T-shirt. He was upset, and she didn't blame him. But she had no choice but to press on. She picked up her pen and her papers and prepared to write down what he said.

It was straightforward enough. She'd got all the material about education and daily routines from Annie. Health and care needs were only complicated for Lucy, and Kit had got most of that from Annie, too. She had managed to get Matt to add some more details, but it was all superficial stuff. None of it was giving her an inkling about the kind of person that Matt Cooper really was. She recalled Annie's reaction to being asked about Lucy's early life and it occurred to her that this might be a means to get the measure of her husband, too.

'It would help me to have your perspective on Lucy's disability. I think that was an area that your wife found it quite difficult to talk about.'

Matt nodded. 'She would have, yes. Annie is a very private person. She's found this whole experience deeply upsetting – we all have, of course. But having to talk to people like you and have our family business trawled through . . . well, for Annie, that's almost the worst part of it.'

'Could you help me with that?'

'Yeah, sure, what can I tell you?'

'I gather from your wife that Lucy's disability was totally unexpected?'

'Yes, that's right. Annie had a normal pregnancy as far as we both knew. It was our first child, we were very excited and really we had no idea what to expect, for the birth or anything after that. You know what it's like, with the first one?' He was smiling at her, eyebrows raised in question. She looked back down at her papers and carried on writing. She wasn't getting into that discussion if she could help it.

'Do you have any children?' He wasn't going to give up; she was going to have to answer him.

'No, I don't.'

'Any plans?'

The question was so direct and personal that Kit looked up at him in surprise.

'I'm sorry, Kit, I've shocked you. That was a bit much, I suppose.' He leant forward in his chair, and she was surprised to see a slight flush to his face. He'd overstepped the mark, but at least he had the good grace to realise it. 'It's just that it's quite difficult to be asked all these questions by someone you know nothing about. It feels a bit robotic, you know? Like I could just tick some boxes and feed my answers into a machine and it could collate the data and come out with pretty much the same conclusions as you probably will. I don't mean to be rude, Kit, I understand what you are doing here. But it was a very difficult time when Lucy was young, and I suppose I've shut it down.'

'That's understandable. You just have to get on with it, I suppose. You probably didn't have much time to think about yourself.' She felt bad for him, now that his arrogance was gone and she could see him struggling.

'You are so right. Not everyone can see that. I didn't have much time for brooding over what happened, and maybe that was a good thing in some ways, but it's not easy to be asked to open it all up by a complete stranger years later.'

Kit found herself answering him before she had even had a chance to think about it. 'It's OK. I know it must be painful to talk about it. I suppose you all seem so fine with Lucy's disability that I didn't really think about that question as much as I should have. I know what you're saying about the assessment, and if it helps you, I don't mind you knowing that I don't have any children. But I do have lots of relevant experience and I know a lot about what makes kids tick.' She hoped he wouldn't ask what her relevant experience was. Next thing, she'd find herself divulging her childhood traumas to Matt Cooper. 'So,' she said hurriedly, 'if it's OK with you, I really do need to know about Lucy. I know it's hard, but I need to understand her history.'

Matt nodded. 'OK. I'll do my best. What can I tell you?'

'Do you have any idea what caused Lucy's disability?'

'No. Annie didn't know she was pregnant, Lucy was unplanned, but Annie's very healthy so I don't think it's anything she did during pregnancy. There's nothing genetic on either side and it wasn't a birth accident.' He looked up and, when Kit lifted her eyes from her notepad, she could see that he was uncertain whether to go on.

'Is there something that's hard to say? Do you want a break?'

'No, it's just that this is quite personal. I may as well tell you the whole thing . . . The pregnancy wasn't planned, Annie and I hadn't been together very long at all, but it felt right to both of us so we went ahead. It was the first grandchild for my parents, and for Annie's mother as well, so you can imagine the fuss. It had all gone like clockwork, Annie even went into labour bang on her due date. It was an easy birth, too. Well, for me anyway.'

Matt laughed slightly but then didn't continue. After a while, Kit glanced up again from her writing and saw he was staring out at the sea.

'Matt?'

Kit saw a movement in the muscles at the side of his jaw. She recognised that twitch straight away, it was what happened to Tyler when he was swallowing hard, determined not to get upset. Then Matt made a fist and rubbed his forehead with his knuckles, as if he had a headache.

'I'm sorry. This bit really is quite difficult. I'll just try and say it as it happened.'

'OK.'

'As soon as Lucy was born the midwives took her away to be checked. They were a while bringing her back. I didn't think twice about it at the time. You're on such a high, you know? They didn't say anything then, and once they handed her over, we were both in love with her straight away.'

He paused again. 'It was the next day before anything was said. Annie was keen to go home. She's not a great one for hospitals, she doesn't like the lack of control, no privacy and all that. She was starting to insist, and no one would really give her any answers, so she was on the verge of signing herself out. Well, you've met my wife, so I guess you know how she can be.'

Kit tried to disguise her expression but knew she'd failed.

'Look, I know you've probably found Annie difficult. But try to see it from her point of view. She was only eighteen when she got pregnant, a few years younger than you are now, I'd guess? But she has fought for Lucy every step of the way, and she's made sure that Chloe and Cameron have a normal life, too.'

Kit hadn't thought about any of this before. She hadn't even worked out how young Annie would have been when Lucy was born. Kit wondered how she would have managed herself if she'd got pregnant at eighteen, let alone with the baby turning out to be severely disabled.

'So, when they tell you something might not be quite right, like they told us the day after Lucy was born . . . well, you don't really want to believe it,' Matt continued. 'They let us go home, but they said she'd need more tests. I'm going to be completely truthful with you now – we ignored them at first. We were delaying tests, postponing appointments, being difficult about it all, telling each other it was nonsense, bloody doctors, what did they know? Lucy looked perfect and so we made up our minds that she was perfect. Does that make sense?'

'It's denial, I suppose.' Kit could see Matt and Annie in this picture, the challenging people that they'd been the first time she'd met them, utterly self-confident. She felt briefly sorry for the doctors who had had to break the news that Matt and Annie had decided not to hear.

'Yes, it was. Total denial. And it worked for a while; we were in a kind of bubble, now I look back on it. We kept convincing each other. And there were plenty of people around us who were willing to confirm what we wanted to believe. Proud grandparents aren't too keen on hearing that things might not be quite as they want them to be.' Matt gave Kit a weak smile. 'My parents were the worst actually. Annie's mother was a lot more practical, more accepting. My mother and father are used to being able to solve any problem by throwing money at it, and for once, that wasn't going to change a damn thing . . .'

He stopped again, and Kit sensed that he was looking for a way to carry on talking about his parents or Annie's mother, or anything except Lucy. He wanted a detour. A part of Kit wanted one too. She felt so cruel. She desperately wanted to back off from this guy, and from what she had opened up. She didn't want to watch him relive all this. But she seemed to have hit on his raw spot, and now she could see that there was more to him than she had realised.

'So, when did you become aware that the doctors might be

right?' She watched his profile and was relieved to see he was composing himself.

'When it got to the point where Lucy hadn't rolled onto her side, then when she hadn't sat up, and all the other babies in the pram group had done those things months ago. She just wasn't reaching her milestones and we couldn't pretend any-more. We tried. My parents got involved again, I'm afraid.' He rolled his eyes. '"Your cousin's youngest didn't sit up until he was eighteen months old and he's a high court judge now." All that kind of thing. You go along with it outwardly but inside you know you're all kidding each other. No one wants to be the one to say it first.'

'Who did say it first?' Kit asked, guessing the answer.

'Annie, of course. It was Annie. She was incredibly strong, and she insisted that we needed to know. She had to deal with my parents, which I can tell you is not easy at the best of times, and she had to deal with me as well. I really didn't want to hear it. What can I say? It was a tough time. Really tough . . .'

His voice trailed away, and he looked down at his lap, swal-lowing hard. On the back of his tanned neck, thick strands of brown hair were glistening with perspiration. Kit felt a momen-tary urge to touch him, to give him some comfort, but resisted it. Instead, she put her pen and her papers down on the floor, then leant forward in her chair, hoping to encourage him to go on. When he looked up to meet her gaze, she realised that she had misjudged the distance, and that their faces were much too close together, close enough for her to see tears welling in his eyes. She forced herself to hold eye contact and he held it too, seemingly unable to go on, waiting for her to take charge.

'Can you tell me about that, Matt?' She slid backwards in her chair, re-establishing the distance between them.

'The thing is, when they tell you the diagnosis, and you begin to realise what's ahead of you . . . It's just words at that point, but after a while you start to see your future. We'd see older kids in the waiting room at the clinic and how disabled some of them were, and I'd say to Annie, "Oh, that's awful, but they must have a different disability to Lucy." Then we'd find out they had CP too, so then we'd agree with each other that they must have a much more severe type of CP. Then you find out that some of them have got the same. You can go on like that for a while, finding different ways to deny it, but in the end, it dawns on you that you've got a lifetime of caring ahead. Annie and I were both ambitious; I was brought up to work hard and succeed and so was she. A disabled child didn't exactly fit our plans.' He glanced at her. 'I know that sounds awful, Kit, and I hope you won't hold it against me because it's in the past now. We've achieved what we planned to after all, and we love Lucy, of course. But that's how it felt at the time.'

'I won't hold it against you at all. I understand.' It was the response he wanted and there was no harm in giving it. But she wondered at his slightly self-satisfied tone, his view of himself and Annie as a success story, in spite of Lucy throwing a spanner in the works. But then again, they were pretty successful. Why would he pretend otherwise?

'Of course, nothing takes away how much it hurts,' he continued, making Kit wonder whether he'd guessed what she was thinking. 'I hear our friends moaning about their kids growing up. It can be hard to listen to at times, if I'm honest. We would give anything to have all that ahead for Lucy. To have a healthy child and see that child grow up and become independent, going out into the world – that's a privilege, isn't it? Excuse me for a moment.'

He got up and left the room quickly. Kit heard a door close in the hallway. She guessed he had gone to the bathroom to pull himself together. A few minutes passed, during which Kit tried to work out what she thought about what had been said and where she could take this next. She realised that her own throat had tightened a little while he'd been talking. This was as close as she was likely to come to an emotional reaction. Kit never really cried herself, so she usually regarded crying as being fake and manipulative. But Matt Cooper's words had affected her deeply, and she knew for the next day or two, her mind was going to be full of the picture he'd painted of Lucy's early years, and what Matt and Annie had faced. She had no idea really, she realised. She felt exactly like the young, naive kid Annie had said she was.

'I'm sorry, I just needed a minute.' He sat down. His face was dry and his eyes just slightly reddened. He had another mug of coffee with him and he sipped at it before continuing. 'Anyway, look, Annie and I went through the stage of wanting to run away, but we were lucky, it didn't last long for either of us.

We're both tough people, and we saw it the same way. We were going to make it work. We wanted more children and a nice life. I provide the money, Jean's organised some of the care and my parents have helped us a lot financially as well. They came around, in time. My father dotes on Lucy actually. And Annie makes everything run smoothly at home. That's the deal. We are living proof that you can have a good family life with a severely disabled child. Of course, we're luckier than most. We're affluent and I know that gives us an advantage,' he added, seeming to have read Kit's mind again. 'But still, the point I'm making is our life is great, including Lucy's. And then all this comes along, and it's threatening everything we've got. You can't really expect any of us to welcome you with open arms, can you?'

'No. Of course not.'

'I could have walked away. I guess some men might have. But I couldn't have lived with myself if I'd left Lucy. She was my little girl before the diagnosis and she still was after it. To be honest, a lot of men don't feel that way. And it's all turned out fine. More than fine. I am quite proud of that. Then this happens. It just seems so unfair. I miss being with my family so much, Kit, and I worry about how they're coping. I appreciate what you did at the legal meeting, making it work so that I could see the children with Annie supervising. I'm not being ungrateful for that, I know things could have been so much worse without your help. But it's just not the same as living in my home with all of them, you know? And we've got no idea how long this could go on for.'

Kit found herself once again struggling to stifle the impulse to say or do something to make him feel better. To make up, somehow, for the damage that she had done to his family and for making him trawl back through Lucy's early years.

'I can't put myself in your shoes, so I'm not going to pretend that I can.'

'No, you're right. You can't imagine what this is like from the outside. I could lose everything. My job, my home, my family. It's all hanging by a thread right now.' His words were coming quickly and his voice was louder. His hands clenched together, kneading each other. 'And it would affect my parents, too. You know what this town is like, everyone's connected, and the fact is that everyone knows us. Our businesses are a big part of keeping Sandbeach afloat, and the town needs people like us if it's going to get the regeneration finished. But you and I both know all that will count for nothing if I get charged and this gets out, even if I'm cleared in the end. "No smoke without fire," and all that. We'd all have to move away, I guess, start again somewhere new.'

He stopped and looked at her, and his voice softened. 'I'm sorry. I don't mean to rant at you. You've made this as easy as it could be and I'm chatting to you, telling you all sorts of things, but then I have to keep remembering that I can't relax, because if I say the wrong thing, if I slip up, you could take my children away from me.'

'Strictly speaking, I couldn't. The court could.' It sounded just as defensive as she felt. His words had put her on edge. It was almost as though she might be personally responsible for bringing the economy of Sandbeach to its knees.

'But that's just words really. It's you that the judge would listen to. You, the police, the CPS – you could tear my whole life to pieces and destroy everything that Annie and I have worked for. It's a hell of a responsibility for you, isn't it?'

Kit bit her lip, feeling again that she was too young, too inexperienced, to have this much power. She decided that the best thing she could do was to leave him alone now. She put her pen and papers together to signal that she was bringing things to a close.

'I'm sorry. I just wanted you to know how it feels from this side. I hope that I've helped, though?' he asked her.

'You have. Shall we leave it there now?'

He glanced at his watch. 'It might be just as well. My parents are due back pretty soon and I wouldn't want to expose you to them.'

She put her things away in her bag and stood up, and Matt led the way out of the room and into the hallway. Halfway down, he stopped at a door.

'This is the room that my parents had fitted out for Lucy.' He opened the door for Kit to step inside. The room contained a bed, complete with hoist, and another bed for whoever was sleeping in with Lucy. There was also all the usual furniture and the same sort of posters that she had seen at Matt and Annie's house.

'We made it as similar as possible to home so that Lucy would feel more settled. She loves coming here for weekends.'

'Do her carers come with her?' This arrangement was news to Kit. She cursed Jean Collins yet again.

'No. Why do you ask?'

'It's just the records don't show anything about her staying over at your parents'.'

'Does it matter?'

'No, of course not. It's lovely for her to have the change. I was just wondering why Jean didn't allocate some of Lucy's care hours to her weekends here – it could have helped them with the overnights?'

'There was no need,' Matt said. 'My mother sleeps in with Lucy. She manages everything at night.'

'How often does Lucy come?'

'Every couple of weeks usually. But she hasn't been for a month or two actually.'

'Oh? Why's that?'

'She decided she didn't want to. It might surprise you to know that she can be quite stubborn. It'll pass.'

Kit glanced around the room again. It was immaculately tidy, but it smelt musty. She saw that Len and Jackie, too, seemed to know all about what Lucy liked. On the wall near Lucy's bed, a calendar showed Taylor Swift, posing next to a Christmas tree, wearing tiny red shorts and a sparkly jumper. On the floor underneath it, this year's Taylor calendar stood neatly propped up against the skirting board, still in its shrink wrap.

Matt had moved out of the room and was waiting for her.

As Kit followed him towards the front door, she saw a large display of photos that climbed up the wall to the side of the staircase, ending in a beautiful studio portrait of Matt and Annie with the three children.

'It's lovely, isn't it?' Matt's tone was warm again as he took a few steps back to stand beside her.

'Yes, it is.' It really was stunning, with Matt and Annie looking photogenic behind Lucy's chair and Chloe and Cameron on either side of their sister, one blond head leaning on each of her shoulders, all three of them giggling over a shared joke. There were other family groups, too, showing Matt at various ages along with a younger girl and a couple who must be the infamous Len Cooper and his wife. The photos of the girl seemed to peter out in her late teens, but there was photo after photo of Matt – holding up sporting trophies, graduating, relaxing on beaches and by swimming pools, and marrying Annie. The couple looked so outright beautiful in their wedding photos that Kit found it hard to stop staring at them. A row of smaller pictures had been cut out of newspapers; they showed Matt and Annie in full evening dress, snapped as they arrived at various functions and clapping in the front row at local award ceremonies and prize-givings.

Matt saw her looking at the newspaper cuttings. 'My mother, I'm afraid,' he said, with a sheepish smile. 'She's rather proud of us. It's a bit embarrassing really.'

Kit's eyes moved across the display and she caught sight of another framed newspaper cutting. This one showed Len

Cooper, in a suit and tie, cutting a ribbon that was stretched across the door of a building. He was surrounded by a crowd of people in the midst of a round of applause, one of them a portly middle-aged man wearing the mayoral chains. Something about the photo jarred in Kit's mind. She knew Sandbeach like the back of her hand, so could see the photo had been taken from the far side of the bay, up high on the road that went out towards the west. The sea formed a gleaming backdrop in the lower part of the picture, only partially hidden by the ugly squat building Len Cooper was presumably opening. But the building itself wasn't familiar to her at all. Then she remembered what Vernon had said about Len building a residential home for older people. It certainly had that institutional look about it, single-storey and nondescript, and she realised it must have been built in the last few years, while she'd been out at Cliffside. She scanned the cutting, but before she could draw close enough to read the print underneath, Matt was clearing his throat loudly and she saw that he had moved away and was holding the front door open.

The sound of crunching gravel filled the hallway. A dark maroon Mercedes swept across the drive and pulled up in front of the door. A man got out, instantly recognisable from the family photos. He was uninteresting to look at, with Matt's lanky build and thick hair but none of his chiselling. He was dressed in nondescript casual trousers and a checked shirt. A small woman got out of the passenger side. She was wearing a black and white floral dress and sunglasses. Kit took in her slim build and glossy blow-dried hair and admired her expensive-looking black suede sandals. The whole effect was to make her look much younger than her husband, until the sun fell unkindly on the marionette lines that rucked up the skin of her lower face. Something about that face seemed familiar to Kit. Even under the thick make-up, it was obvious her skin wasn't good. Kit could make out an uneven surface, a bumpy criss-cross over the cheeks and the slightly thickened nose – facial veins, she'd know them anywhere, through any amount of slap. Mrs Cooper was a drinker, Kit would have bet her job on it. Len Cooper locked the car and walked around to the door, and Kit waited, curious to see how this scene was going to play out.

'Kit, this is my father, Len. And my mother, Jackie. This is Kit, the social worker.'

'So it's you we've got to thank for what's happening to my family?' Len Cooper spat. 'Right, well, I'm glad to see you here, girl, because I've got a few things to say to you.'

Kit felt her confidence rise instantly in the face of this. *Girl* indeed.

'If you've got something to tell me for my assessment, then yes, of course, that would be very helpful.'

'I'll tell you this for your assessment. I want my son back home with his family where he belongs. So, let's hear what you are going to do about it.'

'Your son is facing serious allegations. We can't have him around his own children until we know he's completely cleared.'

Len Cooper had moved close to her now, so close that she could see flecks of spit on his thin, pallid lips.

'So, what you say goes, is it? Because of something that's been said by some little slag? Let's see how long she keeps her story up. You are going to be sorry you ever believed a word that came out of her filthy mouth.'

'Dad, leave it.' Matt was suddenly in between his father and Kit. He put a hand up to keep Len Cooper back and allow Kit out onto the drive. Jackie Cooper slipped past in the other direction, taking her husband's arm on the way, ushering him into the house.

'I'm so sorry,' Matt said. 'My parents are very upset, I'm sure you can understand why. He didn't mean to scare you.'

'He didn't scare me.'

'I'm glad he didn't. Look, Kit, I know you can't do what I want. I want you to promise it's all going to be all right and of course you can't. But for what it's worth, I think you have a very difficult job and you do it very well.'

Out of the corner of her eye, she saw Matt Cooper's hand moving upwards. She put her own out to meet it, thinking that he was going to shake hands. But his rose higher, as if he was going to touch somewhere around her shoulder. She looked at him, knowing that her face showed her surprise. His hand dropped immediately to his side.

'Thank you again, Kit. Goodbye now.' He stepped back and closed the door.

CHAPTER 8

Kit drove away in the direction of the office, but after a few minutes she changed her mind and headed for the promenade. She parked and bought a coffee from the van on the front. She felt cold, so she went back to her car and got her hoody from the back seat before finding her usual bench. Under a flat metallic sky, the sea was grey and lifeless and seemed so low down that Kit felt closed in and breathless when she looked at it. A storm couldn't be far away now.

She sipped her coffee and watched the joggers and the determined holidaymakers on their hired bikes. Her body was as tense as a board and her mind felt thick and slow, just a jumble of images, flashes of what had seemed like great insights at the time but had been replaced by an opposite thought the very next minute. She thought back to Annie. How controlled she had been; haughty, almost sneering at times. An utter cow, in fact. But there had been other notes, and it was these that Kit knew she had to understand. Annie's inability to talk about Lucy's early years was one; it had been genuine, Kit was sure of that. She remembered the small smile that Annie had given her when she'd realised Kit wasn't going to insist. It had been a thank you, an expression of relief, not a smirk, and the only moment when Annie had climbed down and allowed something to pass between the two of them as equals. The pain of what had happened with Lucy was still present, Kit realised. Even Annie's supreme organisational skills had not been able to manage that away. Kit knew she had found the first bit of firm ground in the case – Annie loved her children deeply. She would not allow them to be harmed.

Kit thought, too, about Matt's mother. She doubted very much Jackie would be in a fit state to manage the demanding physical care she now understood from Annie to be what Lucy needed – the hoisting and changing and feeding. Jackie Cooper's skin had told Kit all she needed to know about that. She recalled Christine, dead drunk most nights and barely capable of making it up the stairs. Surely Jackie didn't look after Lucy overnight? So was it Len who did so? Kit tried to check herself; maybe she was just looking for something to justify her instinctive dislike of Len Cooper. She sipped her coffee and dug her free hand into the pocket of her hoody, where it made contact with a piece of paper. She pulled it out. The outside showed Chloe's drawing of her cat, sitting inside the picture of the house Kit had given her to work on. Kit's name was written across the cat. Kit remembered that she had drawn Lucy's bedroom on the other side of the paper. Chloe had added to the picture and then she had given it to Kit. It had been in her pocket ever since.

A splash fell on her face and she sat up straight with a shock. The rain started to fall heavily and within a couple of minutes her clothes and shoes were getting soaked. She shoved the picture back into her pocket, dropped her cup in the bin and ran to the car park. Slipping into her seat, she heard her phone and saw that it was Vernon. She let it ring out while she wriggled out of her hoody and threw it onto the back seat, searched for a band to tie back her wet hair, and then let it ring out a second time so she could light a fag. Only then did she pick up her phone to call him back.

'Ah, good, where the hell have you been? I've been trying to get hold of you for hours.'

'Vern, you've rung me twice. I was on a visit. What's up?'

'The bloody Coopers, what else? Dai's been on the phone with the CPS most of the day. It seems they're not proceeding with the case against Matt Cooper.'

'What? Why not?'

'This is what Dai has been trying to get to the bottom of. He's none too happy, I can tell you. Anyway, it seems one of the women has pulled out before they've even got started. Hang on, I'm trying to find it, I've got her name here somewhere.' Kit waited patiently, knowing it might take some time for Vernon to locate the scrap of paper he needed.

'Stephanie Harman, that's her. Not only has she withdrawn the allegation, she's undermined the whole case. She says now it never happened and swears the two of them made it up.'

'Made it up? What the hell would they do that for?'

'She reckons this other one, what's her name, hang on . . .'

'Nicolette.'

'Yeah, that's her. Stephanie Harman reckons Nicolette Baxter wanted to go after him and persuaded Stephanie to back her up, told her they might get some money out of it, so she agreed, but now she's regretting it.'

'What? Are you serious? What about Nicolette?'

'She says it was actually Stephanie Harman who kicked the whole thing off. Nicolette still insists the allegations are true. The pair of them are contradicting each other left, right and centre already. The CPS don't reckon they've got much chance of a conviction. In fact, as we all know, they haven't got a snowball's with all that hanging over them.'

'Surely Steph will get done for perverting the course of justice?'

'Wasting police time probably.'

'But what about Nicolette's statement? She hasn't withdrawn it yet, has she?'

'The problem is Nicolette was the weak link from the start. She's fragile, mental health not great, bit incoherent. The CPS were already worried about putting her on the stand. So, with Steph withdrawing her statement and undermining Nicolette's at the same time, they reckon they're screwed. It's all about how this might play out in court. Matt Cooper is a big fish and the CPS aren't going to risk it unless they are pretty sure they can reel him in.'

'What about the sister – Katie, isn't it? Can she be a witness?'

'There's no suggestion she knew anything about it. Steph and Nicolette were always at the Coopers' house. But we know that already, so it tells us nothing whatsoever. They didn't make any allegations at the time or tell anyone that anything had happened. The only evidence is what they said in their interviews seventeen years after the event, and this Stephanie's blown that right out of the water now.'

'What next then?'

'Might be the end of it. But get back to the office. We'd better make sure we've covered all the bases. Bring supplies, will you?'

As Kit wandered around Aldi, picking up cakes and biscuits for Vernon and a ready meal for her tea, she felt her fury rising. She'd pushed her way into the Coopers' lives, invaded their privacy and insisted Matt should move out of the house, all based on what Steph and Nicolette had said. And now it looked like it might be just a pack of lies. She thought about Matt: his tears as he described Lucy's birth and early years, his devotion to his family, his warmth and openness. She felt terrible and hoped Vernon wasn't going to send her out to apologise to the Coopers. She didn't think she could face them. What the hell was this Stephanie Harman playing at?

When she arrived in his office thirty minutes later, Kit found Vernon busy on the phone. She gathered he was speaking to someone in Legal. Kit threw him the biscuits and settled down to wait. His tone was flirtatious rather than belligerent, so Kit knew it must be Sue Sullivan on the other end, rather than one of her flunkies. To confirm her suspicions, she leant forward to see what he was doodling on his notepad. Even from upside down, the drawing looked suspiciously like Sue. Vernon was paying a lot of attention to getting the curves of her figure just right. Kit hastily averted her eyes.

'Right, OK then, we'll do that. Let me know and Kit'll have a look at it. Thanks for that, I knew it was best to go straight to the top.' He put the phone down and looked at Kit.

'That was Sue Sullivan.' He started unwrapping the custard creams.

'You don't say.'

'Eh?'

'Never mind. What did she say then?'

'She said you'd better go and look at what's in the interview transcripts. It's not likely to take us anywhere, it's purely procedural, but see what you can find out. After that, come back to me and we'll meet with Sue and have a look at your assessments.'

'What for?' Kit stopped with a custard cream halfway to her mouth. 'He's been cleared. Surely now we just leave them alone?' Kit put her biscuit down on the edge of Vernon's desk, her appetite lost.

'The criminal case didn't proceed. But there's still Nicolette's statement to think about, and Stephanie could be made to come to court and explain why she withdrew hers. You know all about the two different standards of proof, I assume?'

'Maisie was telling me about it the other day.'

Vernon guffawed, spitting biscuit crumbs everywhere. 'That will have been a fat lot of help.'

Kit thought back to Maisie's lecture in the bar, and how it had made her fret about why Steph and Nicolette would make up lies about Matt Cooper, all these years later. 'You'd better run through it for me then.' She chucked her biscuit in the bin, giving up any hope of being able to force it down now she knew her contact with the Coopers wasn't necessarily over with after all.

Vernon cleared his mouth, in readiness for a display of his own intellect. 'Long one short, the criminal case operates on a basis of beyond reasonable doubt. The CPS knew they didn't have that, what with this girl playing silly buggers.'

'Woman.' Kit rubbed her forehead out of pure frustration.

'Yeah, yeah, woman. But the family courts operate to the lower standard – civil law only needs to establish the balance of probabilities. Our Mr Cooper is not quite out of the woods yet. We need to know a bit more about what the two women said. In theory, we could get it into court for a fact-finding. If we think the kids may be at risk, that is.'

'And how am I meant to know that?'

'That's the six-million-dollar question, isn't it? I doubt there's a social worker in the country who knows the answer to how you do it, once the criminal case is kaput. Let's start with what you do know. What's your thinking on this case? What are the kids saying?'

Kit thought back to the visit she'd made to Annie and the

children. 'Nothing unusual. Cam and Chloe are great. She could be a bit of a madam, I reckon. I spent a bit of time with them, did some colouring – I used the house, the fairy, all that. Cameron's the quieter one; he's a little bit jealous of Lucy, I think.'

'That's no surprise. Sometimes the sibs can feel like the disabled child is the special one, everyone focusses on them. We all do it, social workers included.'

'Yeah, I know. Chloe's different, she seems to want to be around Lucy, they even share a room at the moment. They're bright, happy kids from what I can see.'

'You've got to hand it to the Coopers really. I mean, it can't be easy. If they're doing well with Lucy and the other two are stable, they're doing a pretty good job.'

Kit nodded. 'I know. And Annie was so young when she had Lucy. I talked to Matt about that. He described what it was like, having her and coming to terms with it all. He got really upset. He said stuff I'd never thought of. I actually felt like I learnt quite a lot from him.'

'What's your feeling about him now then? Punch or shag?'

She found herself blushing, remembering Matt Cooper's tanned neck, his striking dark brown eyes glistening with tears, and his articulate, emotionally intelligent description of what it felt like to have a severely disabled child. 'There's a side to him I hadn't seen before, that's all. I'm still figuring it out.' She tucked her thoughts about Len Cooper away. She needed more to go on before she could tell Vernon. But at least she wasn't going to have to close the case just yet. Maybe she'd find something to back up her suspicions that something about him didn't feel right.

'We'll wait to hear from Sue then, get a look at the interview transcripts, see what you think. In the meantime, we're going to have to ask Matt Cooper not to move back into the home.'

'They are not going to like that one bit.'

'I know. But it's necessary. Hopefully Mandy Bruce will already have explained to them that the criminal case isn't necessarily the end of the whole thing, so it won't be too much of a surprise. OK?'

'Yes, OK.' She got up and moved towards the door, where she leant against the frame. Vernon was watching her face.

'Have you read any serious-case reviews?' He had got to the bottom of the custard creams now, and, after dropping the packet on the floor near the bin, he started unwrapping the bourbons.

'A few in college, but not since.'

'Then you need to. Get on the NSPCC website, they're all listed. Read them over the weekend. You need to go into this with an open mind. Right now, you can't believe that he did it. It's your default position, it's mine too, it's everyone's. The first thought is "no". Then you see everything through that lens.'

'Yeah. I keep wondering whether an abuser would still go home and notice that the decking needed cleaning.'

'Yes, he would. And Jimmy Savile probably really did love his mother.'

She smiled. 'OK. But there's another thing.'

'Good thing I haven't got any other staff to supervise, isn't it? Go on then, what?'

'It's Annie,' Kit admitted. 'She drives me up the wall, but she would not tolerate anything that would harm the children. And I just feel that she'd know. How could she not?'

Vernon shrugged. 'The single most pervasive bias in human reasoning is that people like to hold on to their beliefs.'

'What does that mean, for Christ's sake?'

'Google it. It means we don't accept new information if it goes against what we already believe. That's been the basis of a fair few serious-case reviews, I can tell you that much. Annie is massively invested in denying it. I don't mean she's doing it deliberately, risking her kids to keep the nice house and the handsome husband. She'd have to be a monster. But what I mean is, if she's got an inkling, she's fighting against it so hard, she genuinely can't see it.'

Kit nodded, even though she wasn't sure she agreed. Picking up a pen from Vernon's desk, she used it to write a note on the back of her hand about the NSPCC website, then picked up her bag and headed for the door, with an unpleasant weekend of reading ahead of her. As she reached it, Vernon called after her.

'You gotta remember, girl – Annie Cooper's got a lot to lose. And having a lot to lose can make you blind.'

CHAPTER 9

The following Monday, Sue Sullivan told the police and the CPS in no uncertain terms that her clients' department needed information about Steph and Nicolette's statements to determine their next move with the Cooper children. Once she'd got her own way, Sue had swept into the team room in person to tell Vernon all about the fight. He'd listened with admiration and then instructed Kit to get over to the police station at once, before anyone could change their mind.

The weather was still damp and drizzly. She decided to walk over to the police station anyway, feeling a sudden desperation to be outside. The route took her past the housing office, some charities and the Community Mental Health Team. A few street drinkers hung around, waiting for the alcohol project to open. A man was lying in the doorway of the tattoo place; Kit got near enough to check he was asleep and not dead. Once she could see he was breathing, she went on her way. This was definitely the less desirable area of town. But it was good to be in the fresh air nonetheless. Kit remembered the promise she'd made to herself a while ago: to get out more, maybe get back to some swimming. She felt cross with herself, because it hadn't happened, of course. All she did was go to work, come home and worry about the Cooper case, or about Tyler. She could have got out to the beach at weekends. But her anxiety was like a prickly kernel deep inside her stomach; she had to wrap herself around it, keep watching it, otherwise she might lose control, miss something, make a mistake, get the whole thing wrong. It made enjoying anything impossible, so it felt pointless to try. She knew she should – she couldn't get this disillusioned and bitter so early on in her career. She couldn't burn out on her first difficult case.

But after spending most of the weekend reading serious-case reviews, her mind was still full of nightmare images. The deaths, the injuries and the abuse. The families in those reports were almost all well known to social services, of course. Drugs and alcohol, poverty, domestic abuse, mental illness. Not vaguely akin to the Coopers. She'd read some of the Savile reports, too. They had made her feel sick and hadn't helped her in the slightest. So many people had suspected, even known about him, but done nothing. He was hiding in plain sight, one report said. He thought about his sex-offending every waking minute of every day. Some people even said he looked like a paedophile. She knew better than to think like that, but she got the point.

When Kit arrived at the police station she asked for Dai Davies at the desk and rummaged around in her rucksack trying to find her ID. She finally located it and was admitted through the security door to the stairwell, where Dai was waiting for her. They started up the stairs together.

'Morning, lovely. You ready for this then?' he asked.

'Yeah, I guess so.'

Dai led the way into his tiny office. His desk was full of stuff, she noticed. Photos, mostly of his beloved nieces, a couple of elaborate paperweights, a few tiny sculptures of cats, some nice pens. Kit barely had room to open the transcripts when he banged them down on the desk. She understood the reason behind the clutter, though. It was the stuff of familiarity: cherished objects and loved faces to ground him and comfort him when he had to face something horrible.

'Give me a shout when you're done.' He gave her one of his kind smiles. 'I'll be next door if you need me.'

When Dai left, she sat at the desk and stared at the documents, dreading what was inside and suddenly regretting how well informed she now was about other cases. She steeled herself, picked one up and started reading. As soon as it was done, she turned to the other one.

She got the idea pretty quickly. Nicolette Baxter and Stephanie Harman both described how they'd met Katie Cooper at the town's one and only private school, where they'd been drawn together at the age of thirteen by their mutual tendency towards trouble. After a while, the three of them had progressed to truanting, leaving in the afternoons after the register had been taken. Steph lived a distance away from school on the Coed estate; she'd got in with a scholarship for bright but

underprivileged kids. Nicolette had a big house but it was a
bus ride away. Katie's house was the nearest, and the other plus
was that her parents worked all day, as did her brother, who
was twenty-three and training to be an accountant. The girls
could have the Coopers' huge house to themselves every day.

Both women described their first contact with Matt. They said
he'd come home from work early one afternoon. Kit remembered what Vernon had said about having an open mind and
she found the only way she could do it was to tell herself it was
a story about someone else, some random man, not the Matt
Cooper she knew and had warmed to. She read about how he'd
chatted to Nicolette and Steph, treating them like adults, asking
about their lives and encouraging them to confide in him. Then
he'd driven them home, saying he was worried about two pretty
girls walking the streets alone and a bit drunk. He'd dropped
them around the corner from their houses, so their parents
wouldn't see. That had become a habit, and then it had started,
just as Vernon had said. Kit flinched when Nicolette described
the first touch. He'd helped her into the car one day when the
drive was icy, his steadying hand on her arm. Just being kind,
concerned. But the boundary had been crossed.

Kit stopped reading for a moment. She could see what was
coming in this story, and, in her mind, she screamed at the
two girls to get away from him, not to get in his car again.
Not to take gifts from him, not to drink the alcohol he gave
them from his parents' massive drinks cabinet. But on it went,
with a horrible inevitability. The way he'd touched Steph's

knee one day, and the next time, stroking her leg through the material of her skirt. Moving his hand under the material and up the outside of her thigh. Casually, while he was talking about something else, almost as if it wasn't happening at all or he didn't realise he was doing it. Impossible, then, to say anything, to be the one to break the spell and draw attention to it. Kit could see how the trap had snapped shut behind Steph that day.

Eventually, Steph had found herself sitting in the Coopers' living room one Sunday afternoon, in one of the armchairs that were half turned towards the huge window, staring out at the frothing sea, and the chilly, bleak beach. She'd asked herself for years afterwards why she hadn't walked away right then, before he came to get her. One part of her had known what was coming but another part of her hadn't believed it, and the non-believing part had won. She was still afraid she might be wrong about his intention. If she made a fuss, how ridiculous would she look then?

Afterwards he'd told her it was a secret. She'd let him touch her so many times, he told her, she must have known what he wanted, and she'd never stopped him. When the girls had spoken about it, they found he'd told them both the same thing: 'No one's going to believe a little scrubber like you over me.' They knew he was right. They'd broken off contact with him and with Katie, and they'd done their best to get on with their lives. They couldn't see any other way.

When Steph's best friend had started working in a new

residential home and hadn't been able to stop talking about the fit son who was the financial director of the company, Steph admitted that she hadn't been able to resist the temptation to find out more about Matt's life. It hadn't been difficult in Sandbeach. She'd asked around and found out that Katie had moved to London. She seemed to have disappeared; no one was in touch with her. But Steph soon tracked down one of Matt's old rugby mates, who had his address. She admitted freely that the Coopers were quite right in thinking she'd been to their home. She had gone along and she'd stood outside and taken it all in. The nice home, the smart wife and the girl in a wheelchair. She said that was what had finally convinced her it was time to do the right thing. She'd spoken to Nicolette, whose own interview was full of her struggles with anxiety and self-harm caused by the abuse, and they'd talked it over and agreed to report him. They felt sure that by now things had changed, and they'd be believed.

Kit closed the transcripts and sat for a minute, trying to work out what she felt. It was as if she was looking at two different versions of Matt Cooper. Her mind shifted from one to the other. Which one was real? Her head was spinning and she needed to get out of the cluttered office. Leaving the transcripts on the desk, she said a quick goodbye to Dai and made her escape.

It was lunchtime, but Kit knew she couldn't eat. She got a coffee in the café near the office and sat at a table in the back for a while, thinking about what she'd read. She hadn't realised until now that Steph Harman had lived on the Coed. She tried to do the maths in her head – Steph had said she was about thirteen when she met Katie Cooper, and that was seventeen years ago. That would make her about the same age as Jazz. Kit tapped her fingers on the table for a few seconds, trying to stop them from straying towards her phone. Matt Cooper was going to be back home in no time, that much Kit knew. There was nothing to prove he'd done anything at all, no matter what Vernon said about thresholds of proof. But why would Steph and Nicolette make those statements? And why had Steph changed her mind? There was no sense to it, and there were too many loose ends. After a few more taps on the table, her fingers went their own way, found Jazz's name in her contact list, and sent a text. Seconds later, the reply came.

Yeah – 56 Canning Road

Kit replied to thank Jazz and to deal with the inevitable questions about when she was going to bother to come and see her nephews and nieces. She did feel guilty about them, especially Amber, eight years old and already surviving her family by pretending to be far less clever than she really was. After assuring Jazz that she would be in touch soon, Kit drained her coffee, put thoughts of Steph Harman to one side, and set off back to the office to update Vernon about events.

CHAPTER 10

As Kit entered the building, Vernon was crossing the reception area, notebook and pen in hand. He gestured at her to follow him into the lift.

'Where are we going?' she asked him as he pushed the button for the top floor.

'I've been summoned by the admin clerk.'

'Why am I coming with you?'

'Well, unless there's something you haven't told me, it's bound to be about the Cooper case, isn't it? How did you get on with the transcripts?'

Kit tried to find a way to answer, but it was too complicated. 'I'll tell you later. Let's get this over with first.' They had arrived at the top floor, where Cole's secretary showed them into his office. He wasn't behind his desk. Instead he was waiting for them at a table in the corner.

'Ah, Kit, good, glad to have you here. Take a seat, both.'

They sat on the other side of the table and Vernon opened his notebook.

'This won't need minuting, Vern, it's just an informal chat.'

'What's it about?' Vernon asked.

'The Cooper children.'

'Then it needs minuting. I'll take a note and attach it to the file if that's all right with you, Cole?'

Cole Jackson didn't like it, but he had no grounds to disagree. 'Right, I'll get straight to the point. I understand that Mr Cooper's been cleared?'

Vernon shook his head. 'No. The criminal case is not proceeding. That's not the same thing at all.'

'Isn't it? Vernon, help me out here. Where do you propose going with this now there is no criminal case?'

'We need to see whether we have any grounds for care proceedings. In fact, that's where Kit has been this morning, taking a look at the transcripts. To see if we can go any further.'

Cole Jackson looked at Kit. 'And can we?'

'I'm not sure. The accounts were very convincing. We could be putting the Cooper children at risk if we close it too soon. I need a bit more time to check things out.'

Cole Jackson sighed. 'With respect, Kit, that is an awful lot to construe from reading a couple of statements, isn't it? Especially statements that have now been withdrawn.'

'Only one of them has been withdrawn.' Kit was looking at Vernon for support out of the corner of her eye but he was busy doodling on his notepad, leaning back in his chair and looking remarkably relaxed. Cole Jackson was continuing as if she hadn't spoken. 'Right, well, in any event, I'm under some pressure to make a decision about all this. The Cooper family have been very patient. We argued for more time to make an assessment and they've borne with us this far. When is this likely to be finished, Kit?'

'I've got another visit to do, to see the children again, especially Lucy. Plus some phone calls, to the schools.'

'Is all that really necessary?'

'Yes.' Vernon's voice was firm. 'She needs to tie it up properly.'

'Well, all right then. I think I can perhaps hold them off for that long. But our legal have been on to Mandy Bruce today to say that, as soon as Kit's done, we will give a date for Mr Cooper to move back home.'

Vernon's head came up at high speed. 'Who have you spoken to in Legal?' he demanded. 'Because Sue is dealing with this personally.'

'Sue's fully aware and she's on board with my plan.'

Vernon paused, seeming to need a moment to gather himself. Kit guessed that Sue Sullivan had been his trump card, and the reason he had been taking the whole thing so casually up to now.

'Right, well, as I said, Kit still has to finish off. If anything comes to light that concerns us during our last inquiries, we'll have to think again. And Mr Cooper does not move back into that house until Kit gives it the OK.' It was a surprisingly weak comeback; the news that Sue was not behind him had undermined Vernon completely.

'Thanks, Vern. I'll speak to Sue now and make sure the Coopers understand. You need to get over there and do the visit straight away, Kit. Councillor Palmer is keeping an eye on this and she is going to want to know it's all finished with as soon as possible.'

'OK.' Kit stood, and Vernon followed her. As he did so, his jutting stomach brushed the edge of the table and knocked his notebook onto the floor, where it lay with the top page clearly visible, showing a drawing of Cole Jackson's head sitting atop a body formed out of a giant paper clip. Cole was standing too; he glanced over to see what had caused the noise and made a move to pick the book up. With an awkward sideways leap, Kit managed to get around to the other side of Vernon where she scooped it up. Cole took a step backwards, alarmed by her sudden movement. Kit tried to smile and look relaxed as a searing pain shot through her calf where she'd banged her leg against the table. She left the office hurriedly, with Vernon following after her. They didn't speak until they were in the lift.

'Thanks, but no need for the acrobatics. I wouldn't have cared if he had seen it,' Vernon grumbled, taking the notebook from her.

'Grow up, Vern, for God's sake. You really have to stop that. It'll get you the sack one day.'

'No chance. Besides, it relieves my feelings.'

'What's gone on then? Why would Sue and Councillor Palmer have backed off?'

'Len Cooper no doubt. He's a powerful man.'

'So everyone keeps saying, but I still don't get it. He's wealthy, so are lots of people.'

'But not the people we usually deal with. That's the point. Len Cooper's known for his charity work, plus he's involved in lots of business deals, big role in the regeneration scheme, local boy made good and wants to put something back into his community, all that. So now, Len's son has brushed up against social services and Len gets a listening ear from some influential people, which most of our families definitely would not get. I'm not saying anyone would stop us taking action if we could come up with something definite on Matt Cooper – even Cole wouldn't go that far. But they're not cutting us any slack either. We are right on the boundary of what we can legitimately do, and Sue and Desiree both know it. They've seen the writing on the wall. If we can't find anything to prolong it, we've had it with this one, I'm afraid.'

They walked back to the office together, dejected. Vernon glanced at Kit. 'You look a bit peaky. The transcripts, was it?'

'Yeah, I think so. I'm a bit muddled now.'

'I had noticed. Go on then, you've got loads of time owing. Go home, call your mates, get a bottle of wine or something.'

'All right. I'll call the schools first, get their views on the Cooper kids, then I'll go.'

Kit smiled at him gratefully. It was true that she couldn't concentrate. And she didn't want to be on her own. She'd text Tyler and see if he could come over. She still couldn't get over the novelty of being able to do that, and the fear he would turn up drunk or high still lingered, but, so far, he was doing OK, she had to admit.

Kit made the phone calls, quickly becoming bored as the head teachers of both schools gave her the usual account of how fantastic the Coopers were. The head of Lucy's school was particularly effusive. Once that was done and she'd entered the recordings into her assessment, Kit gathered her stuff and started for the stairs, sending Tyler a text as she went. He replied at once, and she arranged for him to come over to her flat later. On the way past the reception she passed Older People's Services. She paused, and after a second or two of arguing with herself, opened the door and looked around for the duty desk, finding it at the back of the room. Here a pleasant-looking middle-aged man was fielding calls on his headset. Eventually, there was a pause and he pushed his headset down to hang around his neck and smiled at her.

'A visitor from Child Services. To what do I owe this honour? Has Vernon sent you down looking for a row?'

She laughed. 'Actually, I'm after a bit of info.'

'Go on.'

'Len Cooper. Does the name ring a bell?'

The man made a face. 'Oh God, yes. He owns Cartref Residential Home, that new place on the business park.'

'And?'

'Mystery to me how it hasn't lost its registration. All modern and clean but it's huge and there's never enough staff on. We've had complaint after complaint. Why do you ask?'

'My auntie was thinking about it.'

'I'd warn her off if I were you. Place is rigged up like the Starship *Enterprise*.'

'You what?'

'I mean, we're a bit concerned about his use of assistive technology.'

Kit tried to look knowing.

'You've got no idea what that is, have you?'

'No. Sorry.'

'You know, sensors and cameras and so on. Great in its right place, to keep older people safe, but no substitute for care from a real person, and can be intrusive, if not used properly. We're not sure he's always getting valid consents either.'

The thought of Len Cooper monitoring his residents' every moment made Kit's skin crawl. 'Thanks. I'll tell my auntie to look somewhere else.'

'No problem.'

Kit started towards the door but found she couldn't leave it alone yet. She turned to see the man picking up his headset again.

'Where did you say it was?' she called out.

'On the business park. Monument Way.'

'Thanks. I'll pop over and take a look myself.'

That address didn't seem quite right to Kit. In her mind's eye, she'd seen the home as being somewhere else, but she couldn't recall why. She waved her thanks at the man, whose headset was buzzing again, and went out to get into her car. Monument Way was almost on her route, only a small diversion.

She was curious to get a look at part of the Cooper empire. It only took her a few minutes to reach Monument Way, which was a surprisingly modest location given Len Cooper's ostentatious tendencies. Slowing to a crawl, she passed a row of new office blocks, a car showroom or two, a Costa, a Burger King and a KFC. About halfway along the road she spotted a big building, almost indistinguishable from the office blocks to either side, but with a sign telling her it was Cartref Residential Care Home. She pulled up outside. The building was four storeys high and brand new, covered in a smart grey and blue cladding. Kit wondered about making an excuse to go in, but she spotted the CCTV cameras over the main doors and thought it would not be good for her to be caught on film having a nose around Len Cooper's premises. She thought about what the duty worker had said. It fitted with a satisfying snap. Len Cooper seeing an opportunity to cut corners on care and make even more money. Greedy, not to mention a bit creepy.

Glad to have found what felt like further confirmation of her view of Len, Kit drove home, parked the car and walked down to the corner shop to buy some lagers. Back at her flat, she put the cans in the fridge, drew a deep, hot bath and soaked in it for a while. After she got out, she lay on the sofa and immediately fell asleep, waking with a start when Tyler rang the doorbell.

'State of you.' He looked her up and down, taking in the damp towel she'd wrapped herself up in and the strands of wet hair clinging to her face.

'I suppose I'm allowed to have a bath in my own flat.' She let him in and went to dress while he ordered their food. When she came back, he was going through her DVDs, making a pile on the floor for her to choose from, which she did at random, not caring, just wanting the distraction. When their pizza arrived, they settled on the sofa and Kit did her best to focus on the film for a couple of hours.

As the film ended, Tyler eyed her draining another can. 'And you nag me about my drinking,' he said, smiling at her.

'I know. But I need it.'

'Don't tell me. Another bad day at work?'

'Yeah. And don't you tell me it's my own fault. I know it.'

'I don't know why you didn't stick to the café.'

'I couldn't do that for the rest of my life, though, could I?'

'Why not? Easy job, plenty of time for swimming.'

Out at Cliffside, Kit had kept their old habit of swimming in the wilder, colder water. It had felt like a ritual, a way to keep her connection with Tyler and Danny, with those days on the beach when they'd been able to act like all the other kids, nothing to show that things wouldn't be normal for them when they walked home as late as they could, sandy and exhausted, but reluctant to go. When Menna and Huw had seen how much swimming mattered to her, they'd bought her a wetsuit, so that she could carry on all year round. But Tyler hadn't kept swimming, once she'd gone. She was surprised to hear him mention it now. He was eyeing her closely.

'So, what happened at work?' he asked.

'Just the usual. Stress.'

Tyler turned the TV to a music channel, opened two more cans and sat back down, looking at her expectantly.

'Go on then, tell me about it.'

'I can't, you know that. It's confidential.' She didn't want to get into this with him, not now.

'That's bollocks, you can tell me, just don't say any names.'

She could have made something up, but the idea was exhausting, and her head was so full of Steph and Nicolette that she couldn't get past them to think up a convincing lie.

'It's just this family I'm working with. These two women went to the police. They knew the dad before he was married. They reported him for things they said he'd done. So now I've got to try and work out if his kids are safe. That's it really.'

'What things?'

She might have known he wouldn't let her get away with that. He was way too sharp. 'Sexual stuff,' she admitted.

They both stared at the TV, uncomfortable. 'Do you think he did it?' Tyler asked quietly.

'I really don't think he did. Or I didn't think it. Now I'm not sure. Christ, I don't know, I'm just scared of getting it wrong.' She was on dangerous ground here. This was exactly what she'd hoped to avoid, but she was tired and a bit drunk and she'd walked right into it.

'So, these two girls say he did it to them?'

'Women. But yeah.'

'Well, he did then. Why would they lie about it?'

'Well, one of them's withdrawn her statement. So now everyone wants to drop the case. No one believes it anymore.'

'Yeah. That's about it.' He was annoyed now, looking at her, his face animated and his voice louder. 'No one believes it. You try and tell people and you see it coming, as soon as they get an idea what you're going to say, they do this thing with their faces, like close them up or something. I dunno. Or they just kind of blank you. Then you know not to bother.'

She knew at once that this moment was crucial. That this was a hint, the kind Ricky had told her to look for with the Cooper kids. She knew that what Tyler needed now was for her to open the door. She'd heard his hints before, she had an idea what it might be about, and she'd tried and tried to avoid it, because she didn't want to hear it. It was too hard. But she knew that if she pushed him away this time, he'd never forgive her. She didn't have many friends, she didn't have Danny anymore, she didn't have Jem. She needed to keep Tyler in her life even more than she needed to escape what he was about to say. She drew a breath before breaking the silence.

'Is that what happened to you?'

He looked at her with surprise. 'Yeah. Yeah, it was. Danny told me from the start not to tell, said no one would believe it. I tried a couple of times, but he was right. He knew, see, because he'd tried to tell someone, too. Danny tried to tell one of the social workers a few years after it all happened.'

'Which one?'

'Angela something. Maynard, was it?'

'I don't know.' Kit didn't remember her, but that was no surprise. There had been so many. 'What happened?'

'He wasn't doing great by then and he needed help. But she blanked him, changed the subject. I think maybe that's why he did it, you know? Why he topped himself, in the end. He felt bad, guilty, and he needed to talk to someone.'

'What do you mean?'

He hesitated, but then he pushed himself on. 'We'd been going to this bloke's house.'

'What bloke?'

'Micky Winter. Remember him? All the kids went there.'

'I didn't.'

'No, you didn't. That was you, though, wasn't it? Always staying in to do your homework, never bothering with drugs and that. You weren't what anyone would call normal really, were you?'

'No, I guess not. Who was he?'

'Just some bloke who lived up near us. Not on the estate, though, down the hill a bit, one of those massive houses on The Avenue. He ran the youth centre. We'd started going to the centre to hang around and after a bit he asked us back to his house. He used to choose certain kids to take back there. Everyone knew if you got invited back, you'd get fags off him. After a while he started giving us cans and money. Pills or weed sometimes, too. He was dealing, I think.'

'Why do you think that?'

He shrugged. 'If we were at his house, there would be blokes coming to the door all the time. Sometimes we'd see them in the hall giving him money, he was giving them something back. I never saw what but it was obvious.'

'Sounds likely.'

Tyler was staring at the floor. She waited and finally he started speaking, so quietly that she struggled to catch his words.

'He'd touch us sometimes, nothing much, he'd stroke our legs, stuff like that. It made me feel sick as fuck but we always went together so we weren't worried. We were cocky, us two, we thought we were clever. But then there was this one night, Danny was up the park with Cassie. Remember her?'

Kit nodded. Cassie had been Danny's one and only decent girlfriend. Kit had loved her. She hadn't seen Cassie since the funeral.

'They were off their faces already, but they wanted more cans. Danny asked me to go up and bring some back for them. He texted Winter and told him I'd be up. Winter said for me to meet him at the centre instead, he'd sort me out there.'

'Why?'

Tyler shrugged. 'Like I said, there were always blokes back and forth at his house. I guess he was avoiding them.'

'OK, so what happened?'

'I got up there, the centre was empty. He said he had stuff for me. He gave me some cans, some weed, he asked me to have a drink and a smoke with him before I went. Then he took me into this room. Like a sitting room. It had chairs and a coffee table with plants on it and a big mirror.'

He was going into unnecessary detail to avoid talking about the next bit, she knew that. But his recollection of the mundane details of the room tore at her heart, too, telling her that the memory of that night was frozen deep into his mind. He'd stopped again now and, although she dreaded what would come next, she encouraged him on again. 'Go on. I know it's really hard and I haven't always got it right, but you and me have always tried to look after each other, haven't we?'

'No, I don't want to say no more.' This wasn't like him at all. He lacked her stubborn streak; any stroppiness was a front, part of his banter. Underneath, Tyler was eager to please her and would usually let her take the lead.

'OK, just nod or shake then?' It was a favourite trick that she'd used with lots of kids when they couldn't get words out. But she hesitated then, not able to get the words out herself. She knew that what Tyler needed was for her to say it as it was, to not be afraid.

'Did he rape you?'

He sat for a moment looking at the floor. Then came the nod. 'I ran to Danny after, and he knew straight away. So that was it, I reckon. Danny felt bad for letting me go on my own. That's why he topped himself. And because he'd tried to ask for help later and he didn't get it. It was in his head all the time, about Winter touching us, and about what he ended up doing to me. He thought it was his fault, like he'd let it go on and then he'd sent me up there.'

'Why didn't Danny go after Winter, though?' She couldn't

help herself. It didn't add up and it irritated her mind. It was not sounding like Danny at all.

'I talked him out of it. Like I said, Dan was mental, I thought he'd kill Winter. He'd have gone down for it, for life probably. I didn't want that.'

But something about Tyler's face told her that wasn't the whole of it. 'Come on, Ty. Danny didn't just walk away and leave it. He wouldn't.'

Tyler looked her in the eye then, daring her to disapprove. 'He burnt the youth centre down. He went straight there the night it happened and he just did it.'

She remembered as soon as he said it. The youth centre had sat in the middle of town, a tall Victorian building painted a weird dirty yellow. She remembered hearing fire engines one night when she was in bed, and the next day an acrid smell had risen up to hang over the hill. On the way to school she'd seen the blackened wreckage. It had been burnt to the ground.

'Christ. How did he get away with that?'

Tyler shrugged. 'It wasn't hard. No one was around, no one who was going to tell on him anyway, just the boys. He worked out where the blind spots were on the CCTV, climbed up on the roof and smashed the cameras from up there. Then he lit the fire really good. Danny knew how to do it. We were right pyromaniacs as kids, me and him. Burning it down made him feel better, I think – for a while anyway. Didn't make much odds to me.'

Her stomach was churning now. 'No one got hurt?'

'It was empty.'

'Are you sure?'

'Certain. He promised me he hadn't hurt anyone.'

'So what are you going to do now?'

'What do you mean?'

'We need to report it. I can arrange something for you, I know a few police officers now and—'

'No.' His face was firm and his chin set. 'I am not going through that.'

'Ty, you have to. What if he does it to other kids?'

'Winter's dead.'

Kit felt the churn again. 'How did he die?'

'What, you think Danny did it, do you? No, he died of cancer, while I was away in secure. Dan told me. Said I didn't need to worry about him anymore, he'd got what was coming to him. But I couldn't have done it anyway. Going through all that in front of people, having it all out in court, people blaming me, trying to make out I was the pervert because I didn't stop it.' His face was in his hands now and she couldn't see his expression. His voice came quiet, all the anger gone. 'When I got Miss Morrison for my probation officer, I felt like I could trust her. So I told her about it, because I just wanted to feel better, not feel so shit inside all the time, even after all these years, you know?'

'Yeah.'

'And I told you because I wanted you to believe me. That's all. To have an idea what happened, and to believe me, straight away, no questions asked, no need for the details. No doubts. Because you're my twin sister. You have to believe me, even if no one else does.'

A wave of guilt and regret washed over her. She realised the last thing she should do now was lie to him. 'Look, I know I didn't handle all this very well. But it's more complicated than you think, Ty. I always knew something wasn't right with you, and with Danny, but I never asked you. I had an inkling and I was avoiding the whole thing. It was too hard for me to hear, but that was just me being selfish, I'm sorry.'

He didn't ask how she'd known, and she didn't volunteer it. The truth was that she'd felt the shape of it that day with Danny in the café, enough to know she didn't want to hear anymore, that she wouldn't know what to do, how to handle the full story. There was no need for Tyler to know how badly she'd let him and Danny down.

Tyler rubbed at his eyes. 'I've got to talk to Christine about it, too.'

'Christ. What the hell for?'

'I need to confront her, Miss Morrison says. See what she knew. It's part of my counselling. I'm going over tomorrow.' He looked up at her and his face was full of hope. She knew exactly what was coming. 'You want to come with me? About eleven?'

'OK. I'll have to take time off work. I'll check if I'm free.'

'Don't worry about it, I can go on my own. It's not like it's a big thing. I can handle her.'

She knew then that she couldn't get out of it. She wouldn't put herself in Christine's way for anyone else's sake, but Tyler needed her. There was no way she could let him go on his own. 'Actually,' she said, 'I think the morning's pretty clear tomorrow. Text me when you're on your way and I'll meet you there, OK?'

'OK.' He smiled at her and she could see the relief in his eyes.

CHAPTER 11

Kit got in to work as early as she could the following morning, before even Vernon was likely to be there. She had been awake most of the night thinking about what she could do to help Tyler. She'd finally come up with a plan, and needed to get it done without the risk of Vernon spotting she was up to something and deciding to poke his nose in.

After dropping her bag at her desk, she went down to the reception area. As she arrived, she saw that there was a very drunk woman there already. She watched the woman make several attempts before managing to tear off a ticket from the machine. Once this was achieved, the woman staggered across the reception area and flopped onto a chair, where she immediately fell asleep. The few people sitting around her picked up their belongings and moved to other seats.

Kit looked over at the receptionists behind their glass barriers. She saw that Rita and Carol were on duty, both experienced staff who weren't likely to let her up into the archives alone without checking she had been authorised to do so. But she could see a young man on duty, too. He was quite new, and she saw he was still having to ask the others for help with each person who came up to his desk. She hung back, waiting for him to come free. She considered whether to undo the top buttons of her shirt, but she would have felt ridiculous. Instead, she rummaged in her bag and found a pink lipstick, left over from one of Jazz's attempts to make her over. Kit drew out her mirror and scrubbed some of the dry lipstick onto her lips. That would have to do.

The drunk woman's number flashed up on the screen and rang out on the tannoy at the same time. Miraculously, she came to and stood up straight away. Then she weaved across the reception area to the counter, where she started to shout incoherently at Rita. As far as Kit could gather, she wanted to speak to the Chief Executive personally about her council tax bill. She wanted to know what he was spending her money on.

Kit saw that she was in luck; the young man's counter was free. She walked up to it before any of the people in the queue had the chance, ignoring their glares. She saw from his ID badge that his name was Rhodri.

'Hi, Rhodri, sorry to queue-jump, can you buzz me in? I need to pop up to the archives. I'm here to view a file. I arranged it with Amanda Jones last week.' Kit knew that Amanda Jones was on maternity leave, so it was a safe bet.

'I'll just ring through to her.'

'OK.'

Rhodri made the call, his long thin face becoming anxious as it progressed.

'I'm awfully sorry,' he said. 'Apparently, she is off until September and they have no record of your authorisation. Can your manager sort it out for you?'

Kit did her best to look surprised. 'Perhaps I got her name wrong. But I definitely arranged it with someone for today. My boss isn't in.' Kit forced tears to come into her eyes; a handy trick that she'd learnt in the homes. 'I don't know what I'm going to do. I have a court report due in on Friday. My boss is going to go mad if it's not in for checking by the end of today.'

'I'm not sure what we can—' He started looking around for help. Kit knew she needed to stop him from doing that. She leant forward, as close as she could to the glass barrier, and lowered her voice.

'Look, I can pop in and get it. It's only one document I need. If you buzz me in and give me the door code, I'll soon find it and get it copied. I'll be in and out in five minutes.'

He hesitated. He looked around, but the other two receptionists were both trying to appease the drunk woman, who was now leaning heavily on the counter and raising her voice even more. As Kit and Rhodri watched, the woman started to wobble, before falling sideways off the end of the counter, hitting the floor with a resounding smack.

'Rhodri!' Carol shouted. 'We're going to need some first aid here.'

'That's me.' He looked at Kit, his face terrified.

'I guess you're needed over there then, Rhodri. I don't want to take up any more of your time.'

He threw another glance at the drunk woman, who was now face down on the floor making retching noises. 'Go on then,' he said. 'The code's nineteen forty-five.'

She gave him another smile. 'Thanks so much. You've saved my life.'

Kit left before he could change his mind. She crossed quickly to the security door by the stairs, and, after Rhodri had buzzed her in, made her way up to the second floor, where she found the archive room and punched the code in on the keypad. She saw a computer terminal in the corner but knew she couldn't access it without leaving a footprint on the system. Anyhow, she was fairly sure most of Danny's records would predate computerisation. She moved across to the paper files and started working her way along the stacks.

It didn't take her long to find the Goddard family files. A bundle for each of them: Jasmine, Josette, Krystal and Tyler. And there was Danny's. She pulled it out from the shelf. It had 'Deceased' written across the cover of the top file in heavy black marker. Of course it did. What had she expected? But it still took her breath away. She knelt on the floor and put his files down in front of her.

It was only when she pulled the elastic bands off the bundle and picked up the first file that she realised the enormity of what she was doing. She didn't even know what she was looking for. And she was risking her job, maybe even her registration. Even though it was her brother's file, and he was dead, she shouldn't be reading it. Not to mention the means she had used to get at it. But, she told herself, she needed to know what had gone on. She went back over all the reasoning she had put together the night before. If Danny had asked for help and hadn't got it, then perhaps social services had been at fault, whatever the official inquiry report had said about his suicide. And if there was anything on the files to suggest that social services hadn't removed Kit and the boys from Christine early enough, leaving Tyler to run wild, exposing him to all sorts of risks, he might have a case for compensation. Winter might be dead, but maybe there could still be some justice for Danny and Tyler.

Pushing aside the thought that she was using her position to get information against her own employer, Kit shuffled the files and found the one that related to the right dates. She decided to start from the beginning and work through the file from the first referral. She was reluctant to read it – it had been bad enough living through it – but it was the only way to be sure she wouldn't miss anything. She opened the cover, found the case-recording section and began to skim read.

It was hard work. Some of the handwriting was almost illegible. And painful, too, to see her childhood described by others. After a few pages, the descriptions became repetitive, just like their lives had been for all those years. Christine drunk. All five of them removed to foster care, in two or three or more different placements. Then, a while later, Christine reappearing, sobered up and lawyered up, demanding her babies back. A few months of her keeping it together, the cases hastily closed with tangible relief on the part of the unfortunate social worker. Then another referral and the cycle starting again. Different social workers, some moving on to easier jobs, some simply having done their turn with the intimidating nightmare that was Christine Goddard, gratefully passing the case on to another member of staff.

There were things Kit remembered vividly. One social worker, when Kit and Tyler had been eight, had commented on how Kit looked after Tyler, making his packed lunches for school, and slept on the floor next to his bed in case he had nightmares. And an incident a couple of years later, when Tyler had fallen out of a tree in the park and broken his collarbone. Christine had refused to take him to A & E, until Danny had lost it and threatened her with a broken bottle. She'd reported him to social services for that, and Kit could see now how instead of questioning her about the injury, they were only interested in Danny having anger problems. Of course, that would have been the path of least resistance, but it made her furious to see where the labelling of Danny had begun. No one had asked why he was so angry.

A lot was said about the coming and going of men at the Goddard house, the suspicion of prostitution. Suspicion on the part of social workers, that is. Absolute certainty on the part of the kids. But they'd kept it to themselves, not knowing what it actually was at first, but knowing that the coming and going was good, because it meant food in the cupboards and, sometimes, new clothes, or even a trip to the dilapidated funfair on the pier if Christine was in a particularly good mood.

Most of this she had expected. But none of it helped her at all. Nothing much about Danny; plenty that was inaccurate. The recording even described Jazz going missing for three nights, when Kit remembered clearly that it had been thirteen-year-old Josie who had gone, after Christine had slapped her face having caught her trying her hand at generating her own money for the slots. The better things were missing altogether. No one had asked the kids whether there were any good times, of course. The days when the five of them had some cash and could go to the bus station and toss a coin to choose which bus to ride to the end of its route, leading to adventures in mountains and forests as well as on their beloved beaches. The closeness between them just didn't feature. There was nothing about the way the older three looked after Kit and Tyler, read them stories and got them ready for school.

Kit sighed. She'd rather stop now. And how likely had it been, anyway, that the file was going to give her a clue? They'd had some good and some bad social workers, but if Danny had given any indication that Tyler had been abused, surely even the most incompetent amongst them would have done something about it, not just written it down and moved on?

She skimmed a few more pages. A transfer summary caught her eye. The social worker was Angela Maynard. Tyler had mentioned that name. She looked at the date. Danny would have been sixteen and Tyler would have been fourteen. It was the year after they had all been taken into care for the last time. She began reading.

Meeting with Danny at Redbridge House. This was my last meeting with Danny. I have explained to Danny, Krystal and Tyler that their cases will be transferred to a new social worker because I will be leaving the department tomorrow.

Danny was initially resistant to speaking to me, as usual. However, after some persuasion, he was able to reflect upon his time in residential care and the reasons for him being there. I reiterated to him that this had come about because, in spite of the fact that mum had made substantial inroads in terms of her alcohol issues and had attended parenting groups as she was asked to do, Danny and Tyler had continued to be beyond parental control at home and mum had become stressed. The situation had then broken down again, bringing the children back into care. Since their admission, the boys' behaviour has presented a significant challenge to staff. I explained to Danny that it is time for him to take stock. He is due to leave care in two months' time and needs to address his behaviour in order to achieve a successful transition.

Danny made reference to himself and Tyler when at home having spent time with a man who would take them to his home and provide them with alcohol and cigarettes. It therefore appears that mum may not always have exercised proper care over the boys' whereabouts when they were living with her. Danny became distressed during the session, but time constraints did not allow me to explore this issue any further with him. I telephoned Christine Goddard afterwards and she confirmed that she had been aware that this man had befriended the boys when they were aged around eleven and thirteen. She was also aware that he had supplied them with alcohol and cigarettes even though they were underage. Her collusion with this is a concern.

Kit closed her eyes. She saw the whole picture immediately. Angela Maynard, who clearly hadn't wanted to hear Danny out. That one chance to find out where his furious anger had come from, the guilt at the heart of it, a chance to get him help, and she had blown it. She had been burnt out and exhausted probably, and just wanting to end the job and get away to something easier. Or only half convinced by what Danny had hinted at, and not wanting to delve any further. Finding it hard to believe, or plain distasteful. The shutters coming down, just like Tyler had said they did. Leaving Danny even more ashamed, afraid to talk about it again for fear of getting the same reaction, and finally, three years later, unable to cope with the ball of fear and pain and guilt inside him any longer. And Micky Winter, who had bribed her brothers with alcohol and fags, waiting for his chance to demand something in return. But most of all, Christine. Fucking, fucking Christine. Had she known? Would even Christine have actually turned a blind eye to that?

Kit stood up and put Danny's files back into the bundle, snapping the elastic bands onto it. She put the files on the shelf and then made her way quickly out of the room and down the corridor. She crossed reception, making sure to avoid Rhodri's eye, and once outside, fumbled in her bag and lit a cigarette as soon as she was clear of the building. Her phone buzzed; glancing at it, she could see Tyler's text. He was on his way to their mother's already. She knew she needed to get up there before anything kicked off. She half ran to her car.

As she drove towards the Coed, Kit thought back to when she'd last seen Christine. It had been Danny's birthday, when Kit, Tyler and their sisters had accompanied Christine on a miserable family outing to lay flowers on his grave. Kit had let the others deal with Christine, as per her usual strategy. She'd got past the stage of hating Christine long ago. But she'd had a long think about things when Danny had died, and she'd worked out that with the anger gone, she could easily start feeling sorry for her mother. That would lead straight on to feeling responsible for her, and then the next thing she'd find herself looking after her. She couldn't take that risk, so from then on, she just kept her distance.

Kit met Tyler in the street outside Christine's. They found the front door open as usual, to allow her friends in and out with their dramas and complicated feuds over lotto shares. Tyler followed Kit along the hall and into the kitchen, where Christine was standing in her favoured spot, leaning against the sink, smoking. The house was small and sparsely furnished. It was painted in creams and muted pastel tones and, for the first time, it struck Kit that it bore some similarity to her own flat, the same neutrality and lack of cosiness. The house was immaculate, though. Christine had always spent large parts of the day cleaning, sometimes until her fingers were red raw or, if she was feeling particularly anxious, until they bled.

She was looking at the door as they came in, expecting one of her mates, no doubt. When she saw who it was, she was speechless with surprise. But not for long.

'Well, Jesus bloody Christ, you two are still alive then, are you?'

'Looks like it. Nice thing to say, though, Mam, when one of your kids isn't.' Tyler sat down at the kitchen table and regarded her with disgust. Kit took the chair next to his and waited to see what he would do. She knew it would be for the best if she kept quiet as long as possible.

Christine's face was even more yellow and rutted than it had been the last time Kit had seen her, almost six months before. Every time she saw her mother, it reminded Kit that she really ought to give up smoking, for fear that she would end up looking like her. Christine was painfully skinny, too. Apart from her stomach, which was swollen and rounded, stretching the thin fabric of her worn black leggings almost to bursting point – the tell-tale sign that cirrhosis had finally appeared, the fluid building up in her abdomen. She was only forty-four, but she probably wouldn't make fifty. Kit knew that death from cirrhosis was a terrible thing, and, in spite of everything, she dreaded it for her mother.

She had been pretty once. Kit didn't remember it herself, but Jazz had told her; as the eldest she'd always had more recollection of the early days. They were the better times, when Gino and Christine were still getting on and having a good time together.

'What's this about then?' Christine's voice brought Kit back into the moment. 'I don't see either of you from one year to the next. I could be dead myself, for all you two'd know about it. Your sisters are no better. Only our Dan I had, look, and now he's gone too.'

'Yeah, well, let's not start about that, eh?' Tyler brought her to an abrupt end. They both knew how long she could go on once she started on the subject of Danny, who had turned into a saint in Christine's eyes now he was safely dead and unable to demand anything from her.

'All right, go on then, boy, what's it all in aid of?'

'As I said, I need a word.' Tyler kept his eyes on Christine's face.

'What's she doing here then?' She gestured in Kit's direction. 'Not up the duff, is she?' Christine had always reserved her worst treatment for Kit. Danny's theory had been that it was because she was Gino's favourite, though if that was the case, Kit had seen precious little evidence of it over the last twenty years.

'I asked her to come. I wanted her to hear it too.' Tyler's voice was calm. Kit was impressed, but she doubted he was going to be able to keep it up.

Christine had turned away and was rummaging around in a cupboard, finally pulling out a bottle of cider. She put it on the worktop and started to unscrew the lid. Tyler stood up and crossed to where she stood. He picked up the bottle, took the lid off and tipped the lot down the sink with one hand, holding Christine out of the way with the other, his muscled arm outstretched and his powerful hand gripping her scrawny shoulder.

'What the hell are you doing? I'm in my own home, I'm entitled to have a drink if I want one.'

Tyler laughed at that. 'Do what you like when we're gone,' he said. 'But I've got something to talk to you about, and I don't want you pissed for it.'

Deprived of alcohol, Christine made do with another fag. 'Fire away then, boy, I'm all ears.'

'Micky Winter.' Kit knew Tyler had come out with it like that because he wanted to see if he would get a reaction. Kit was studying her mother's face closely, too. Something was going on there, a flinch around her mouth, a widening of her eyes.

'What about him?' This was a surprise. Kit had expected her mother would deny she had ever heard of a Micky Winter and would stick to that story come hell or high water.

'I think you know what I'm going to say, don't you?'

'I haven't got a clue what you're on about, boy.'

Tyler sighed. 'All right then,' he said, with exaggerated patience, 'you want me to spell it out, do you?'

Christine took a few more drags of her fag. She regarded Tyler carefully, then turned to Kit: 'Go and lock the front door. I don't want anyone walking in and knowing our business.'

Kit was so surprised to be given this order that she did as she was told. Then she returned to the kitchen, where Christine was locking the back door. This done, Christine turned to face Tyler.

'What about him?' she repeated.

'You remember him then?'

'Of course I do. Everyone knew him. He lived down The Avenue. He was a very important man, Micky Winter. He used to run that youth club down in town.'

Usually, Kit could read her mother pretty well, but this time she just wasn't sure. Was Christine faking it, or did she really not have any idea where this was going?

Tyler had dropped his face into his hands. Kit didn't know whether he was crying or furious. Even Christine seemed to recognise that she shouldn't say anything. Finally, Tyler raised his head. 'Where did you think we were getting the money from, Mam?'

'What?' Christine's face was set hard. She wasn't about to admit to anything.

'Where did you think we were getting the fucking money from?'

'What money?'

'The money we used to bring back from Micky Winter's house. And the booze and the fags. You should have stopped us going there. You should have reported him. But Danny used to give you some, didn't he? And you didn't want that to stop. You wanted the booze and the money.'

'I don't know anything about that. I never even knew you went in his house.'

'You knew,' Tyler insisted.

'I am telling you I didn't. I never even knew. Take it or leave it, that's the truth.'

Kit looked at her twin. His jaw was rigid, and she recognised the look he got when he was trying very hard not to cry. Just like when he was young, and he used to wake up from a nightmare and he wouldn't want anyone except Kit to know he was upset. She had been the only one who could calm him. She had looked after Tyler, and Danny had looked after her. That had been the deal. Now, she understood that this mattered to Tyler. She didn't completely understand why; it was hardly news that Christine had always put herself first. But it did matter. He needed to prove that Christine had known something. Kit hesitated, knowing the trouble she might be about to cause for herself, but she couldn't stay silent. She took a deep breath.

'It's not the truth,' she said.

'What's it got to do with you?' Christine spat it out, her anger coming to the surface easily as soon as Kit was involved.

'A social worker called Angela Maynard phoned you about it, a few years after it happened. Danny had said something to her, when he was in Redbridge House. And you admitted to her that you'd known all along that Ty and Danny were going to some man's house and he was giving them alcohol.'

'How do you know that?' The words came from Tyler. Kit knew she couldn't afford to answer that one in front of Christine, who wouldn't think twice about reporting Kit for accessing her dead brother's file. So she ignored him for now. Time enough for that explanation later.

Christine continued to smoke. If she was surprised by what Kit had said, she didn't show it. 'I never spoke to any social worker.'

'I can give you the date and time she rang you, if you like.' Kit said.

Christine shrugged. 'Don't make no odds to me. I never spoke to her. If she says I did, she's a fucking liar.'

Tyler got up at that point and crossed to Christine and put his face right up close to hers. She tried to draw away but he had her backed up against the sink. Kit jumped up and moved towards them. She'd been worried about this. Tyler had never completely lost it with Christine, but it could be the first time. Christine tried to turn her head to the side to get away from Tyler's gaze, but he took a firm hold of her chin and pulled her face back to look at his.

'We all know who the liar is, Mam.' He let her go and walked out of the door.

Kit left Christine bent double, choking into the sink, and ran after him. He was already outside, waiting for her, kicking a beer can around the pavement. As she came out of the gate, Tyler kicked it hard, so high into the air that it shot into Christine's garden, falling just short of her kitchen window.

'Fuck it. Missed the bitch.'

'Ty, she was never going to admit it, was she? You must have known she wouldn't.'

'It's not that.'

'What is it then?'

'Jesus, you're a bloody social worker, haven't they sent you on a course or something? Can't you work it out?" he said. He was pacing up and down now, unable to stay still.

They were becoming exasperated with each other, moving beyond their usual banter. This hardly ever happened, and when it did, it usually got bad. Kit tried to figure out how to calm it down.

'Look, it's different when it's your own family, isn't it? You're not a client. I need you to tell me, that's all. Why does it matter so much to get Christine to admit she knew something?'

Kit saw that her question had quietened him. He was still now and staring at the pavement.

'I just kept hoping maybe she didn't know. That she'd be able to say where she thought the cans and the money and all that came from. She never asked. She must have had an idea, but she didn't want to know.'

It took Kit a minute to recognise the sensation in her eyes as tears. She'd given up on Christine long ago herself, but she saw now that Tyler hadn't. He'd been let down again and again, but he still kept hoping to find his mother doing the right thing.

'Yeah. Of course. Look, you'd better get off home. Or do you want to come to mine?' she asked him.

'Maybe.' He shrugged. 'By the way, how did you know? About the phone call?'

Kit knew that there was no way out of this. 'I went into Danny's records.' She tried to say it as if it was nothing, but Tyler was way too bright for that.

'You what? Is that allowed?'

'Well, no, obviously not. I'd probably get sacked if they found out. But I did. I wanted to see if Danny did speak to a social worker about it. He didn't say much but it should have been enough for her to think Winter was dodgy. She did fuck all about it, but she did ring Christine. And Christine admitted she'd known you two were going there and drinking. Angela Maynard seemed more worried about that.'

'So I was right. Danny did tell her.'

'Not all of it, but enough that she should have asked more about it. He gave her a clue, you know?'

He nodded. 'Yeah. I know.'

'If she had—'

He stopped her. 'No, don't. Let's just get away from here.'

The unfinished sentence sat between them as they walked to the car and they left it where it was. Neither of them needed to fill the silence. It felt just like it had after Danny died, when their wordless understanding of each other's grief had been their only comfort.

Kit knew now that Tyler needed to be alone, because she felt the same herself. She drove into town and dropped him outside his flat, the two of them exchanging nothing but a quick goodbye as he jumped out of the car. Then she drove home, wondering if Danny would still have been alive if Angela Maynard had made a different choice.

CHAPTER 12

The following morning Kit left the flat early and went to the café at the end of the road. Tyler wasn't answering her texts and she'd spent a restless night worrying about him. She was starving and realised she hadn't eaten anything the day before. She ordered a large cooked breakfast with extra fried bread, and a mug of coffee. After she'd eaten, she ordered a second coffee. She kept thinking about Micky Winter. The worry nagged at her mind – Tyler had said Danny hadn't hurt anyone with the fire, but was that true? Was it possible that Winter had been in there, and that he'd died? Danny's anger was diamond-hard and he never forgot a grudge. She reached into her bag to get out her phone and in a second found the births and deaths page of the *South Wales Express*.

Scrolling through the notices for the surname Winter, she found him almost at once. She saw with relief that Michael Winter had died following a short illness. The funeral details were given and donations were asked for in lieu of flowers, for a local cancer hospice and for the activities fund at Sandbeach youth centre. The date of his death was 12th October 2008. Kit frowned. That couldn't be right. She remembered again the smell of smoke that night and walking past the wreckage of the fire the next day on her way to school. Her last year in Sandbeach Primary. But by October 2008, she had been out at Cliffside for more than two years.

As she tried to work it out, she noticed a middle-aged woman sitting at the next table. She was vaguely familiar, and she was smiling at Kit. Kit smiled back. Much to her annoyance, the woman picked up her cup of coffee and crossed to Kit's table.

'Mind if I sit down?'

'I'm sorry, do I—'

'I'm Fay. I'm Lucy's carer. Lucy Cooper. You're the social worker, aren't you?'

'That's right.' Fay was settling herself at the table now. Kit thought this was dead cheeky. She finished her coffee in a couple of gulps. She wasn't in the mood for a chat.

'How's it going, love? With Lucy?'

Was the woman for real? 'I can't go into that,' Kit said firmly.

'Confidential, is it? I understand. She's a lovely girl, though, isn't she?'

'I expect she is.' Kit started to gather up her stuff.

'Well, you've met her, so I'm sure you know.'

'It's hard to get to know her, though, isn't it? With her being non-verbal.' Kit felt bad about being so irritable, but she had wanted her coffee in peace.

'Yes, I know what you mean, love. She does a few signs, though. I manage with those.'

Kit stopped in the process of doing up her bag and stared at Fay. 'What signs?'

'Makaton. I taught her back last year. Only the basics, you know. I use it with all the kids I work with. She really took to it. And I taught little Chloe, too, so she could speak to her sister. Thick as thieves those two.'

'Lucy can do Makaton? How can she manage the hand gestures?'

'Well, I only taught her the easy ones, and one of her arms works better than the other, you know? It's not so tight, she can use it a bit. And she can follow some signs, too.'

Kit sat back down. 'Why didn't you mention this before?' she asked.

'No one asked me.' Fay was starting to look put out.

'I'm sorry, Fay, of course, you are quite right. I didn't ask you. I should have. I just expected that, if there was a way to communicate with Lucy, the Coopers would have said.'

'Ah, well, perhaps they wouldn't, though, see.'

'I'm not following you. Why wouldn't they tell me?'

'Mrs Cooper's got very set ideas, you know? About how she wants Lucy looked after. I don't blame her, mind; I'd be the same if she was one of mine. Mrs Cooper didn't feel the Makaton was helping. Felt she could look after Lucy just fine without it.'

Fay was looking put out again now. Kit took a guess at what might have happened. 'Was she annoyed with you about it, Fay?'

Fay nodded. 'The thing is, when they found out I'd been

doing it ... well, Mrs Cooper, she had her hair off with me. Said her husband didn't want me teaching it to Lucy, he reckoned it stressed her out. Nothing like that has ever happened with them before, they've always been very happy with my work. So I told the other kids not to do it anymore. Me and Lucy kept it a secret then. But I think it's a shame, I do really. Then I heard Mrs Cooper, that day when I was in the kitchen and you had been in with Lucy, do you remember?'

Kit thought back to her first visit to Lucy, and remembered Fay quietly drinking coffee at the kitchen table in the kitchen while Annie and Kit were locking horns over Lucy's communication.

'Yes, I remember.'

'She didn't tell you the truth. Not completely. It is possible to communicate with Lucy and there's more going on in her mind than anyone knows, let me tell you.'

'Is that right?' What was Fay getting at?

'Oh yes. Don't get me wrong, I'm not saying Lucy's not well looked after. Mrs Cooper's devoted to her. It's just ...'

'Go on,' Kit encouraged her.

'Well, I found it funny. It might just be me, mind. The younger girls who used to work there, they all loved him to bits. Thought he was handsome. But I never quite took to Mr Cooper myself. Very charming and all that, but there's something not right if you ask me. I mean, why wouldn't he want Lucy to learn to sign? Even if it's only a few words, it's something, isn't it?'

Kit smiled at her. 'Yes. Yes, it is.' She pondered for a minute. 'But the school didn't tell me either. They said they had never really found a way to communicate with her. They said they'd tried communication boards, iPad, the lot. Surely they would have at least tried to teach her Makaton?'

'That's what I mean about Mr Cooper, though, see. I've been in meetings with him, and he's got that dozy head teacher wrapped right round his little finger if you ask me. If he says jump, she asks how high, you know? And that social worker, too – Jean Collins, is it? All over him like a rash that one. Always going on about how fantastic he is. But it's Mrs Cooper who does all the donkey work with us carers. No one's got anything to say about that, have they?'

'No, they haven't.' Kit smiled at her. 'Thank you, Fay. I am so glad I ran into you.'

'Well, that was just luck, wasn't it? I mean, you're welcome, but perhaps next time you'll think to ask the carers straight off, eh?'

'Yes, I will. Definitely. Thanks, Fay, goodbye.' Kit picked up her bag and went to the till, where she paid for Fay's coffee as well as her own breakfast. Then she went back to the flats to collect her car and drove straight to the office. The usual queue of cars was waiting to get into the car park, overspilling onto the road. After a few minutes of waiting, she became exasperated and pulled out from behind them. Passing the queue, she drove to the back of the building where she parked in a loading bay, crossing her fingers the security guy wouldn't come for a walk round just yet. After locking her car, she made her way into the building and up the stairs to the office.

There was no sign of Vernon yet. She made him coffee, knowing she wouldn't get any sense out of him until he'd had one. When he arrived, she clocked his grim expression and added a couple of custard creams to his saucer before following him into his office. She put the coffee and biscuits down on his desk.

'You're keen this morning,' he said. 'What's up? Best get straight to the point, I'm not in the best of moods. I've just found out I'm being taken to Torquay next year.'

'Doesn't sound like too much of a crisis.'

'It's right in the middle of the Six Nations. Me and Dai always get tickets or else we watch the rugby in the pub. Martin and Nell are a menace with that bloody Groupon, I kid you not.'

'There's pubs in Torquay, you know, Vern.' Kit realised she was going to have to work hard to avoid becoming sidetracked into Vernon's anxiety.

'But Torquay's in England,' he snapped.

'I know that. I'm still pretty sure they have pubs.'

'Dai reckons they won't have the rugby on. The English only bother with football, so he says. Do you think that could be right?'

'I couldn't say. I expect you'll find a way. Can I ask you something about the Coopers?'

'Oh, all right, if you must.'

'I found out Lucy knows some Makaton. The Coopers never said a word. What do you make of that?'

'How do you know it?' Vernon asked, starting in on his custard creams.

'Her carer told me. Fay.'

'When?'

'I just saw her in the café. She says she taught all the kids a bit. She said the Coopers didn't like it. And they certainly never told me.'

'Perhaps they just didn't think to mention it.'

'Don't be so bloody soft, Vern.' Kit could see that his mind wasn't on what she was saying at all. The Torquay plan had rattled him.

'All right, I give in, what do you make of them not having mentioned it?' Vernon was making an effort to focus on the matter at hand.

'They know I've seen Lucy and that I couldn't communicate with her much. They could have mentioned it then. They know exactly what the assessment is about – I went through it with both of them and they never said a word. I think they deliberately didn't tell me. They don't want me to talk to her, Vern. They were hoping it wouldn't come up. Why? Are they hiding something?'

Vernon tipped his chair back into his thinking position. He regarded her with his eyes narrowed.

'What?' she asked him, feeling self-conscious.

'How many other cases have you got besides this one?'

'Fifteen, I think. Why?' She knew exactly where this was going.

'How much time are you spending on the Coopers?'

'Quite a bit.'

'Right. You need to calm down. I told you to keep an open mind but now you're falling too far the other way. You are losing your perspective.'

'I'm not,' she said, knowing she was. Kit kicked herself for revealing it. It was always disorientating when Vernon decided to stop playing silly buggers and switch on his perceptive brain.

'Yes, you are.' Vernon's voice was firm. 'Maybe they are not being any more cooperative than they need to be, but don't go over-interpreting that. Parents don't tell us lots of things. It doesn't mean they are hiding anything sinister, it just means they are angry and resentful about us being in their lives. They probably aren't going to go out of their way to help. That doesn't mean he's an abuser, Kit. It just means he's human. I might well do the same myself. It's a little bit of power, isn't it?'

'I suppose.'

'Now, you need to get this case closed, and get on with your others. How much have you got left to do on it?'

'It's the final visit this afternoon, to see Lucy again.'

'OK, so go and get that done and then close it down. In fact, have the closure in my inbox by tomorrow morning. We've done our best, Kit, but the system has exonerated him and now you are relying on gossip, and, what's worse, you are blowing that out of all proportion. There is nothing on record to say that Matt Cooper has ever put a foot wrong, and if we don't get this finalised and get him back home, there's going to be such an almighty ruck that even the lovely Councillor Desiree Palmer won't be able to save my neck this time. Now bugger off, I need to get on to Dai and see if we can come up with a plan. And do not go asking Lucy any leading questions, all right?'

'I would never do that.'

'Yes, you would. You've got the makings of a half-decent social worker, unlike the rest of the deadbeats in this team, so don't jeopardise it. No fishing, Kit. I mean it. Time to let this one go.'

Kit spent the rest of the day catching up on her recording. She put all the information she'd gathered about the Coopers onto the electronic assessment record, and then went for a late lunch. When it got close to four o'clock, she went out to her car, smoking a fag on her way and two more on the drive to the Coopers', arriving with her heart racing from the hit of nicotine.

Chloe was waiting at the front door when Kit pulled up outside the house. 'Are we going to do more colouring, Kit?' she asked excitedly, as soon as Kit set foot on the drive.

'Not today, sweetie. It's Lucy's turn to talk to me, isn't it?'

Chloe pulled a face. 'I want to do some more,' she said.

'Well, maybe if I'm not too long with Lucy, I can do one with you afterwards. Just a quick one, mind.'

'The fairy again?' Chloe was hanging in the doorway, reluctant to let Kit in until she got her own way.

'If you like. Lucy first, though. But before that I need to talk to your mum. Where is she?'

'In the kitchen.' Chloe turned and went to sit on the bottom stair while Kit went into the kitchen. Annie was standing at the worktop with her back to the door. She didn't turn around. Kit's irritation grew by the second as she waited in silence for Annie to acknowledge her presence. Finally, after a lengthy period spent repositioning ingredients in a tagine, Annie threw a quick glance over her shoulder.

'Oh, hello,' she said. 'What can I do for you?'

'I have an appointment to see Lucy today. Had you forgotten?'

'Looks like it.' Annie turned back to the tagine and resumed her fiddling with the contents.

Kit decided to get straight to the point. 'Annie, why didn't you tell me that Lucy knows some Makaton?'

The back of Annie's shoulders lifted in a shrug. 'I didn't think it was important.'

'Well, of course it's important. You know I've already tried to do some work with her. You know that I need to get her views as part of the assessment. I explained all this to you. You told me she was totally non-verbal.'

'She is.'

'But she can sign. She can communicate.'

Annie sighed. She turned around and leant back against the kitchen counter and crossed her arms in front of her. 'And can you use Makaton?'

'No.'

'Well, there you are then. No point in telling you.' Annie

picked up the tagine, opened the fridge door, and placed it carefully inside.

'But I could have brought someone else with me, someone who can use it.'

Annie closed the fridge and turned back to Kit. She shrugged again. 'I doubt that you'd get much out of her anyway. Fay taught her a few signs, but it was a while ago now and she hasn't used it since. Matt felt it was too much for her. We don't need signs to communicate with her. We understand her needs perfectly well. And quite frankly, I'd rather you didn't troop anyone else through my home. The children find it unsettling. But I suppose then you will say I'm not cooperating. So it's up to you. Lucy's on her own just now, the carer isn't due for a bit. I am taking a record of everything you do and say, and it will all go in the complaint at the end. Do what you like, as long as you are prepared to face the consequences.'

'Thanks, I will. I am going to try and speak to Lucy again. If I can't manage it, I'll have to think about what to do next and what action we can take.' Kit was lying through her teeth, hoping to rattle Annie's composure. 'I need to communicate with her somehow, Annie. I'm not happy to close this assessment until I've done so, now that I know that it is possible.'

Annie rolled her eyes upwards but didn't answer, so Kit turned to leave the kitchen, knowing this was best, before Annie's rudeness needled her so much that she said something unprofessional. Annie would delight in that. As Kit moved into the hall, Annie banged the kitchen door shut behind her.

Kit found Chloe still sitting on the bottom of the stairs. She sat down next to her and Chloe leant in close to Kit's side.

'Hi, sweetie, you still here?' she asked her.

'Yes. I'm waiting to do our colouring,' Chloe said. 'Cameron is out with his friends all the time and Daddy isn't here like he used to be. And Mummy's always cross. She says it's all your fault, but she won't tell me why.'

'You sound sad,' Kit said.

'I am.' Chloe dropped her eyes and Kit saw she was fighting back tears. She reached out to touch her hair but remembered just in time that Chloe didn't like it. Close up, she could see that Chloe's hair was even wilder than it had been the last time she'd seen her. In fact, it looked a bit matted. Surely Annie wasn't letting things slip so much that she wasn't making sure Chloe brushed her hair?

'Look, honey, I really do have to see Lucy first. I'll come and find you as soon as I'm done.' Kit dug in her bag and got out her pack of gel pens and a crumpled copy of the fairy exercise. 'Why don't you go upstairs and put all this ready for us in your room, and I'll be up in a bit.'

'OK.' Chloe started off up the stairs very slowly. As soon as Kit turned the corner into Lucy's room, she could hear Chloe's footsteps returning.

'Chloe?' she called.

Chloe appeared at the door immediately. 'My room's not upstairs now. It's here.'

'I'm sorry, I forgot about you and Lucy sharing. Why don't

you come in here and colour while I talk to Lucy? Then you can show me the fairy at the end.'

'OK.' Chloe came in and threw herself on the floor by Lucy's bed. She started work on the fairy straight away.

Lucy was in her chair again, watching TV. Kit came closer and touched her hand. Lucy turned slightly towards Kit and Kit smiled at her.

'Hi, Lucy. Do you remember me? I'm Kit. I'm your social worker.' Lucy stared at Kit for a few seconds, her beautiful blue eyes unblinking, and then turned back to the TV. Kit sighed. She was starting to recognise when Lucy was not going to cooperate.

'Lucy,' she said, 'I need to talk to you. Remember how I told you that it's my job to visit children and ask them what they think.'

Lucy continued to stare at the TV, without the slightest change in her expression. The room was warm and airless, and Kit was beginning to feel tired. But she couldn't walk away yet.

'It must be very hard for you at the moment, Lucy. Because your dad isn't living here.' Lucy didn't move, and her expression didn't alter, but something in the room had changed. The tiniest of shifts.

Kit tried again. 'I expect you miss your dad, don't you, honey?' This time Kit was ready, and there it was – Lucy's breathing had altered, Kit was sure of it. It had come just a little faster, for a few breaths, then settled down again.

'Would you like your dad to come home?' This time Lucy turned her head. She looked directly at Kit and she made a guttural noise.

'She likes Mum better.' Kit jumped slightly. She had half forgotten Chloe was there.

'Does she? Really?' Kit remembered what Vernon had said. She knew she shouldn't push this too far. But she couldn't just leave it either.

Chloe sat up, cross-legged. 'Yes. Everyone thinks Lucy likes Dad best. But they're wrong. I know. Mum's her favourite.'

'How do you know that then, Chlo?' This was news to Kit. All she had heard from everyone was that Matt Cooper had the fantastic relationship with Lucy.

'Lucy told me, of course.' Chloe's tone suggested Kit was possibly the most stupid person she had ever come across.

'How does Lucy talk to you?'

'With her hands. Fay showed us.'

Kit paused and wondered whether to go on. She glanced at the open bedroom door. The hallway was empty and silent, no sign of Annie. She decided to risk it. Bugger Vernon and his warnings. 'Chloe, would you like to help me talk to Lucy?'

'OK. She won't do it if she doesn't feel like it, though.'

'That's all right. Let's give it a try, shall we? Will you ask her if she will talk to me and tell her about why I'm here?'

Chloe got up and squeezed onto the chair next to Kit. Lucy turned to her and Chloe lifted her hands up and made some gestures, speaking clearly as she did so. 'Lucy, do you want to talk to us?' she asked. Lucy's eyes followed the movements, but she didn't move herself.

'She's not answering. I expect she's not in the right mood.

I did say that she might not be, actually. Can we do my colouring now?'

'Will you ask her again?'

Chloe sighed heavily, but she nodded. 'I suppose so. But if Lucy had anything to say, she'd tell Mum, not you.' She repeated the question and made some more hand movements in Lucy's direction. Lucy's eyes were still following Chloe's hands, but again, she made no response.

'My sister doesn't feel like talking today,' Chloe said, with finality, and then, in order to close the matter, she turned away from Lucy and bent down to pick up her colouring.

The room was quite dark now and the heat was continuing to build. Kit's head was starting to ache, and she was desperately thirsty. She didn't want to stop trying but she needed a minute to think. She reached out to take Chloe's colouring from her.

'It's lovely, Chloe.' The fairy was resplendent in shocking pink once again.

'Thank you. Can we do it again next time you come?'

'Oh, I'm sorry, honey, I'm not coming again. This is my last visit. I came to talk to Lucy but then I've finished working with you three. We need to say goodbye today.'

Chloe looked devastated. 'I don't want this to be your last visit,' she said.

'I really am so sorry. Remember I told you I would be visiting to find out what you and Cam and Lucy thought? And now I've finished doing that, so I won't need to come to you anymore. Life will go back to normal now, Chlo.'

'Does that mean Daddy is coming home?'

Kit hesitated, but there was no reason not to tell Chloe the truth. It was time to admit defeat. 'He's going to be coming home soon.'

Chloe turned back to Lucy and made some more gestures. 'I'm telling Lucy.'

'OK, good girl.'

Chloe had picked up her pens again. 'I'm going to do you another drawing. A goodbye one.'

'That would be lovely.' Kit looked over at Lucy. She noticed Lucy's breathing was fast again, rasping in her chest. She definitely seemed agitated. Kit got up and moved closer to her, stepping around Chloe, who was still busy with her colouring on the floor.

'What is it, sweetie? It's my last visit so if there's anything you want to tell me, it needs to be now.' Kit bent down next to Lucy's chair. She reached out to touch her strong hand, but as she did so, Lucy raised her hand into the air and made a movement, close to her face. Kit looked at Chloe to ask what it meant, but Chloe was looking towards the door, following a sudden noise from that direction.

'I think you've finished here now, haven't you?' Annie stood in the doorway. 'It's time for Lucy's change. Her carer will be here to help me any minute.' Kit wondered how long Annie had been in the hall, and how much she had overheard.

'I think it's important that I understand what Lucy is saying. She made a sign and she seemed upset as well. It seemed to start when Chloe told her about Matt coming home.' Kit braced herself for Annie's reaction.

'Don't be ridiculous. What sign did Lucy make, Chloe?'

'I didn't see her make a sign.'

'Chloe's only six, you know. I'm not sure it's appropriate for you to be using her to communicate with a severely disabled child actually. It's hardly reliable.'

'I am reliable.' Chloe was sulking now.

Annie took no notice of her and continued to address Kit.

'Now, Miss Goddard, if your so-called assessment is over, I think it's time for you to leave.' Annie stood back and waited. Kit could see she was not going to win this one. She decided to retreat, for the time being.

'I'll have to go and take legal advice,' she said.

'You do that. It hasn't really helped you much so far, has it? I don't suppose we'll be seeing you again, so goodbye.' Annie turned and walked ahead of Kit down the hallway. Annie didn't say another word, but opened the front door, placing her attention upon her fingernails while she waited for Kit to leave. Kit did so, having failed to come up with a suitable parting shot.

As Kit got to her car, she heard her name being called. Chloe had come around from the back of the house and was running after her.

'I'm sorry, I didn't say goodbye, did I?' Kit said.

'No, you didn't. That was really mean. Can I sit in your car now?'

Kit wanted to get away. She was desperate for a fag and a

coffee and needed to speak to Vernon. But she saw that Chloe's face was sad again.

'Five minutes. Then I really do have to go.'

Chloe grinned. Kit unlocked the car and they both got in. Chloe settled herself in the front seat and started rummaging through Kit's glove compartment. She found a half-finished packet of fruit Mentos.

'Can I have these?'

'Go on then.'

Kit thought about the hand movement she had seen Lucy make just before Annie arrived in the room.

'Chloe, can I ask you something?'

Chloe nodded, her mouth full of sweets.

'Lucy did make another sign. I know you didn't see her, but I did. What does this mean?' Kit demonstrated roughly what she had seen Lucy do.

Chloe watched Kit's hand carefully and then she chewed for a few seconds.

'Show me again,' she said.

Kit repeated the sign while Chloe swallowed her sweets.

'It doesn't mean anything. I don't think that's even a sign. Sometimes Lucy makes mistakes.' Chloe opened the car door. 'I have to go in for my tea now. Goodbye, Kit.' And with that, she was gone, before Kit had the chance to reply.

CHAPTER 13

Kit arrived back at the office in fifteen minutes flat. Once there, she saw that the car park was packed. She drove round it twice without finding a space and then gave up and parked in the duty social worker's slot. She knew it wouldn't make her popular, but she needed to move quickly.

She took the stairs two at a time. Arriving in the team room, she ignored Ricky's questioning look, and headed for Vernon's door. She prayed he was in there, and, when she put her head in, saw she was in luck. He was at his desk, updating his allocations book.

'Bloody hell, you're a bit sweaty, and you're all red,' he said. 'What's up?'

Kit couldn't speak immediately. She flopped into a chair and took a few seconds to regain her breath.

'You want to give up those fags, girl.' Vernon pointed at her with his pen. He looked down at the allocation list again. 'And by the way, how are you getting on with those two new ones I gave you last week? I've got twenty referrals waiting and I need to get them allocated – when are you likely to have some space? There's a nasty-looking medical exam coming up tomorrow, I was hoping you'd take that for me. I can't send Maisie; the paediatrician's refused to have her in his clinic again.'

'Vern, shut up a minute, I want to tell you something.'

He stopped talking abruptly. 'Oh, all right, no need to get in a strop. What's the problem this time?'

'It's the Coopers.'

'For God's sake Kit, Jesus, not them again. Didn't I tell you not two hours ago to get that closed today?' It was the first time he had ever spoken to her with real exasperation in his voice.

'You did, yes. But something's changed. I spent some time with Lucy.'

'And?' Vernon sighed, but he leant back and waited.

'I got Chloe to do some signing. We asked Lucy questions. She seemed scared or stressed or something. She said something else, too, but I don't know what that was. I asked Chloe, and she said she didn't recognise it, but I'm pretty sure she was fibbing. Something doesn't feel right. Then Annie Cooper came along, and she threw me out.'

Vernon stared at her, struggling to take it all in. 'Why did Annie Cooper throw you out?' he asked, going straight to what was clearly the least important issue as far as Kit was concerned.

'Oh, I don't know. You know what she's like. She was complaining about me using Chloe to talk to Lucy, saying it wasn't appropriate because she's so young.'

'Remind me how old Chloe is?'

'She's six.' Kit could see that Vernon was not impressed. She started to feel less sure of her ground.

'So, what are you trying to tell me?' He was speaking slowly, as if she was daft.

'Well, surely now we can push it a bit further? Can we go back in with someone who can do Makaton? Maybe we'd better get legal advice, too.'

'So, what you're telling me is this: We've got a severely disabled girl with learning disabilities and very limited communication, mental capacity unknown, who's been taught a couple of Makaton signs by an unqualified carer, against the parents' wishes, and you want me to go for legal advice for care proceedings based on something you think she might have said, using a fibbing six-year-old as an interpreter. Are you trying to make us a laughing stock with Legal?'

Kit looked down at her lap. She couldn't argue with him. But then she thought back to Lucy, in that dark, stuffy room, her hand fluttering in the air, the first time Kit had seen her really animated.

'I know you're right about how it looks. But I'm so sure there's something more to find out with these girls. I just feel it. What do I do? I can't just move on and pretend it's all OK, can I? How could I live with myself?'

He smiled at her, his exasperation slipping away as he saw how upset she was. 'I'm not saying you're wrong. Your judgement's good, and I trust it. I'm saying I don't think you can do anything else but move on to the next family. You're always going to get cases that stay with you, Kit. I've got a list going back thirty years. Some I should have handled better, and plenty that I couldn't do a damn thing about, no matter how hard I tried. They keep me awake at night to this day. You have to learn to live with that. But focus on the children that you *can* help.'

'Can I make a suggestion?' Ricky's voice came from the doorway.

'Eavesdropping, were you?' Vernon snapped.

'You left the door open. The entire office heard every word.'

Kit smiled, pleased to see Ricky standing up to Vernon as she had told him numerous times he needed to do. Vernon was stunned into momentary silence, and Ricky took the opportunity to edge his way into the room.

'I just thought maybe . . . there's another way round all this.' Ricky's voice had become uncertain now, his nerve draining away as Vernon glared at him.

'Why don't you sit down and tell us?' Kit said, ignoring the look Vernon now shot at her. Ricky looked like he would rather not, now it came to it, but did as she suggested and sat in the chair next to her own.

'Come on then, lad, let's have the benefit of your expertise,' Vernon said.

'You don't need to speak to him like that,' Kit snapped. She turned to Ricky, making as much of a show as she could of the kindness in her voice.

'If you can think of something that would help me, Ricky, I'd really appreciate that. You can see why I can't just leave it, can't you?'

Vernon gave an exasperated grunt at this, but he didn't speak.

'You see, it seems to me that you're taking all the responsibility here,' Ricky started tentatively.

'Go on.' She encouraged him, making sure that she avoided catching Vernon's eye.

'You've ended up being Annie Cooper's enemy, haven't you?'

'I'm not sure I'd say that exactly.'

'But you're on opposite sides, aren't you?'

'Well, what do you expect? The woman is an absolute nightmare. I don't think it was my fault. Anyone would have struggled to work with her.'

Ricky was looking at Kit, his eyes kind. 'Kit, I have noticed that you often hear criticism where it doesn't exist. I wasn't making any comment about your ability, I was just describing things as they are. But you get defensive quite easily and sometimes it stops you hearing what people are actually saying.'

'Right, OK, sorry,' she mumbled, taken aback.

'What I'm saying is, does Annie Cooper love her children?'

'Yes. Absolutely.'

'And does she want the best for them?'

'Of course.'

'Then there's really only one person who can do anything about this situation. And that's Annie herself. You've got no evidence, Kit. No criminal conviction and nothing at all for care proceedings. But it seems to me that if there is anything to know, then deep down, Annie Cooper already knows it.'

'But she'd never admit that. She's defended him all along.'

'Because the system has put her in that position. I'm not saying that's your fault, before you get all defensive again.'

Kit's mind was ticking over. She was starting to see what Ricky was getting at. 'I follow you, but I'm not seeing where it gets us.'

'I'm seeing it,' Vernon said. He had his eyes closed now and was leaning back in his chair. 'What Ricky's saying is that, while we take all the responsibility, Annie doesn't have to ask herself the big question. She can leave it to us. If we don't find anything, and the police don't, well, then she can tell herself it can't be true. She can hate us and say we're incompetent and it's all rubbish, and she doesn't need to look right in front of her own face. It gets her off the hook.'

'Exactly.' Ricky was thrilled with Vernon's implicit approval. 'So what do I do?'

Ricky glanced at Vernon, who said nothing. Taking this as permission, Ricky continued. 'I think you need to go back there, Kit. You have to speak to her. Somehow you have to put this in her lap. Then you have to hope that she'll do the right thing.'

'But how do I put it in her lap? I've got nothing new to say to her. I can go and see her, but the way she sees it, he's been cleared, and that's that.'

'Now hang on, I don't think you can go over there again—'
Vernon was interrupted by his phone ringing. 'On my way.' He
jumped to his feet and headed for the door. 'There's a father
kicking off with Maisie in the car park,' he called out to the
team as he went. 'Someone call security and the police.'

Kit and Ricky followed him down the stairs. Kit was slightly
ahead of Ricky and saw Vernon's retreating back as he took the
shortcut through the boiler room and out of the back door into
the car park. The sound of his labouring breath reached her as
she gained on him. Up ahead, she could see Maisie cowering
against the side of her car as a man stood over her. He was
yelling, but Kit couldn't make out the words.

'Oi!' Vernon shouted, and he grabbed the man's shoulders
and pulled him backwards, away from Maisie. The man was
struggling in Vernon's grip. He was younger than Vernon and
very muscular, and Kit could see Vernon was losing hold of him
already. As Kit reached them, the man wrestled himself away.
He jumped backwards and stood, bending slightly forwards,
his hands out to his sides, open-palmed, ready to go for Vernon.
Kit knew Vernon was in trouble. As usual there was no sign of
the security guard. Furious rage glittered in the man's small
eyes. Kit ran through Maisie's caseload in her mind, trying to
work out which angry father this might be. If she could identify the kids, maybe she could find a way to reason with him.

'You can fucking keep out of it,' the man was yelling at
Vernon. 'This is nothing to do with you.'

'If it's about your kids, then tell us what the problem is,

and we can talk it over.' Kit kept her tone even. But the man turned on her.

'There's no problem with my kids. The problem is this useless fucking bitch.' He turned back to Maisie, only to find she had taken the opportunity to slip away across the car park. Ricky was helping her towards the back door, and she was dragging furiously on her asthma pump.

'Kit, it's Pete Croft!' Maisie managed to call out. Kit had it now; she'd heard Maisie talk about this guy, a father of two whose contact had recently been suspended by the court after one of the boys disclosed to Maisie that his father had been hitting his mother. Maisie had never said she'd had any problems with him herself, though. The man was looking from Maisie to Kit, and back again now, deliberating. For a moment, he seemed about to go after Maisie, but then he changed his mind and, with no warning at all, he came at Kit.

'Get away from her!' Vernon shouted. Kit saw Pete Croft's angry, jutting jaw, and she heard Vernon's footsteps as he ran towards Croft's back. Croft heard it, too, and swung round, his right arm coming up in readiness. He threw his fist out but was punching thin air. Kit took a few moments to register that Vernon had fallen to the ground, his face turning crimson, his hands grabbing frantically at his own throat.

'Vern!' Kit started towards him, but the man swung round again and stood firmly in her path.

'There's something wrong with him, get out of my way!' she screamed.

'Shut up, bitch.' His mouth curled into a snarl. Vernon was making gasping noises now.

'Undo his shirt! I know what do to!' Cole Jackson was getting out of his Porsche in the senior staff's section of the car park. He jumped the dividing barrier with surprising athleticism and ran towards them, taking his jacket off as he ran.

'Call an ambulance,' Kit shouted at Ricky.

'It's going to be too late by the time they get here. He's having a heart attack.' Cole came level with Kit's left-hand side. Pete Croft was blocking their way. He was squaring up again, putting himself in between them and Vernon. Cole stood rooted to the spot, clearly not willing to try and pass him.

'Who the fuck are you?' Pete Croft growled. 'Are you the boss? Cos if you are, I've got something to say to you.'

On the ground, Vernon was gasping louder now, and his body was convulsing as he curled his arms around his chest. Fear and rage rose in Kit's stomach. She could see Ricky coming towards Pete Croft from the side, but she put her hand up to tell him to stop. She didn't need help. Pete Croft had stopped being a person to her now and had become an object, something that simply had to be moved. She moved closer to him and, before he could go for her, she gathered all the nicotine-flavoured spit she could muster, and shot it straight into his face, aiming at his open mouth. It was a neat trick Danny had taught her, in case she was ever in danger; no one ever expected women to spit. As he put up his hand to wipe his eyes and mouth, making a choking noise full of disgust, she put her hands tight on his shoulders so that her nails dug into his flesh through his thin T-shirt, and brought her face as close as she could to his.

'You stop it. Right now. The police are on their way. That man is dying. If you don't let us help him, I will make sure that you go down for a very long time. Daisy and Ryan will be grown up by the time they see you again.'

He stared into her eyes, but she didn't flinch. Physical violence didn't scare Kit. After a few seconds, he took a step backwards and started away across the car park, still retching from the taste of Kit's spit in his mouth.

Kit ran to Vernon's side. He was still gasping; she knelt down next to him, but she didn't know what to do. Then Cole Jackson dropped down beside her, and ripped Vernon's shirt open. He started to bang on Vernon's chest. Vernon was not making any noise now. He wasn't moving either. Cole Jackson took Vernon's head and tipped it backwards; he put his fingers in Vernon's mouth and moved them around, then leant over and started giving him mouth to mouth. Kit took Vernon's hand and held it, rubbing his fingers between her own and watching his motionless face each time it appeared between the rise and fall of Cole Jackson's head. She felt Ricky's hands on her shoulders from behind, trying to reassure her.

'Don't die, don't die, don't die,' she whispered. 'What would Nell do without you?' Cole Jackson's head went down again and again until suddenly she heard a retching noise and Cole shot back on his haunches in an attempt to save his expensive suede shoes, as Vernon opened his eyes and brought his morning tea and biscuits up all over the tarmac.

Kit was aware of vehicles pulling up nearby and footsteps coming towards her, but she couldn't look up from Vernon's face. She kept hold of his hand. He was deathly pale now, but his eyes were open, and he was trying to speak.

'Shut up for once, for fuck's sake,' she told him. As the paramedics reached them and took over, Kit was pushed out of the way. By the fire escape, Maisie was being tended to by a paramedic. Cole Jackson was putting himself back together, picking up his jacket and dabbing at his vomit-splashed shoes with a tissue. When he glanced up, she smiled at him.

'Well done,' she said. She felt self-conscious, but she had to acknowledge what he'd done somehow.

He shrugged. 'No problem. Couldn't let him die on the premises, could I? Think of the paperwork. I'd have to design a new form for that.' He grinned at her, something she had never seen him do before. She wished Vernon could have witnessed the sudden appearance of Cole Jackson's sense of humour. 'And well done to you, too,' he continued, adding to the surprise. 'You handled that really well. You're ... er ... quite *tough*, aren't you?'

She laughed. 'Yeah, I am.'

Then she found herself looking around for Ricky. He was talking to a police officer a few feet away, but his eyes were fixed on Kit. He smiled at her, and to her own surprise, she immediately started to cry. Ricky left the police officer mid-sentence and reached Kit in a few strides. He put his arms around her and held her while she shook and sobbed, until finally the warmth of his tight grasp started to calm her. He reached into the pocket of her hoody then and took out her cigarettes and lighter. He lit one for her and put it in her hand, then took her other hand in his and started to lead her towards his car.

'Where are we going?' she asked him.

'I think you need to go home. I'll drive you, we can get your car later.'

'No, It's fine. I'm fine. I've got something I need to do.'

Ricky was appalled. 'I really don't think you should be working.'

'I have to. It can't wait. I'll call you later.'

Kit walked away quickly before Ricky could get the chance to stop her. The paramedics were now manoeuvring a complaining Vernon onto a stretcher. Kit felt calm enough to smile at how he was going to react to the news that he'd been saved by the kiss of life from Cole Jackson.

After collecting her bag from the office, Kit sat in her car for a few minutes, thinking about what Ricky had said. He was right about giving responsibility to Annie, but, at the same time, she wasn't sure it would be enough. What could she say that would shift Annie's thinking? She thought again about Steph Harman. Then she picked up her phone, flicked on to Jazz's text to check the address she'd given, started the car and set off for Canning Road.

Kit didn't let herself think about what she was doing until she pulled up outside number 56. It was a few streets away from Christine's, one of the houses that had already been done up in the refurb programme. Kit knew these houses inside out, knew the design and capacity of each type. She could see Steph's was a mid-terrace with two bedrooms. She must have children then, but no more than one, or maybe two if they were quite young. It was a neat house, freshly dashed in a dark creamy colour. Steph had picked the green front door from amongst the choices provided by the housing association. It was a good decision, Kit thought, far smarter than the reds and blues on the other houses. Judging by the outside, Steph was looking surprisingly together. But then Kit thought about Christine's immaculate kitchen, and the way she would sit after a long cleaning session, nursing her sore fingers and drinking vodka.

As she got out of the car, the front door of the house opened, and a woman came out. She was medium height, and had cropped hair dyed a flaming shade of red. Kit wavered for a moment, but she was buoyed by the feeling of being on her own stamping ground, and much more confident than she ever felt in the offices and meeting rooms of the civic centre. Plus, she had Steph's association with Jazz to give her an intro, after all. Kit walked over to the house and stepped onto the path. The woman looked up from locking her front door. She was well made up, thin-faced but still pretty, and dressed in a shapeless blue tunic of some kind; not a nurse's uniform but something similar.

'Steph?'

'Yeah?' She was on the alert at once. She glanced at Kit's chest and Kit wished she had thought to remove her council badge and lanyard – the sure sign of trouble for anyone on this estate, whether it emanated from Social Services, the Council Tax Department or Noise Control.

'I'm Krystal Goddard. You used to know my sister Jasmine – Jazz.'

Steph stared for a few seconds before a wary recognition overtook her face. It was only at this point that Kit thought to wonder whether Jazz had ever had cause to give Steph Harman a good slapping over some bloke or other.

'Yeah, Jazz. I know her. You're Krystal? Thought you moved away?'

'I did. I came back. Can I speak to you for a couple of minutes?'

'I'm on my way to work. I'm working for a home care agency, I'll have all my calls waiting for me. And they dock our pay if we're late.'

'I'll be quick. Can we go inside?'

'I haven't got the time for that. What do you want?' The badge was still causing a problem, Kit could see that. She moved up the path towards Steph, determined to herd her into the house.

'It's quite personal, Steph. It's about your case. The one against Matthew Cooper.'

'I got nothing to say about that bastard. Who sent you

234

anyway?' She was peering at the badge now, her hackles well and truly up.

'I've been asked to call out to see if you are OK. Whether you need any help or anything, after the case not going ahead, you know?'

It was too vague, and it was wasted anyway. Steph Harman saw through it at once.

'Have you bloody bollocks been sent out to see me! You always were full of yourself, even as a kid. Jazz used to say that. Don't lie to me, I know what's what and social workers don't come out to help people like me over something like that. Now what do you want, Krystal? Let's have the truth.'

'All right, look, the truth is this: I've been involved with the case, I can't tell you how, but it's important. The criminal case can't go ahead without you. Why would you say all that about him and then drop out?'

'The police know you're here, do they?'

'No.'

'No, I bet they don't. They wouldn't be happy, would they? But it's not going ahead anyway, so I'll tell you the same as I've told every other fucker who's asked me. There is no point. People like him don't end up paying for what they do. Why should I waste my time?'

'You were happy to waste it at the start.'

Steph's face was impassive. 'Yeah, well, Nic talked me into it.'

'No, she didn't. Come on, Steph, it's important.'

'Why?'

'I can't tell you.'

Steph's eyes narrowed, and Kit knew she'd been read. 'You think something's happened, like maybe he's done it to his kid as well?'

'I really can't tell you. It's confidential.'

'So that means yes then.'

Kit didn't answer, knowing Steph would take that as confirmation, but comforting herself with the thought that she hadn't actually said it, and so she hadn't breached the Coopers' confidentiality as such.

'Right, so the case has been dropped and now you're worried about the girl in the wheelchair, yeah?'

Kit was taken aback, but then she remembered from the transcript that Steph had been to Matt's house and had seen Lucy from the street.

'I can't answer that either, Steph, and you know it. But I just want to know whether you were telling the truth.'

'I was telling the truth.'

'So why withdraw your statement then? Why get that far and then not go through with it? Did Len Cooper threaten you? Did he bribe you?'

'I wouldn't touch that bastard's money. And I'm not afraid of him neither. He couldn't do worse than his son's already done to me.'

Steph leant back against the front door and started to open her bag. She was buying time, which could only mean she was wavering. Kit quickly felt in her pocket for her own fags and held the packet out to Steph. She took a cigarette and let Kit light it for her. Kit knew she had her then. She waited, letting Steph squirm, knowing that to speak now would be to risk losing her again.

Steph pulled on her cigarette for a few seconds. 'Look, I couldn't go through with it, all right? It's what I told you just now, no one was going to believe me. That's what he always said, and I thought for a bit maybe that wasn't true anymore, but after a while I could see it on their faces, the police and that – once they'd met him it all changed. I could see them thinking, "Nah, he wouldn't do it, not him."' She looked Kit in the eye. 'They went along with it all fine, then they saw him and straight away they stopped believing me. Everyone thinks he's too good, why would he need to do that? That's how he gets away with it. They're all too stupid to understand – he doesn't need to do it. He just likes it.'

'Steph—'

'Before you start, the answer's no. I'm not changing my mind. I'm not going through it. I am pissed off with seeing it written all over their faces. I've got two kids myself, I just want to forget it and get on with my life. If you're as clever as you reckon you are, you'll find a way to make sure his kids are OK. But this conversation never happened, so don't bother telling anyone, because I'll deny it. But you won't tell anyway, will you? Because you're not even supposed to be here.'

Kit had nothing left to say. She shrugged, feeling exhausted.

She had given it her best shot, but there was nothing she could do. Steph was fumbling in her bag again now, retrieving her car keys. Looking up, she glanced at Kit's face. 'I'm sorry, kid. I don't mean to have a go at you.'

'I know. It's fine, thanks anyway.'

'How's your Josie by the way? Still a head-banger? And what about Tyler?'

'Yeah, thanks. Josie's doing good actually, and Tyler's OK, too.'

'I won't even ask about your mam.'

Kit smiled. 'No, don't bother. It's been hard on her, you know, since Danny died.'

Steph stopped fiddling with her car keys. She looked uncomfortable. 'Yeah. I heard about Dan. He was a good lad. I was sorry to hear it. I'm sorry I can't help you, too. I know you're only trying to look after those kids.'

Steph started to move forwards now, meaning to make Kit turn and go back down the path. As she came close, she looked intently at Kit's face.

'I recognise you now. Your face hasn't changed, but it's all that long hair threw me off. Mine used to be like that, do you remember?'

Kit didn't remember Steph at all actually, but she sensed it was best not to say so. She'd manipulated things with the mention of Danny and it had changed the air between them. It was going to be hard for Steph to just walk away now.

'I've kept mine short since it happened,' Steph continued. 'Had it all cut off the next day.'

'Why?' Kit was completely unable to put together what Steph was getting at.

'It reminded me. When it was long, I mean – it reminded me of him.'

Kit waited, but nothing more came. She put her hand on Steph's arm, feeling sharp bones through her uniform, seeing her struggling and feeling awful for her. All those people not believing her. She remembered what Tyler had said, about the closed faces. 'It reminded you of what, Steph? Tell me.'

Steph was flushed now, her brassiness gone. Up close she was tired-looking under her make-up, and Kit could see that she really was much too thin.

'He used to like long hair. That's how he started it, touching my hair, just a brush at first. Then one day he started playing with it. Like this.'

She put out her hand and took hold of a strand of Kit's hair. She wound and wrapped it around two fingers, then let it drop and took up another piece and repeated the motion. 'He had a real weird thing about it. Sometimes I used to think that was the worst bit, you know? Not the other stuff, that was bad enough, but the playing with me – like I was a doll. Making sure I knew he could do it if he wanted, that what I felt didn't matter.'

Kit thought back to the transcripts and remembered there had been something about Matt Cooper touching the girls' hair. She'd skimmed it, finding it hard to bear the thought Steph's words made her remember, too, a line from the Savile reports: *At the end of the day, he did it because he could get away with it.*

Steph dropped Kit's hair and gave her a pat on the shoulder. 'Gotta go, I'm late now. Good luck, girl.'

She brushed past Kit and hurried down the path to her car, jumping in without a backward glance. As she drove away, Kit's phone buzzed in her pocket. She pulled it out.

> Heard there was trouble at your place – r u ok

It was Tyler. She texted back.

> How did u know

A few seconds later the reply came.

> News gets around. Crofta nutter keep away

> I plan to. Can I see u

She waited, standing on Steph's path, not caring if anyone was looking and wondering why, passing her phone from one hand to the other. A few more seconds and the phone vibrated again.

> need to get my head round it maybe in a bit

She typed an OK and sent it, and then she stood still, relief washing over her. She had been so afraid. She'd already lost Danny, but to lose Tyler, too – she found she couldn't even bear to take the thought any further. Whatever happened now, she could face it, as long as he was all right. The fear of losing her job over the Cooper case suddenly seemed insignificant. She knew it was time to confront Annie Cooper.

CHAPTER 14

The next day, Kit woke shaking with anxiety. She couldn't get rid of the image of Vernon falling to the ground. She stayed curled up in bed until the shaking subsided enough for her to pick up her phone and ring in sick. The whole building was full of the news of Vernon's heart attack and the duty manager accepted her explanation without comment. She slept on and off all day, and during her wakeful times she tried to sort out the tangle in her head. Around 4 p.m., she got out of bed and, seeing that the sun was still bright outside, sat in her favourite spot on the living-room windowsill and let it fall onto her back, warming her and relaxing her tight muscles. She had to take one bit of it at a time, she realised. She had to choose which bit to sort first and stick with that until she had it tidied up. Work first, both because it had to be the priority and because it meant that she could delay thinking about her brothers a little more. After an unenjoyable meal of spaghetti on toast she went to bed early and fell back to sleep at once.

Friday came around and she dragged herself into the office early. After texting Ricky to check his plans for the day, she busied herself with paperwork. When Ricky came back from his visits at four o'clock, she was waiting for him outside and jumped into the front seat of his car while he was still trying to park it.

'Hello. What's going on then?'

'Do you fancy a trip to see Annie Cooper? I could do with the back-up. I was thinking about what you were saying and I reckon maybe you've got a point. I think it's time to put her on the spot.'

He agreed readily, clearly taking the invitation as a compliment. Kit directed him to the Coopers'. As he pulled up outside their house, Kit was relieved to see that only Lucy's adapted vehicle stood on the drive. It looked like they had a chance to see Annie alone. They walked up the drive in silence and Kit rang the bell. She could see Ricky was nervous now. She felt a fizz of anticipation in her own stomach, but was determined, too. She had to give this one more shot. If it didn't work out, she promised herself that she would do what Vernon had told her to: she would move on and focus on her other cases.

After a few seconds, Kit heard movement inside the house. Through the glass panel to the side of the front door, she saw Annie coming out of Lucy's room. She was carrying a tray with a bowl of water on it. She looked at the glass panel as she came towards the door and her eyes met Kit's. She put the tray down on the hall stand and marched towards the front door, swinging it open so hard it banged back against the wall. She stood in the doorway, waiting for one of them to speak.

Something looked different about her, and it took Kit a few seconds to realise it was the first time she had seen Annie with her hair down. It hung to her shoulders, a soft sheet of blonde light. She was dressed up in a fitted green silk shift dress and high heels. The house was strangely quiet; there was no sign of Chloe and Cameron. Maybe the Coopers were all set to go out and celebrate the end of their ordeal. She could hardly have picked a worse time to challenge Annie.

'Annie, this is a colleague of mine, Ricky Diallo. Can we speak to you for a few minutes, please?'

Predictably, Annie gave an incredulous laugh. 'You are absolutely unbelievable. I had to throw you out of here only two days ago, because of your unprofessional behaviour around my children. And here you are, back again. You've got some cheek, I'll say that for you.'

Kit had been prepared for all this, but she still felt a sting of irritation at the remark about the children. Annie wasn't done, though.

'So, no, you can't have a word with me. I'm expecting my husband home any time now. As far as we are concerned, your involvement in our lives is over and done with. You, on the other hand, will have plenty of reminders about us in the coming months. I've spoken to your professional body already today and they are very interested in what's been happening here, I can assure you. "Gross professional misconduct" is the term they used. So perhaps you'd like to go away and focus on how you are going to defend yourself, because I will tell you quite openly, I intend to finish your career and I won't rest until I have done so.'

Kit was thoroughly riled now. In spite of the fact that this felt like the billionth time that she had been subjected to Annie's grandstanding, it still pushed her buttons. She felt her voice rising.

'Annie—'

Ricky put his hand on Kit's arm. 'Mrs Cooper,' he said, his voice gentle, 'we appreciate you have no reason at all to let us in. You are completely correct. The children's cases are due to be closed and, strictly speaking, we have no right to even be here, and certainly no right to insist you to talk to us.'

Annie fell silent. Kit kept quiet, too, amazed at how easy it had turned out to be to take the wind out of Annie's sails.

'Mrs Cooper,' Ricky continued, 'the honest truth is that there are aspects of what has happened that are still a worry to us. Cameron, Chloe and Lucy are your children and so it would be wrong of us not to share those worries with you. What you do about it . . . well, that is up to you, and we have no part in that. So, you will be rid of us once we leave here, one way or the other. All we are asking for is the chance to speak to you one last time, as the children's mother, because we are confident that you love them and want to protect them. Send us away right now if you like, just say the word and we're gone. But then you'll never know why we came.'

It was a gamble, but to Kit's amazement, Annie Cooper gave a quick nod, and stood back to allow them into the hall.

She closed the front door and led the way into the sitting room, indicating the sofa, to show that Ricky and Kit should sit down.

'I need to speak with the carer for a moment first,' Annie said. She left the room, giving Ricky and Kit the chance to exchange a glance.

'Nice one,' Kit whispered.

'Thanks. See what happens when you stop fighting everyone in sight?' He was grinning, but Kit felt irritated, and she found herself thinking that Jem would never have said that to her. But then, Jem was gone, and it was the fighting that had been the cause of that.

'I have fifteen minutes, no more.' Annie Cooper's voice was stiff as she re-entered the room and crossed to the fireplace, where she stood waiting. Kit looked at Ricky, hoping he knew how to handle this.

'Would you sit down, Mrs Cooper?' he said. 'I'd find it easier to explain this if you did.'

Annie sat in the armchair opposite them. Kit knew it would have cost her a lot to do as she was asked, and that she wouldn't tolerate much more of this. Ricky needed to get on with it.

'Well?' Annie demanded.

'We realise you've been through a great deal of trauma,' Ricky started.

'Spare me all that. It's your colleague here who has been the cause of our trauma, along with that incompetent old fool who supposedly manages her.'

'It's understandable that you're angry. Anyone would be in your position.'

'You really are as patronising as hell.' For once, Kit agreed with Annie. She knew Ricky was completely genuine but he wasn't coming across well. It was time to get back to the straight talking.

'Let's get to the point and then we can get out of here and leave you alone.' Kit had Annie's attention now. 'The truth is that the criminal-justice system can't convict your husband of anything. We all know that.'

'Because he's done nothing wrong. He's been totally exonerated, just as I said he would be.'

'But he hasn't been, has he? That's the whole point. No prosecution, no care proceedings, no fact-finding. This case was never tried, it collapsed because Stephanie Harman withdrew her statement. No one knows why she did that.'

Kit waited a moment to let that sink in. Annie didn't reply and Kit found herself unsure where to go next.

Ricky filled the gap caused by Kit's silence. 'So what we are saying is the system can't proceed any further against your husband. That's it for us, we've done our best to get to the bottom of things, but now that's impossible.'

Annie shrugged. 'And?'

Ricky sat forward again, looking at Annie earnestly. 'So now it's up to you.'

'What is that supposed to mean?'

'It's up to you to decide whether your husband committed

those offences. In actual fact, you're probably the only one who really knows whether he is capable of that.'

Annie stood up. 'This is getting us nowhere,' she said. 'I gave you a chance, but I can see that was a mistake. This is the same old nonsense that we've been through over and over again. Matt did nothing wrong, I am a hundred per cent confident of that. You appear to be determined to prove the opposite, but you have no evidence whatsoever.'

It suddenly occurred to Kit to wonder just how much Annie knew about what was in the transcripts. 'Did you ever get to hear the full allegations against Matt?'

'No, why would I? Matt dealt with all that, and he told me what I needed to know.'

'Which was what?'

Annie shrugged. 'Matt remembers those girls, but he never had much to do with them. They were friendly with his sister, that's all. Then they come along all these years later with this ludicrous story that he interfered with them. I mean, why now? Surely if there was anything like that going on, they would have reported it at the time?'

Kit wanted to answer that question, to explain why it would have been so hard for Steph and Nicolette to tell anyone. But she knew it would become a detour, and she needed to keep pushing Annie along the path they were on.

'But do you know what it is that they said he did?'

'Why would I want to know that?'

'For Christ's sake, Annie, what I am asking you is, do you know it? And if not, why not?'

It was clear Annie didn't want to answer. Kit knew that if Annie was resisting the question so strongly, it could only be because the answer had already occurred to her.

'Matt felt it would upset me,' she said eventually. 'And what was the point? It's a pack of lies, the whole thing.' For the first time since Kit had met her, Annie's voice lacked conviction.

'So what that means is that you don't even really know what the allegations were?'

'As I said, Matt was protecting me.'

'But why does he need to protect you from it, if it's all just a load of lies? You're not exactly the frail type, are you?' Kit waited for a reaction to this, but it didn't come. 'He would have known exactly what they claimed – he would have gone over the interviews with his lawyers. They don't make for easy reading, I can tell you.'

Annie sat down on the edge of the chair and looked at Kit. 'You've read the interviews?'

'Yes, I've read them.'

'Why?'

'To see whether we had grounds for care proceedings.'

'Then you can tell me what was in them.' This was suddenly a different Annie, open in a way Kit had hardly ever seen. If she could find the right words, maybe she could get Annie to think the unthinkable, just for a moment. And if, deep down, Annie knew her husband was guilty, that moment of acknowledgement would be enough to bring all of her denial crashing down. Surely then she would do whatever was necessary to protect her children?

Kit hesitated. Out of the corner of her eye, she could see Ricky looking at her, and the look contained a warning. She knew what he was worried about, and she began to regret having brought him along. The quickest way to give Annie everything she needed to hear would be to tell her what was in those transcripts. Annie was asking to know, and her receptive frame of mind would be gone the second Matt arrived home and was back in charge. But to tell Annie what was in the transcripts would be a serious breach of confidentiality. She couldn't justify it when there was nothing to prove the kids were at risk. Kit would risk the sack and the loss of her registration if anyone found out. And it would mean an investigation, in which Ricky would be the main witness. Kit thought she might well have taken the chance on her own account, but she couldn't put Ricky in that position. No, she'd have to find another way, and just hope Annie would do the right thing.

'I can't tell you what was in those transcripts. I don't have the grounds to disclose it to you. Matt's the only one who can tell you that. You could go and get legal advice on it, but I'm pretty sure I'm right – it's up to him to tell you, and no one else can, as things stand.' Kit knew Annie wouldn't do it. Matt would be home before she even got an appointment with a lawyer, and that would be the end of that.

Kit thought quickly. 'There is something else you could try.'

She knew this was not going to go down well, and she struggled to find a way to say it. 'You could speak to Lucy.'

Annie's mouth twisted a little. 'Speak to Lucy about what, exactly?' Annie was slipping away, back into her refuge of hostility. Kit could see that soon she was going to lose her altogether.

'I think you know the answer to that. You know Lucy said something to Chloe. All you have to do is ask her about it. If there is anything to tell, Lucy would tell you. You are the one person she would tell. Chloe said so.'

Annie's face was set rigid now, her mouth a thin, tense line. 'We had this discussion yesterday. You seem to be implying that Matt has molested his own severely disabled daughter. That is disgusting.'

'Mrs Cooper,' Ricky intervened, 'if you really are sure that your husband doesn't present a risk to your children, then great, have him back and get on with your lives. Put it all behind you. But be very clear, that is not what we are telling you, or what the police or the CPS are telling you. We are saying we couldn't catch him. We cannot and are not saying to you that he didn't do it. We just don't know. So now there's a decision for you to make, and you and your children will have to live with that decision for the rest of your lives. Lucy is especially vulnerable, we all know that.'

Annie's expression remained neutral. Kit couldn't judge whether the point was going home, or whether Annie was just biding her time before she exploded and chucked them both out onto the street. She took the chance to pick up as soon as Ricky stopped.

'I know exactly how you feel about the conversation Chloe and I had with Lucy. But are you really telling me you are not going to talk to Lucy and check it out? Just in case? Matt's never going to know you did it. So just speak to her and see what she says. That makes sense, doesn't it?'

Annie's face was taking on a shuttered look. They'd nearly got her, but it wasn't enough to overcome her reluctance to ask Lucy directly whether anything had happened. And now Annie's attention was wandering. She turned her head at a noise from the hallway.

'It's time for the carers to hand over. So if you don't mind . . .'

Fay appeared in the doorway, her coat on and her bag over her shoulder, arriving for her shift. She acknowledged Kit with a quick smile, then looked away awkwardly. Annie stood up, her back straight and her face composed. She went to the doorway and waited, ready to usher them out.

Kit thought quickly. 'Before we go, could I use your toilet, please?' she asked.

Annie was obviously reluctant, but she couldn't say no. 'Yes, all right, I think you know where it is?'

'Yes, I do.' Kit turned to Ricky. 'You go down to the car, I won't be long.' He did as he was told, putting out his hand to shake Annie's at the door. She didn't offer her own in return and Ricky left, looking disappointed.

Kit headed for the downstairs toilet, in which she locked the door and then rested her hands on the sink, staring at herself in the mirror. She had to think for a minute. She had to find a way to persuade Annie to talk to Lucy. With Ricky out of the way, maybe she could risk disclosing something from the transcripts. But what? She knew she was only going to have a few seconds before Annie would manoeuvre her out of the house. And Annie was not going to want to listen. Still with no idea what to say, she opened the toilet door.

Annie was standing by the front door, waiting. She was half turned towards Kit, but was staring out of the window, absent for a moment. She was playing with her hair where it fell over her right shoulder. She cupped a thick strand in her palm, twisted the end in her fingers, then let it drop. The motion of Annie's fingers running through her long hair triggered a picture, which flickered in Kit's mind and made her stomach flip with disgust again. The picture wouldn't stay still enough for her to see it properly.

Then she had it. She remembered Steph Harman reaching out and picking up a strand of Kit's hair. And Nicolette's transcript. 'He'd touch our hair. Just reach out and play with it, wrapping it around his fingers. He said he liked long hair. He did it afterwards, too. Touching my hair and telling me not to cry.'

Kit remembered something else, too. Seeing Annie standing at the door reminded her of her visit to Matt Cooper at his parents' house. How she'd been leaving, and he'd reached his hand out towards her in the doorway. Almost as if for a handshake but aiming too high. Had he actually been about to touch her hair?

Kit hated to hurt Annie, in spite of everything. She felt cruel, and a part of her wanted to back off, to leave it alone and close her mind to what Matt might have done and might yet do. To get on with her job and help all the other children who needed her. Or to get out altogether and just do something easier. But she knew that if she walked away at this point, she would never forgive herself.

Annie turned then, realising that Kit was there and got ready to see her out for the last time. Kit felt her way towards the right words, knowing she had only one chance. She crossed the hall. She stopped in front of Annie, standing uncomfortably close, so that she couldn't get hold of the door handle without leaning in and brushing her arm across Kit's back, which she was willing to bet Annie wouldn't do.

'I'm going now, Annie, and I don't suppose you'll see me again. Please think about speaking to Lucy.'

'Just go.'

'Yes. But there's one thing that I want you to know. Nicolette and Steph said something in their interviews about Matt. Do you know what it was? He used to touch their hair. They both had long hair and he liked it. He used to take it in his fingers, play with it. It seemed innocent enough to them at first. I don't know if you recognise that habit of his, Annie, but if you do, then you really do need to speak to Lucy. Because later on, he played with their hair again. After he'd assaulted them.'

Annie said nothing. In fact, it was as if Kit hadn't spoken. Kit knew it was best to go before she recovered and asked any questions. She had taken enough of a risk already by disclosing this much. She stepped back to allow Annie to grasp the door handle, and as soon as the door was open, she left. She was careful to look relaxed as she walked down the drive towards Ricky.

'That seemed to go OK, didn't it?' he asked, as soon as she got into the car.

'Yeah, it did.'

'What did the trick, do you think?'

'I guess it was what you said.'

Ricky looked pleased. 'You see? I knew it would be possible to reason with her. Maybe she'll push him to tell her about what Steph and Nicolette said now?'

'Yeah, maybe.' But she knew it wasn't true. It hadn't been enough, or maybe the thing about the hair hadn't been the right choice. Maybe she hadn't made the connection with Annie at all.

Ricky started the car and set off in the direction of the office. Kit felt a tremor of anxiety at the memory of what she had disclosed to Annie, and what Matt could do to her and her career if he ever found out.

CHAPTER 15

After a troubled weekend, Kit arrived at the office on Monday morning, where she saw Ricky driving around in the car park desperately trying to find a space. Eventually he pulled up onto a grass verge, spraying his car with mud in the process. He slammed the door irritably and joined her as she stubbed her fag out under her heel. They took the stairs together in silence; Kit's mind was full of Vernon and she wondered how they were going to manage without him. At the entrance to the team room, she almost walked into Ricky's back. He had stopped dead and was looking across at Vernon's open office door. Kit could see the computer screen was lit up, and a briefcase was lying by the desk. They looked at each other. Surely Vernon couldn't be back? No, Kit realised straight away that that was ridiculous. Even Vernon wouldn't be back in work straight after a heart attack, and Nell would never tolerate it anyway.

A woman moved into their line of vision. She was pinning things up on Vernon's memo board. The memos Vernon had left up there, most of them dating back ten years or more, had been taken down, and were nowhere to be seen. Vernon's to-do pile, a tottering heap of papers he frequently tripped over but otherwise largely ignored, had been removed from the floor next to his desk. A sticky floral smell reached them as they arrived in the team area. Tracing it, Kit saw it came from a plastic plug that sat in one of the wall sockets, periodically giving out a swish of something vaguely akin to the scent of lavender toilet cleaner. Maisie was sitting bolt upright at her desk, her face a picture of pure alarm, and the rest of the team were keeping their heads down in a way that confirmed trouble was in the air.

A cough came from the direction of Vernon's room. Kit walked over and put her head round the door, to find a slender woman in her early thirties on her knees on the floor. She was reorganising Vernon's bookshelf, which for the most part had contained dusty textbooks relating to legislation so old it had already been superseded at least twice. Kit saw these were now in the bin, and the woman was replacing them with a row of departmental procedure manuals. Kit knew Vernon had some of those, too, but they were in use propping up wonky desks in the team room. In the rare event that Vernon ever decided to revert to procedure, there would always be a palaver while he crawled about on the floor trying to locate the right manual without bringing half the office furniture down on everyone's feet.

The air was filled with clouds of dust and the woman raised her head to cough again, holding a tissue to her mouth. She spotted Kit and dropped the tissue. 'Can I help you?' she asked, without the hint of a smile.

'I'm Kit Goddard.'

'Ah, Kit, good to meet you.' The woman stood up and offered her hand. 'I'm Georgia Pritchard. I'm your new manager.'

Kit opened her mouth to question what this could possibly mean, but as she did so, there came the sound of the main office door swinging open and shut. Georgia Pritchard's eyes strayed over Kit's shoulder and became fixed on whoever had come through the door. The next moment, a waft of musk and coconut arrived to compete with the toilet cleaner.

'I see you two have already met.' Kit turned to find Cole Jackson behind her. 'I expect Georgia has explained that she has very kindly agreed to help us out in the interim.'

'Interim of what?' Kit asked.

'Until we can get a more permanent arrangement.'

Kit didn't like the sound of this at all. 'Until Vernon's back, you mean?'

'Kit, yes, of course. I didn't mean to be insensitive, I know you view Vernon as a mentor. And don't we all? A man of his experience is valued in my department, I'm sure you know that. But someone needs to take the helm in the meantime. And of course, we don't know how things will go with Vernon. People can change their minds after time off, you know. A bit of gardening leave. He might find he starts enjoying it. There's no saying Vernon will even *want* to come back.'

'Mmm.' Kit thought how Cole Jackson clearly knew nothing whatsoever about what made Vernon tick.

'Anyway,' Cole Jackson continued, 'luckily for us, Georgia

was available. We are old colleagues. She's just finished a stint in another authority, working on their performance-indicator framework, and I managed to persuade her to come and slum it with us for a few months. Before she goes on to greater things, eh, Georgie?'

Behind Cole Jackson's back, Maisie was mouthing something which, after a few repeats, Kit identified as, 'They're shagging.' Kit managed not to laugh and waited with trepidation to hear what might come next.

'Anyway, I'll leave you all to get on. If you've got five minutes later, Georgia, perhaps you could pop up and we could go over your thoughts about the PI framework?'

'Yes, Cole, I'll see you shortly.' When he'd gone, Georgia Pritchard came out into the main office and propped her thin behind against a desk. She had straightened black hair. Her eyebrows sat high up on her forehead and they, too, were jet black. Her skin had the tell-tale orange tone of a fake tan. She gave Kit and Ricky a quick smile which didn't go anywhere near her eyes.

'So, I called in and spoke to the rest of the team late on Friday afternoon, but you two weren't here. I wasn't sure where you had got to, if I'm honest, because you hadn't signed out on the board.'

She indicated the whiteboard. Kit and Ricky fidgeted, neither of them quite sure how to explain that the board was never actually used for keeping track of anyone's movements. Its only purpose was for Vernon to have a list of the team's names, so as to reduce the confusion caused to him by the turnover of agency staff, who would often arrive and then leave again within a few days.

'Anyway,' Georgia continued, 'I'll need to speak with both of you. Kit, you first?'

Maisie and Ricky pulled faces of sympathy as Kit followed Georgia into her office. She sat down opposite the desk and stared at Georgia's eyebrows, wondering if someone at the brow bar had been having an off day when those had been created. Georgia picked up Vernon's allocation book and flicked through it.

'I'm doing my best to get on top of the systems here,' she said. 'I'm amazed to find that allocations are still being recorded manually. I intend to get that sorted as soon as. So I'll be able to send you a weekly list of your allocated cases electronically, and you can then update it. All your closures to demonstrate throughput, obviously, and statutory visits to comply with the performance requirements. I can see you've a few cases here that have been hanging around for quite some time.'

'I've been very busy with one complex case.'

Georgia Pritchard looked at Kit in silence, her face betraying a complete lack of comprehension. 'Well then, you need to get that case tidied up and get on. I've only glanced at your caseload and it's already pretty clear to me that you're missing targets left, right and centre. Take this one, for example – the Ripton case. You haven't proceeded to conference, you haven't taken legal advice. You've already set up support services, so you are doing nothing active. Why haven't you closed it?'

'I was hoping for a chat about that one.' Kit had kept the Riptons in mind for her next supervision with Vernon.

'That's what I'm here for.' Georgia Pritchard made a steeple with her fingers and rested her chin on it, which Kit took to be her 'I'm listening to you now' pose.

'Well, it's just that everyone's happy with Corey. Mum seems cooperative, she's been through all the domestic-abuse work, she's done all the right things, the boyfriend's off the scene as far as I know. But I don't feel I've got to know Corey very well, and he seems quite guarded to me. I think I need to spend some proper time with him.' Kit's brain told her to stop, but her mouth ran on regardless. 'He loves his Xbox. I plan to call over after school this week and play a few games with him. Then maybe I'll take him out for a Big Mac, see if he'll relax and open up with me.'

Georgia Pritchard couldn't have looked more appalled if Kit had smacked her in the face. 'And would Vernon Griffiths have found that an acceptable use of your time?' she finally managed.

'Well, yes, Vernon likes us to spend time with the kids. To build a relationship with them.'

Georgia Pritchard stared at Kit for a few seconds more, then cleared her throat. 'Right. I can see we are going to have to go back to basics. The purpose of this team, if I have understood Cole correctly, is to assess, then take immediate actions. Close down where possible or get open cases into proceedings or to conference and transfer on to the long-term teams as soon as they are stable.'

'Yes, it is. But we need to make accurate assessments first. How can we do that if we don't get to know the children?'

'Look, Kit. I know from Cole that you and Vernon had a special understanding. But Vernon comes from a particular generation. Things have moved on since then. You're newly qualified and he's not done you any favours by encouraging you to think the way he does. I understand you're considered to have potential. You could do well in this department. But you need to realise that Cole is all about an effective service. Task-focussed, minimal intervention – that's the best way to help these families and it's the best use of public money. I've looked at the referral rates into this team, and they are through the roof. There's no time for you to be playing on Xboxes and eating junk food. You need to get the Ripton case closed. You've put in support, the child's not made any allegations, you've covered your back. OK?'

'OK.' Kit knew the time had come to concede defeat, at least on the surface. Mentally, she made a note to call and see Corey and Jemma Ripton as soon as she could.

'You'd better send Ricky in now,' Georgia Pritchard continued. She glanced at her watch. 'No, actually, I'll see him later. I need to have a word with Cole.' She reached into her desk drawer, took out a make-up bag and started to add even more dark powder to the sharp arches of her eyebrows. 'You can go,' she told Kit, without looking at her.

Kit went back into the team room. Ricky was nowhere to be seen. Maisie was staring intently at her computer. Kit wanted to go for a smoke, but she guessed that unscheduled fag breaks would probably not go down well under the new regime. She logged on to her computer and spent a few minutes flicking through her emails while she waited for Georgia to leave. Finally, Georgia swept out of her office. Kit kept staring at her screen until the team-room door banged behind her. Kit and Maisie looked at each other.

'What do you reckon?' Kit asked.

'I reckon she's trouble. She's Cole's spy. He's wanted Vernon out from the minute he arrived here, and between the two of them they can easily find the grounds. She's all over our cases already, she's only been here five minutes. Cole's lining her up for Vernon's job, that's obvious.'

'Yeah. Of course he is. But Vernon won't let that happen,' Kit insisted, although inside she felt doubtful.

'Get real, Kit. Vernon's sixty-two. He's got thirty years in, a full pension waiting for him, and he's just had a heart attack. They've got a couple of months at the least to collect evidence against him. Then they haul him over the coals and give him the chance to go quietly, avoid a fuss. He's bound to take it. Then we're all stuffed.'

'I didn't think you even liked Vernon?'

'Better the devil you know, kid. I'd start looking for something else if I were you.'

Kit felt miserable and she still didn't think she could risk a fag. She spent the day working on the Cooper case, getting all the recordings up to date and finalising her assessment. At lunchtime, she drove Ricky and Maisie to McDonald's, where they all sat in a sombre mood. The sky had clouded over and as they ate their fries in silence, they watched the holiday-makers flocking in, shivering in their summer gear, stuffing their kids with chicken nuggets and pretending to have a nice time. Back at the office, Kit carried on grimly with her admin. At four forty-five, she was closing down her computer when Ricky put his head round the team-room partition.

'Kit, I think you'd better come upstairs.'

'I was just going home.'

'Seriously, Kit. You need to come now. Georgia's looking for you.' Kit could see that Ricky looked worried. She joined him at the bottom of the stairs.

'What's up now?' she asked him.

'I don't know. But she doesn't look pleased. She said to go straight up to Cole Jackson's office.'

'Christ. Not my day, is it?' Kit pretended to laugh it off, in the hope of reassuring Ricky, but she had the jitters. Had Annie told Matt what she had done the day before? If Matt Cooper had been on the phone with a complaint, she could be about to be suspended on the spot.

Ricky left her at the first floor. She continued to climb the stairs to the top of the building, and made her way into Cole Jackson's suite, where his secretary ushered her into his office. Kit found Cole Jackson, Georgia Pritchard and another woman waiting for her. The woman was grey-haired and overweight, with an air of self-importance. She was making a great show of leafing through what actually amounted to no more than three pieces of paper.

'I'm Clare Donald,' the woman said, without looking up at Kit. 'I'm the senior complaints officer.'

This was it then. Kit knew there wouldn't have been any complaints on any of her other cases; she'd done so little work on any of them, she'd had no chance to do anything wrong. It was the Coopers, she was sure of it.

Cole Jackson indicated that Kit should sit down and leant forward and cleared his throat. 'Kit, I'm sorry to have to drop this on you. I know you've had a very difficult time recently and this is not going to be pleasant, I'm afraid. We've received a serious complaint about you today.'

Kit did her best to look surprised.

'It's no surprise to you then?' Clare Donald said. Kit was taken aback at Clare's ability to read her, but she thought it best to keep up the facade now she'd started it.

'Well, it is actually, I can't imagine what it's all about.'

Clare Donald picked up her papers and started reading from them. 'It's from a Mr Matthew Cooper. I gather he was accused of some quite horrendous offences and was exonerated.'

Kit felt a spasm of absolute frustration. Was she really going to have to explain that Matt Cooper had not been exonerated at all? She had just enough presence of mind to keep quiet, before Cole Jackson rescued her by intervening.

'Kit, we've talked about this case before, haven't we? I thought the plan was to get it sorted and closed ASAP. From my memory, we had no grounds to be involved anymore.' His tone was surprisingly kind.

'Yes, that's right. And that's what I did.'

'So what's the nature of this complaint, Clare?' Cole Jackson asked.

'I spoke with Mr Cooper myself this afternoon. He called in to the office. It seems this gentleman has been through quite an ordeal. He feels that there has been an unjustified determination on the part of the local authority to pursue him, even though he didn't commit any crime.'

'And what makes him think Kit did that?'

'Well, for one thing, he saw her leaving his house on Friday afternoon, along with someone else. Turned out she had been to see his wife. He claims she had no reason to be there, it was all due to have been closed. He feels this is just one example of Ms Goddard overstepping the mark, which apparently she has done a number of times.'

Bugger, Kit thought. She hadn't spotted Matt Cooper near the house when they'd left. But she couldn't decipher from what Clare Donald had said whether Annie had dropped her right in it or not.

'So, where were you exactly on Friday? You and Ricky Diallo? Because we've already established that you two weren't signed out on the board, haven't we?' Georgia was chuffed at being able to lob this into the conversation.

Kit thought quickly and decided the best policy was to be honest – up to a point. 'I did call in to see Annie Cooper. Just to let her know that we were closing the children's cases, that's all.'

'Is that normal practice in the team? To let people know in person? Sounds like a gold-standard service to me. Surely a simple closure letter would have done the job?' Georgia was looking at Cole as she said this, vying for his approval. Kit thought longingly of Vernon, and his trust in her. At this point Vernon would have been doing his best to help her cover her tracks, at least until he could find out what she had been up to and give her a bollocking in private. But she was on her own now. It was lucky that she was a bloody good liar.

'Well, no, we don't usually go in person. But I didn't think a closure visit could do any harm. Annie Cooper's been through quite an ordeal as well, you know?'

'So, you were being supportive? Well, that sounds appropriate to me. There's nothing to prove that Kit did anything she shouldn't, is there?' Cole Jackson was looking at Clare Donald, who was gawping at him. Kit couldn't fathom it out either. Surely he wasn't defending her?

'Why take someone else with you? That's a shocking waste of resources,' Georgia Pritchard snapped.

But Kit was ahead of her. 'Annie Cooper can be difficult. I wanted to smooth things over with her, end things on a good note, but I thought it would be best to have a witness, just in case she made any complaints afterwards.'

'Well, it looks like that was a good judgement, Kit,' Cole

Jackson said. 'As it turns out, you were right to be cautious.'
He looked at Clare Donald. 'This doesn't need to get too complicated, does it, Clare? Surely if Ricky Diallo bears out what
Kit is saying, we can get this wrapped up? I can't afford to lose
her for long – if something's going to blow up, it's going to be
in that team. I need competent staff down there.'

'Lose me? Lose me where?' Kit asked, but no one bothered
to explain. Clare Donald was sucking the end of her pen
thoughtfully.

'Well, you may be right, Cole . . .'

'Can we really afford to take Ricky Diallo's word?' Georgia
had spotted Clare Donald's hesitation and she was in like a
shot. 'I can't imagine Mr Cooper being satisfied with that.
Surely this should go for full investigation? And we'd have to
explore what Mrs Cooper has to say about the purpose of this
so-called closure visit?'

Clare Donald nodded. 'Mr Cooper is pressing for an independent investigation. I think we need to cover every angle.
Plus, they've always got the option of the Ombudsman, not
to mention Social Care Wales. This could rumble on for a bit.
Frankly, Cole, you might want Ms Goddard to keep a low profile for the next six months or so. I understand the Coopers
are quite well connected.'

'Yes, they are. They could stir things up a lot. We don't need
that right now.' Cole sat back, looking anxious. Kit decided she
had had enough of this. Something was going on and she was
not a party to it. She didn't like it one bit.

'When you say "keep a low profile", what does that mean exactly?'

She directed her question to Clare Donald, but it was Georgia who replied. 'Cole could suspend you right now,' she said, in a tone which implied that she would be thrilled if he did just that.

'Is that what you're doing then?' Kit asked him, irritated beyond belief. 'Because if you are, then fine, I'll go and clear my desk.'

Cole was looking at Clare Donald now, and Kit could see he was appealing to her. But her heavy face was set like a slab. Cole sighed.

'Yes, Kit, I'm sorry, but it's for your own sake. You need to be right out of the picture. Look on it as a chance to have a break. I'm sure we can get you back into work in no time.'

Cole Jackson was smiling at her, but his tone was firm. Kit was furious. Without a word, she got up and left the room, slamming the door on the way out, not caring that it made her look childish. She headed for the office to collect her bag, a serious intention to go and get very drunk already forming in her mind. The office was empty, for which she was grateful – no explanations necessary. Ricky would find out what was going on soon enough. She collected her bag and headed for the car park. Then she got into her car and sat there, not even feeling like she wanted a fag.

She stared out of the window at the drizzle that had gone on and on all afternoon. Should she drop the car at home and go to the pub as soon as it opened? The idea still appealed, but she didn't think she should be alone. She couldn't tolerate Ricky right now; their friendship was too new and she'd have to keep thinking what she was meant to say and do next. She couldn't bother Vernon, even if she could get past Nell. Her thoughts turned to Danny, but she pushed him away; no point in wishing he was there to look after her, that was just going to make her feel worse. Tyler had his own stuff to deal with, she was worried enough about him already, he wasn't up to helping her. When it came down to it, she was just a kid from the care system, and like a lot of them, she had a useless family and hardly any good friends.

The self-pity of this snapped Kit back to her senses. She did have somewhere to go. She had been luckier than most, after all. She threw some clothes into a rucksack along with her toothbrush, phone and charger. Then she went out to the car and drove to the pet shop, where she bought a bone and some of Jess's favourite biscuits. She lit a fag, turned the car in the direction of the coast road and set off for Cliffside.

CHAPTER 16

An hour later, Kit pulled up outside Huw and Menna's house. She got out of the car to open the gate, holding it carefully at the top with her fingertips to avoid splinters. She paused to look out over the sea. This was a wild and isolated part of the coastline; the cliff paths were rudimentary and outright dangerous in places and the weather was dramatic in the winter months. But Kit preferred it to the manicured gardens and twee beach huts that featured on the more expensive bay where Matt Cooper's parents lived. Even breathing the air here made her feel a little better. The rain was stopping as she got back into the car and drove up the long, stony lane to the house. As she pulled up outside, Huw opened the door, his folded newspaper in one hand and a bottle of beer in the other. When he recognised Kit, a wide smile appeared on his face.

'Hello, stranger. You OK?' He opened his arms and drew her into a hug.

'Not really.'

'Better come in then. I think Menna's about to inflict dinner on me.'

As he led her into the hall, the kitchen door opened, and Jess leapt out, nearly knocking her off her feet. Menna followed behind, smiling with delight.

'It's good to see you, girl. Come and have some food. You don't look like you've been eating enough to me.'

'I am, trust me. Just not as much as I did when I was here.' The amount that Huw and Menna could eat had always amazed Kit. Yet they both stayed wiry and lean, which she guessed must be due to their daily walks on the cliffs. Since giving up fostering, they'd managed to keep themselves busy with the walking and the dogs and their numerous hobbies, along with their pretty constant bickering. But Kit sensed how much Huw and Menna missed having a houseful of kids. They'd loved every bit of it, never saying no to a placement and getting taken advantage of by desperate social workers on a regular basis as a result. In spite of the chaos, she'd always felt safe in their house, no matter what was going on with the other kids there. Huw and Menna always knew what to do and she trusted them completely. It felt good to be back and she was glad that she'd come.

'Could I stay tonight?'

Menna glanced at her. 'Of course. Anything wrong?'

'Yeah, sort of.'

'Hang your coat up and come and eat. We'll soon sort it out.'

Kit disengaged herself from Jess and did as Menna said. Then she followed her into the kitchen, where Menna handed her a bottle of beer. Kit sat down at the table and stared out at the sea glowing in the early evening sunshine.

'What's up then?' Huw landed clumsily on a chair on the other side of the table. Menna made an exasperated face at Kit.

'I'm surprised we've got any furniture left.'

'Shut up, woman. Can't you see there's something wrong with the girl? She doesn't need to hear you bloody banging on.'

'Your language. That's what finished our fostering career,' Menna sniffed.

'It bloody wasn't. It was your poor hygiene standards. Animals on the beds and all that, they said.'

'Actually, it was both of those things,' Kit pointed out. 'Plus, you two telling that social worker to get off your property or you'd set the dogs on him.'

They all laughed together then, although Kit recalled it hadn't been funny at the time. The social worker had come to tell Kit that it was thought best she should move to a new placement, one with younger carers who were more compliant with modern fostering standards. He had received short shrift, so the fostering agency had gone ahead and de-registered Huw and Menna, which everyone thought would force Kit to move. It hadn't worked, though. Huw and Menna had refused to turf her out and she had refused to go, much to the disapproval of the social worker, conveyed from a safe distance down the phone line. With no fostering allowance coming in, Huw and Menna had simply used their own pensions to keep Kit until she finished school. She was grateful to them in a way that she had never yet managed to articulate.

Huw was looking at Kit expectantly.

'It's a long story.'

'Go on then. We've nothing better to do.'

'It's work. They've suspended me.'

Huw snorted. 'Well, they're idiots then. Why did they do that?'

'I've been working on this case. Middle-class couple, three kids, nice house. Allegations of sexual abuse, historical stuff, against the dad. Nothing we could prove but I think the wife's got her doubts. Now he's made a complaint. They want me to stay off work for a bit, while it's investigated. They're all pretty scared of him.'

Huw frowned. 'Do you think he did it?'

'I don't know. I think he might have. And I think something's not right with the oldest girl. She's severely disabled and she can't tell me, or maybe she won't. There's something weird with the grandfather, too, I don't think she wants to be around him. It's a muddle, but I don't feel I can just leave it and close the case.'

'Sounds like a nightmare. What are you supposed to have done wrong?'

'I pushed the wife a bit, probably shouldn't have.'

'So they want you out and hopefully it will all blow over?'

'That's the idea.' Kit decided not to admit that Annie Cooper could easily ensure she got the sack if she chose to. Kit wanted Huw and Menna to think well of her. 'But even if they do have me back, Vernon's gone off with a heart attack. There's a new woman, I'm not sure I want to work for her. I'm starting to wonder if it's all worth it.'

Menna put a plate of stew in front of Kit and then sat down on the other chair. Her face had barely aged in ten years. Kit loved them both, but it was Menna who really understood her and had always been able to give her advice when no one else could.

'Listen to me, flower. You worked hard to get that job and it's obvious you're good at it. You're going to have plenty of problems in your career. You can't afford to let it get to you this badly. It sounds like you've done your best to look after those kids. Surely a few weeks off can't be that bad, can it? You're just going to have to grit your teeth and get through it.'

'I wish I could. But I honestly don't know if I can. Maybe I should go back to the café, ask Alex for my old job back. That's what Tyler says.'

Menna was the one snorting now. 'Yes, because that boy's full of good advice, isn't he?'

Kit laughed. 'Good point well made.'

Menna got up and went over to the cabinet in the corner. She held Jess's lead out to Kit.

'Go on. As soon as you've finished, get down the beach. Clear your head. Have you got a coat? It'll be chilly down there by now. Take one of mine.'

'I will. Actually, no, it's OK, I think I've got a hoody in the car.'

Kit finished her stew, took the lead and headed out the back door. Jess came bounding after her. Kit stopped at the car and found her hoody on the floor in the back. She must have dropped it at some point. It was still warm out so she tied it around her waist for now. Then she clipped the lead onto Jess's collar. They walked across the fields, slightly uphill, heading into the brighter light that lay over the cliff, reflected up from the sea below. Her nose and throat tingled with the fresh peppery scent of wild garlic underfoot. Jess pulled impatiently, and after checking for sheep, Kit reached down and let her off the lead, and they began to make their way down the path towards the sand.

In the distance, she could see the Cliffside Café. She wondered whether to walk over and see Alex. Her stomach lurched at the thought of him but she was too shy to do it. Maybe it was best left anyway. She had great memories of the café, she'd loved working for Alex, but it was all in the past now. She had a new life, her own flat and a good job. She needed to keep moving forwards.

As she reached the sand, the sun was reappearing. The sky was glowing with streaks of peach and apricot. She walked across to the far side of the beach and found her old spot, a well-worn ledge on a small rock, just wide enough for her to squeeze onto. She sat for a while and watched the sunset and enjoyed the sight of Jess running frantically in and out of the amber-tinted rock pools. She started to feel calmer and clearer. The muddle in her head was still there, but she felt she could pick at some of the threads of it now.

She'd changed her mind so many times, that was the thing. Maybe she needed to get it all in the right order first. She thought back to the very start, when she'd fretted over why Jean Collins hadn't known that Matt took turns in caring for Lucy at night. But then she'd spent time with the kids, and with Matt himself, and she'd totally changed her view of him. His love and care for Lucy had sent her off in a different direction – so much so that, when Steph had withdrawn her statement, Kit had felt outraged on Matt's behalf, and ashamed of the part she had almost played in destroying the Cooper family. And there was certainly nothing sinister in Jean not having known about Lucy's overnight care, after all. She hadn't known the first thing about Lucy spending nights with her grandparents either, which Lucy had suddenly refused to do anymore, leaving Kit to wonder why. But her lurking suspicion that Lucy might be avoiding her grandfather had been swept aside in turn when she'd spoken to Steph Harman, and seen the pain in her thin, strained face. That was when Kit had started to believe that Matt could have abused Steph and Nicolette. And there she was, back at the start, with no clue what might have happened to Lucy in either of the Cooper households.

She closed her eyes and rested for a minute, but a shiver rose up her back. It was starting to get chilly. She untied her hoody from her waist. It smelt a little damp. She thought back to the last time she'd worn it; it had been the day she'd heard the case against Matt Cooper wasn't proceeding. She'd been sitting on the promenade and got soaked in the rain; she'd taken the hoody off and thrown it into the back of the car and forgotten to pick it up when she got home.

She was really cold now, so she shook it out and put it on anyway; it definitely smelt weird but she'd chuck it in Menna's washing machine when she got back. She pushed her hands into the pockets where the fingers of her left hand connected with a folded piece of paper. She remembered she'd found it in there when she wore the hoody that day on the promenade. But then there had been a storm and she'd put the drawing away without looking at it. She remembered Chloe, intent on her picture of the house, insisting on an extra room for Lucy. Kit didn't feel like looking at it now. In fact, she felt sick of that bedroom, and of trying to work out what might be going on in that house.

She closed her eyes again. Her mind had gone into a groove now and images of Lucy's room filled her head. Then there was the near-replica at Len and Jackie's, the stuffy room that Lucy hadn't occupied for a while. A couple of months, Matt had said. But no one had replaced the calendar, even though there was a new one there ready and waiting. Something about this still didn't feel right – why have the calendar there for Lucy and not put it up? Unless . . . had Lucy not actually been at her grandparents' since December? If she wasn't due a visit, maybe no one had bothered with the calendar.

This rang a bell somewhere else, too. Annie had said that Chloe had been sharing Lucy's room since Christmas. Kit had accepted the explanation about Chloe being scared of Santa without question at the time, but actually, it didn't sound like Chloe at all. Lucy and Chloe were very close – thick as thieves,

Fay had said. Fay had taught the girls to communicate; had Lucy managed to tell Chloe that she was afraid? She could easily see Chloe as a tiny sentinel, keeping watch.

But none of this would explain why Lucy was avoiding going to her grandparents' house. Even as she thought this, Kit knew that she was stretching to keep Len in the frame, such was her instinctive dislike of him. There was no way to fit Len and Matt together in one picture. It was an either/or. She needed to stop skewing it with her bias against Len. If she took him out of the equation, looked at it a different way, maybe she could make sense of it. If Lucy wasn't avoiding Len, why was she so determined to stay at home?

An answer began to rise in her mind, out of focus but insistent. She pulled Chloe's picture out of her pocket and opened it up, smoothing it out on her knee. She had remembered that it showed Matt, a stick figure on the put-up bed in Lucy's room. Lucy's bed had been empty and it still was. But the drawing showed something else, something Kit didn't remember seeing before. Kit recalled how Chloe had carried on scribbling after she'd been asked to stop. She'd added something to the drawing. Kit remembered how she had spoken to Lucy that day alone in her room. Saying things she shouldn't have, practically inviting the child to say something about her father. And how she had heard footsteps in the hall and wondered if Chloe had been listening. Then, at her next visit, Chloe had dismissed the sign Lucy had made when Kit showed it to her. Kit thought of the way she'd got out of the car and run off quickly. Too quickly, she saw now. Sweet little Chloe, so desperate for attention.

Understanding came to Kit then, arriving in a flood of adrenaline before the words could form. And she realised in an instant that she had misread the Cooper case completely. She had failed to see the clues.

She stood and called Jess to her, and they ran across the beach together and started up the cliff path. Kit struggled but she hurried on. Reaching the top, she stopped to put Jess on the lead and catch her breath, and then they ran to the gate, through the garden, and in through the back door, where she dropped Jess's lead in the kitchen and then sprinted up the stairs into Huw's office.

Huw had left his computer on after checking his racing results. Kit sat down and brought up a Google Image search. She typed in 'Makaton signs' and began scrolling through the pictures. Nothing looked quite like the sign she'd seen Lucy make. To her frustration, she found most of the websites required a hefty paid subscription before one could get at the main content. She found a free website that showed some basic signs and checked all the ones that seemed possible, all the words that she thought Lucy might have been trying to say. But still nothing looked right.

And in any case, what help would it be? She was rushing about as if she knew what could happen next, propelled by her sudden realisation. But actually, what could she do? She had no one to turn to. She imagined trying to explain the whole thing to Georgia Pritchard or Cole Jackson. She knew there was no way that could turn out well. She couldn't bother Vernon with it. Once again, it all came down to Annie. Kit knew she couldn't risk so much as setting foot in the Coopers' street with this complaint hanging over her. Annie would have her job off her then, for sure.

'Bollocking, bollocking fucking bollocks,' she muttered to herself.

'Your language is getting as bad as mine. What's the problem then, Kitty?' Huw had slipped into the room behind her, a glass of port in his hand. He slumped into the armchair next to the desk, stretched out his wiry legs and regarded her with amusement.

'It's the family I was telling you about. I just realised something. It's a bit of a long story, but I need to find out what the daughter was trying to say – she's very disabled and she made a sign. I think she was saying something about what was going on. I should have followed it up at the time, but I didn't, and now I think it was important. In fact, I think I had the wrong end of the stick all the way along. I've done something very stupid and I need to put it right.'

'What kind of a sign?'

'Makaton.'

'Go on then. Show me.'

'Why?'

'I've picked up a bit of Makaton in my time. We fostered a fair few kids with disabilities, you know?'

Of course. She had forgotten all about that. Huw and Menna had been respite foster carers, too, giving families with disabled kids a weekend break once a month or so. They could have helped her understand more about Lucy all along. She kicked herself for not having thought to ask for help, for thinking she could do it all herself.

'OK, well, it was something like this.' Kit made the sign as best she could. It had been hard to see, and Lucy had been very quick in her movements, but she thought she had it pretty close.

Huw narrowed his eyes and sipped at his port. 'That doesn't look quite right. Are you sure it wasn't more like this?' He made a slightly different movement, tapping at his nose twice, and Kit saw at once that this was the sign that Lucy had made.

'That's it. I'm sure that's it. What does it mean?'

'Well, that is the sign for "sister". Is that any help?'

'Yes, it is. She does have a sister. And if my theory is right, that makes sense.'

'Well, there you are then.'

'But it's weird at the same time. Why would she refer to her as "sister"? Why not just sign her name?'

Huw thought for a minute, enjoying the intrigue. 'Kids often use just an initial to sign someone's name, like someone in the family or someone they see a lot of. So, I was always 'H', you see? Easier for them to learn than spelling out a whole name, and quicker for them to do as well. But it only works up to a point, because obviously sometimes people have the same initials. So Menna was never "M" because the kids we had with us on respite already had a "Mum" at home. We had to use her middle name. G for Gladys. She always hated it. Moaned like hell. Anyway, could that be it?'

'Yes. You're right. Thank you. That is it.' Kit could barely take it all in. She realised Lucy knew the truth. Lucy had known all along.

'So now you know what she was saying, what are you going to do next?'

'I have no idea. I'm completely screwed. I've closed the case and I'm not even in work at the moment, technically. The parents hate the sight of me and they are just looking for an excuse to get me sacked. I can't go near them right now.'

'Sounds like you're right then. You are screwed. Maybe you should leave it, eh?' Huw got up and padded over to the door. 'Now I'm off for a refill.'

Kit knew she couldn't leave it. Because she had got it wrong, and now she had to put it right. There was nothing she could do tonight. She needed to think it through. She went down to the kitchen for a glass, and, after a few minutes spent saying goodnight to Jess, got herself a strong vodka from the drinks cabinet and went up to bed. Even after the vodka, she lay awake most of the night, turning everything over in her mind, and by the time she sat up and watched the first trickle of light silvering the beach, she had decided she had to take a risk. Ricky had not been totally wrong when he said she had made an enemy of Annie Cooper. But she had to communicate with Annie somehow, and there might be a way to do so.

Kit got up and left a note for Huw and Menna. Then she wrote her mobile number on the back of Chloe's drawing and went out to the car. She drove back to Sandbeach. The traffic was light and she arrived in the town far too early. She was starving and on top of the sleepless night, it was making her feel thick-headed and slow. She stopped at the services at the motorway junction and bought a Subway and a Costa. Then she headed for the Coopers' estate.

When she arrived, Kit saw that Matt Cooper's car was on the driveway. It made no difference anyway. It wasn't as if Annie would have asked her in for coffee and a chat if he hadn't been around. Kit parked diagonally opposite the house and put her hood up. She sat and drank her Costa and ate her meatball marinara and stared at the house.

After half an hour, the door opened. Kit slid further down in her seat and watched as Matt Cooper came out, carrying his briefcase. She caught a glimpse of Annie Cooper in the doorway behind him, dressed in her usual smart but sombre clothes: black trousers and a plain black top. Kit waited for a while, to be sure Matt had gone. Then she got out of the car and felt in her pocket for Chloe's drawing. She unfolded it carefully as she walked over to the Coopers' drive and then up to the door, forcing herself to knock straight away so she wouldn't have the chance to bottle out. Although she'd seen Matt leave, she couldn't help glancing around behind her, anxious he would come back for some reason and catch her here.

After a few seconds, the door opened. Annie stood and

stared at Kit, her face the usual picture of puzzlement followed swiftly by outrage. From the kitchen behind her, Kit could hear Chloe and Cameron engaged in a loud argument. Kit knew she had to get in quickly, before Annie started performing.

'I'm sorry to disturb you. I don't need to come in. I just wanted to return something.'

As Kit had hoped, Annie was caught off guard by this unexpected opening. Kit held Chloe's drawing out to Annie. She knew Annie might well shut the door in her face, and that would be that. But on the other hand, she might be curious enough to look at it. Kit waited, every muscle tight and her breath held in her mouth. Annie glanced at the picture. She was engaged; not hooked completely, but showing just enough interest to give Kit a window to get in there.

'It's Chloe's drawing. I came to return it. I'm not here for anything else, it's just I thought Chloe would be upset if she didn't have it. After she spent so long on it, you know?'

Annie had gathered herself now. 'What nonsense is this?' she snapped. 'You do know we have made a complaint about you? You are not to come near us, we have made that perfectly clear. Our case is closed, and we won't be having anything to do with you or your department again. Why would Chloe want this, for God's sake? What on earth are you up to?'

Kit held the paper out to Annie again. 'As I said, it's Chloe's drawing. I thought she would want it back. Perhaps you'll want to take a look at it yourself before you give it to her, though. Chloe drew the picture very carefully. It explains why Chloe wanted to sleep in Lucy's room, and why Lucy wouldn't go to her grandparents' anymore. She didn't want to leave Chloe alone.'

Something hit home. Kit felt it in the air between them, and she saw it on Annie's face, a click, a fitting together. Annie looked down at the paper again and Kit held it further towards her.

'Just look at the drawing. Listen to Chloe. Chloe's telling you now, Annie, not me.'

Annie's hand came up to the level of Kit's. For a moment, it looked as if she would just let the paper drop. It fluttered in between their fingers, but then Kit felt it tugged away from her, and saw Annie had taken hold of it properly.

'And there's something else. That sign that Lucy made, the last time I visited?' Kit demonstrated the sign quickly. 'Do you know what that means? I looked into it, and it means "sister." Lucy wasn't asking me to help her at all. She was asking me to help Chloe. If you look at Chloe's drawing, I think you'll see the same. I just thought you ought to know what Lucy knows. For both their sakes.'

The door closed on her but Kit had seen Annie's face and she knew it was enough. She should be pleased, but instead she found her heart racing and her limbs shot through by bolt after bolt of stinging adrenaline. She had convinced Annie of what she believed to be true and now the family was going to come apart. Matt Cooper would probably go to prison. And she'd been the cause of it. She got into her car and started to drive back toward Huw and Menna's, trying to calm down. After forty minutes, her phone buzzed. She pulled over and saw a text from an unknown number.

please come back I need your help

She hesitated, unsure whether this was some kind of a trap and Annie and Matt would be waiting ready to give her another dressing-down or looking for some way to get her into even more trouble. But she knew that was unlikely. The text could only mean that Annie had finally caved.

She turned the car round and headed back. When she arrived, she saw that Matt's car was on the drive and she began to see what Annie was going to do. As she walked up to the front door, she was reminded of the first visit she had made with Dai and Beth, just three weeks previously. She remembered Matt's face appearing at the window, and the way she had felt sure he had known they were coming. The image was stamped on her mind, and as she re-examined it now, she knew she had been right in her first instinct. In that brief moment, his chin had been lifted just a touch too high, betraying his arrogance. Cocky, that was the word. He'd known they would come, he'd known why, and he'd thought he could win.

Annie opened the door to Kit's knock. She stood aside wordlessly to let her in and Kit could see that in spite of needing her help, Annie was still no great fan of hers. It didn't matter. They had a job to do and the silent agreement between them was that they would do it together. They didn't need to like each other.

Kit waited for Annie to close the door and followed her into the living room. Matt was sitting on the sofa, still dressed in his suit and tie. He was sat back against the cushions, his body spread out and relaxed. His face fell into a frown when he glanced up and saw Kit behind Annie.

'What are you doing here?' He sat up straight as she came into the room.

Annie indicated for Kit to sit down. 'I asked her. I told you to come back from work because I have something to say to you and she is here to witness it.'

'Witness it? What do you mean?' Matt's composure was teetering. Annie felt in the pocket of her trousers and took out Chloe's drawing. Kit remembered it as Matt scanned it. A stick-figure Matt still sitting on the bed, but now with the addition of a tiny figure next to him, which could only be Chloe. A child's drawing, but with one careful detail. Matt's fingers laced in Chloe's hair.

Kit watched Matt take it in and she registered the pause before he lifted his head. The pause that was too long by a fraction of a second. He'd had to stop and think. The master manipulator, hesitating over which switch to throw. Game up.

'What's this about? I don't understand. What's going on here?' he asked, half smiling. Too late, mate, Kit thought, looking over to Annie, who was standing by the mantelpiece.

'Don't bother,' Annie said, her voice calm. 'I'm not going to argue with you about it. That's not the purpose of this conversation. I am going to tell you how it is and how it is going to be. Kit's going to listen to it all, just to make sure she knows I can protect my children and myself and so that there's no argument later down the line about what I said. I don't want any problems in the divorce court. Or any other court, as a matter of fact.'

Matt opened his mouth to speak.

'No. I am not interested.' Annie cut across him. 'We all know what that picture is telling us. But in case you think there's any doubt, I've spoken to Lucy and she told me what she could. She doesn't completely understand, but Chloe told her enough and she knew something wasn't right. She knew Chloe needed her help.' Annie held up her hand as Matt tried to speak. 'No. You may think that Lucy isn't a reliable witness, but I've spoken to Chloe, too. I showed her the picture and I talked to her about telling the truth. I told her that I would always believe her and that was all it took for her to tell me. I know what you've done, and I know how you manipulated her.'

Kit thought about cute, funny Chloe, and let herself understand all this properly for the first time. She felt her eyes brimming with tears. The little girl who wanted so much to be special, an easy target for Matt's manipulation, especially when everyone thought Lucy was the vulnerable one. She'd turned to her older sister for help, moved into her room to keep herself safe. And that was why Lucy had stopped going to her grandparents; she wasn't avoiding Len. She was looking after Chloe. Kit had almost got it completely backwards, just because she had had a stupid hunch about Len Cooper.

Matt sat up now, leaning forward and with his eyes fixed on the floor as Annie continued.

'I have asked myself whether I knew. I suppose I'll ask myself that for the rest of my life. The truth is that I fought it. It wasn't hard for me to ignore what Kit had to say, and you certainly encouraged that, didn't you? All those things you said about her, the young girl with no life experience. I remember you joking, asking who would turn up for work dressed like she was off to hang around McDonald's with her mates on a Saturday afternoon. I didn't like her to start with, and you played on it, and in the end, I couldn't take her seriously. Job done, eh, Matt?'

Kit thought about Chloe again, and Steph and Nicolette, and took in the sight of Matt's bowed head, committing it to memory so she could enjoy it later. She wanted to see him hurt now, to see him brought down.

'And do you know, it was unnecessary. I could fool myself quite easily without your help.' Annie gave a small laugh, and Kit saw a flash of her shame, her contempt for herself and her own stupidity.

'Even when Kit came here and told me about you touching those girls' hair, I still wouldn't believe it. You've done that to me, lots of times. But I just blocked it out. Even when Chloe wouldn't have her hair brushed for weeks on end, just wouldn't let anyone touch it, I refused to put two and two together.'

Matt got up suddenly and strode across the room. Kit thought he was going to grab his wife so she jumped up too, but Matt had come to a standstill, and taken Annie's hand.

'Annie, please, none of this is true. Chloe makes things up all the time, we both know that. We've talked about it, haven't we? How she does it for attention, how she's jealous of Lucy?'

Annie let him go on holding her hand, but her voice didn't waver. 'Yes, we have. That's because you're always saying it. Now I think about it, I'm not sure that I've ever known Chloe lie, not about anything major. It's all been you, you saying *she made this up, she made that up, we need to be very careful, Annie, she's really got a problem with fibbing*. Bit of a safety net for you if she ever did say anything. Obvious, really. Not very sophisticated, are you?'

Kit remembered her first visit, when Cameron had taunted Chloe about her fibbing. Saying Matt had told him. Another sign that had passed her by.

Matt had dropped Annie's hand now and he turned to Kit. 'I'd like you to go,' he said. 'This is a conversation we need to have in private. I can assure you it will be sorted out.'

'She's going nowhere,' Annie replied before Kit had the chance to speak. 'I'm not finished yet. Sit down, Matt.'

He was furious, but he sat and crossed his arms, waiting for Annie to go on.

'Of course, I was very young when we met. You liked that, didn't you?'

Matt threw a horrified glance in Kit's direction. Kit very nearly threw the same back. She hadn't expected to have to hear this type of thing. But Annie ignored them both. She was staring out of the window now, her face incredulous. Kit could see that she was realising some of this for the first time, that she was speaking her growing understanding out loud as it came to her, second by second. Then she looked at Kit and seemed to decide to change tack. 'You wouldn't give up, would you? Standing in my own kitchen, arguing about why we wouldn't let Lucy learn to sign. Marching into her room, trying to get her to say things. I heard you, you know? I was outside the door. I don't like you at all, that will be no surprise to you, I'm sure. You're not even half as clever as you think you are. But I do owe you. They'll be safe, the children, I can promise you that. I think you might want to make a phone call now?'

Kit nodded, knowing exactly what Annie meant, and she went into the hall and fumbled for her phone. Before she made the call, she paused to listen for a few seconds longer, not wanting to miss the death blow. Annie's voice came to her through the half-open door.

'I will have the children and the house and enough money to look after all of us, including all the care that Lucy is used to. The four of us are going to continue to have that nice life you are so proud of. You won't be working for a long time to come, if ever again, but I am sure your father can cover the financial side for you. I expect him and Jackie to pay through the nose for me and the children for the rest of our lives, so make that clear, won't you?'

Kit heard a response to that from Matt, quick and angry. She couldn't catch it, but she heard every word of Annie's crisp reply.

'I don't think you are quite understanding me. Whatever the police do or don't do, this is the end of it. You are cornered now, one way or another. We can have it all out in the divorce court if you like. Your sexual habits, things you liked, things you would say. I'm sure I'd see some things I'd recognise if I had those transcripts, wouldn't I? I don't mind telling it all, I've got nothing to be ashamed of. Those other two cases might be opened again now too, and, even if they aren't, I'm about to make sure the police speak to Chloe. You're caught now, and you will pay, Matt. You will pay for what you did to my little girl.'

Kit opened the front door and went out to make her call and then she waited for Beth Mackay to turn up, which she did after just twenty minutes, Dai Davies in tow and casting concerned looks at Kit's face, which she realised must be showing signs of her lack of sleep. She sat on the Coopers' garden wall and attempted to pull herself together. After a while, Dai put his head out of the front door and gestured for Kit to join him.

'Can you have a word with Mrs Cooper? I think it's more of a job for a lady.' He pointed down the hall towards the kitchen.

Kit went in and found Annie sitting at the table. Her face was in her hands and she was sobbing. Kit sat next to her, not knowing what to do. After a while, when she had not subsided, Kit put her hand on Annie's back and she raised her face. It was a mess of tears and running mascara. She looked at Kit, and when she spoke, her voice was shaking.

'It's disgusting . . . my girls . . . I should have known. He's my husband. I didn't know, I should have but I didn't know . . . I can't stop thinking about it, what he did.'

Annie started to retch then, and Kit jumped up and hauled her to her feet and half pushed her to the sink where she leant her head down and threw up violently, over and over again, releasing an odour that told Kit that she had had to steel herself with alcohol before she could confront her husband. Annie straightened then and reached for the kitchen roll. She wiped her mouth and then she pulled her handbag out of the corner of the worktop. She produced a compact mirror and started to tidy her face. She was still trembling.

A noise came from the hallway and Kit looked up to see Matt moving towards the front door, with Beth Mackay behind him, her hand hovering close to the small of his back, ready to usher him out. He stopped when he reached the door and turned, and Beth stood aside slightly, allowing him a last glance back into his home. He looked into the kitchen and Kit was aware of Annie straightening herself up and looking back at him.

'Goodbye, Matt. Tell your parents to get their chequebook out. And don't ever try to contact me or my children again.'

When Kit got home it was mid-afternoon. She got straight into the shower, images of Matt Cooper running around in her head. She felt filthy and creeped out, seeing a monster now where she had seen a quite beautiful man. She'd spent the morning speaking to the police and then she'd had to go over the whole thing again at length with Cole Jackson and Clare Donald, after she'd rung Ricky to tell him the story and he had marched into Cole's office in a flaming temper demanding Kit should be reinstated at once.

Clare Donald had not made it easy for her, still shuffling three pieces of paper about in a display of her extreme reluctance to let Kit off the hook. In the end, Cole Jackson had turned to face her.

'Clare,' he had said, his irritation finally bubbling over. 'It really doesn't matter whether Kit did some things that strictly speaking she shouldn't have. She was right, and we were wrong. I don't imagine Matt Cooper's going to be pursuing his complaint now, do you? So let's just drop it. Now, send Georgia up, would you?'

Once Clare Donald had left and Georgia had arrived, with her nasty mouth glued shut, Cole Jackson had turned to Kit.

'We both owe you an apology, Kit. I'm going to have to tell you not to go out on a limb like that again, but we can let it pass this time.' He had put his hand up to stop Georgia from interrupting. 'Please go home now and take a few days off to recover. You can resume your duties next week.'

Kit had agreed readily and left, but not before she had secured a promise from Cole that Lucy's case would be reallocated from Jean Collins to a new social worker who would look into every possible type of assisted communication for her. Once that was done, she made tracks, not missing the opportunity to irritate Georgia with a smile on the way past.

After her shower, Kit got herself a Coke and a bar of chocolate and sat on the sofa, but she couldn't settle. Now that she'd done what she could about Matt Cooper, she finally had some space in her mind to think about Tyler. She couldn't avoid it anymore, and besides, there were things sticking up in her mind and catching at her thoughts, and she needed to flatten them. Maybe she could do it one point at a time, like she had with the Cooper case.

She reached for her bag and rooted around for a pen and her notebook. Then she wrote a list of the things she didn't understand. The first was Micky Winter's death notice – why had it asked for donations to the youth centre after it had been burnt down? She sipped her Coke and thought about this, before picking up her phone and googling Sandbeach youth centre. When her search returned an address, she put it into Maps, picked up her denim jacket and her fags and went to her car.

Fifteen minutes later Kit drew up in front of a single-storey grey building set high above the bay. She exited her car and walked around to the front, where she spotted a brass plate. It had been badly vandalised, battered and scratched and covered in a sticky grey-white substance she'd rather not think too much about. But she could just make out that the building had been officially opened by someone in January 2006.

So the youth centre had been rebuilt in a different spot three years after Danny had burnt it down. It was that simple. Kit laughed at herself. She was definitely getting paranoid. She'd been away in 2006 and so had Tyler, so neither of them had known the centre had been rebuilt. It was no great mystery after all.

Relieved to have ticked one item off her list, Kit looked around and saw that, on the opposite side of the road, there was a small park set into the hill. She crossed over and climbed the steep path through the park towards a bench at the top. The sparse lawn of the park was littered with rubbish and the bins were overflowing. There was a small playground halfway up, with a broken roundabout and a couple of tatty swings, the paint peeling from their frames. But she could see there ought to be a decent view of the bay from the top, and she wanted to get a look at that while she pondered the remaining items on her list. As she reached the bench, she saw a silver plate set into its back. A memorial, dedicating the bench to Micky Winter, in honour of his work for the young people of Sandbeach. It made her feel angry and shivery. For a minute she didn't want to sit on it, but she told herself that she was being stupid, sat down, and leant forward to get her breath back.

After a few seconds her chest eased and she lifted her head, staring down at the youth centre. In her mind, a shadow sat over the whole thing about Tyler and Micky Winter. Something she couldn't understand or just couldn't see. She pulled her list out of her pocket and looked at the next item: *Why youth centre?* It still didn't make sense to her that Winter had told Tyler to meet him at the centre that night. She'd drawn a line to connect this with the next item on the list: *People at house*. This made no sense either. It wasn't the explanation for Winter's choice of location, she felt sure of it. Even if there had been people back and forth to Winter's house, as Tyler had said there were, why would that stop him? Surely, he would have just locked the front door and that would be that? There had to be another reason why Winter had wanted Tyler in the centre that particular night. The night he was forewarned Tyler would be coming alone. No crazy Danny to protect him.

She let her eyes rest on the view of the bay and, as she did so, realised she recognised the view. A single-storey building, sitting high up over Sandbeach with the bay behind it. She knew instantly where she had seen that view before – in Len and Jackie Cooper's hallway, in the newspaper cutting she thought had shown Len opening his residential home. That was why she'd thought the residential home was in a totally different place to where it actually was. The building Len Cooper was opening in the picture was the new youth centre. She felt there was a connection here, but the pieces were too far apart – she couldn't pull them together yet. Then she thought again about the room in the old Sandbeach youth centre, with the potted plants and the chairs and the mirror on the wall. She'd thought the details were trivial when Tyler had told her, that it was sad to hear how the trauma had fixed them in his mind, but that they hadn't mattered in themselves. Now she wasn't so sure.

She got up and headed back down the hill and over the road, pushing open the glass door and walking into the reception of the youth centre.

A pretty pink-haired young woman sat behind the reception desk, yawning and fiddling with her phone.

'Hi. Can I help you?' She dragged her eyes away from the screen with considerable effort.

'Yeah. I'm a social worker.' Kit showed her badge. 'I was just wondering what facilities you've got. I was hoping to bring some of my teenagers up here, get them doing some activities maybe.'

'No problem. What are they into?'

'The usual, I guess. Could I take a look around?'

'Sure. Help yourself.' Her eyes flew back to her phone at once.

Kit wandered through the centre, glancing into rooms as she went, passing a gym, some changing rooms and a big room with a climbing wall in it. The place was deserted. In a corridor towards the back of the building she passed a row of doors with glass panels. She saw they were offices and that this was where the staff were hanging out, so she passed them quickly. At the far end of the corridor, just past the staff kitchen, were two doors without glass panels. One was unmarked and the other one had a sign that showed it was the counselling room. She felt a dart of adrenaline pulsing in her chest as she pushed it open a crack to check the room was empty.

She walked into a room which she saw at once was pretty

similar to the one that Tyler had described: two armchairs facing one another with a coffee table in between them. The room was done out in muted greys and pinks and it felt bare and stuffy, as if it wasn't much used. Kit sat on one of the pink chairs and looked around. Her eye was caught by a ridge that ran just below eye level along the wall opposite her. She got up and crossed the room and ran her hand over it, following it across the wall and then upwards at a right angle. She could see that the ridge traced a large rectangle. It was the outer edge of a panel of MDF, which had been attached to the wall and then painted the same colour as the rest of the room. Something had been blocked out. She leant her forehead against the panel and breathed in through her mouth a few times, fighting back the bitter taste in her mouth as the picture finally started to come together in a nauseating rush.

A voice came from behind her. 'Are you OK?'

Kit looked around to find the pink-haired woman standing in the doorway with a steaming mug of coffee. 'Yes, sorry, just felt a bit faint for a minute. It's the heat, I think.'

'Oh, OK.' She turned to go, having already lost interest.

'I was just wondering – what's your name, by the way?'

'Amy.'

'I'm Kit. Sorry to be nosey, Amy, but I was just wondering what this is?' Kit tapped the rectangle of wood.

Amy turned reluctantly. 'Oh, that. They used to do family therapy in here.'

'So this was . . .'

'The one-way mirror, yeah. They blocked it up when the council pulled the funding. Not appropriate for our role, apparently.'

'Did you have a therapy room at the old centre, too?'

'Yeah, we did, pretty much the same as this one.' She turned and hurried back up the corridor before Kit could bother her with anything else.

Kit made her way out into the corridor after Amy. She pushed open the door to the unlabelled room. It was the viewing room, the other side of the one-way mirror, where professionals would gather to observe a family in therapy and to direct the therapist via a telephone. Kit recalled that this particular humiliating experience had been inflicted on the Goddard family once, with predictably explosive results. The room was small and dark and obviously now used for storage; boxes of files and packs of printer paper were piled up against the walls. Kit stood and stared at the rectangle of wood covering this side of the mirror; she thought about Tyler in a replica of this therapy suite and her skin crawled as the final piece of the puzzle clicked into place and she realised why Winter had wanted him in there. It had been nothing to do with privacy at all. In fact, it had been quite the opposite.

Kit closed the door and made her way back to the reception, where she found Amy sipping coffee and studying her Insta. Kit thought quickly as she approached her. She was going to need some proof, just enough to get the police to take an interest, and she didn't have a shred as yet. She leant on the reception desk.

'So, Amy, some of my kids aren't that sporty . . . What about making films? Could they do some live streaming maybe? They're all big into YouTube. Do you do any of that here?'

'Not really. Our last manager was into it. But after Micky died it never got going again.'

'Why's that?'

'We didn't have the equipment anymore, and it was too expensive to replace it. The first lot got destroyed in a fire actually. The old centre burnt down completely. Everything went.'

'That's a shame.'

'Yeah.'

Kit stood for a moment, watching Amy's fingers as they resumed their position on-screen, turning her words over in her mind until she found the gap in them that she could push through. 'Sorry, did you say the first lot of equipment?'

'Yeah.'

'So you had another lot?'

'Yeah – to replace the stuff that went in the fire.'

'What happened to that then?'

Amy looked up, an ugly knot forming beneath her cerise fringe. Kit ignored it, smiling as if she had no idea she was really starting to get on Amy's nerves.

'When Micky got ill, he gave it back to whoever it was who'd donated it.'

'That's a bit unusual, isn't it?'

'The person wanted it back apparently. It raised a few hackles here, but Micky packed it all up and took it away. Pretty much the last thing he did before he went off sick actually.'

'Who donated it?'

'No clue, sorry.' She was becoming outright uncooperative now, but Kit had to get just a little more.

'I'm just wondering if that's something that I ought to report. It doesn't seem right to me that someone takes a donation back. Especially as you're saying that the donor can't even be traced. No audit trail, you see? The council won't like that.'

It was far from being one of Kit's best lies, but Amy's fear of getting into trouble combined with her uncertainty about the meaning of an audit trail did the trick.

'I think there's a list of donations here somewhere. The name might be in that.' She reached into her desk drawer and immediately brought out a large notebook. She leafed back through it. 'There you go – 2006. It will be in there, I expect.'

She turned the book around for Kit to see. Kit leant over it and ran down the page that listed donations to the centre, mainly money and sports equipment. Then she got her phone out of her pocket and took three photos of the entry showing a very generous donation made on 8th January 2006, including a computer, a webcam and a DVD burner. She emailed the photos to her own account and to Ricky's before going outside and climbing back up to Micky Winter's bench, where she sat for a while. She picked up her notebook, turned over a new page and drew two overlapping circles. In the first she wrote

Micky Winter's name. In the overlap she wrote *youth centre* and *webcam/cameras/tech*. And in the other circle she wrote *Len Cooper*. Then she walked down the hill to her car, so fast she stumbled and turned her ankle on the crumbling tarmac path, her welling anger and disgust so strong she didn't even register any pain.

Tyler opened the door to his flat, clearly having just woken from a nap, his hair on end and his face thoroughly hacked off.

'I need to talk to you.'

'OK.' He stepped back and let her in, and she went into the living room and sat down. He disappeared into the kitchen and appeared a few minutes later with two mugs of coffee.

'What's up then?'

'We need to speak to the police.'

'What? Not this again. I've told you, I'm not doing it. What's the point? Winter's gone.'

'I don't think it was just him.'

'What the fuck does that mean?'

'Let me ask you something.'

His face changed as he heard her tone. 'What's it about?'

'Let me ask you first. Then we can go from there. When you went to the centre that night, you said Winter took you into a room. You said it had a mirror on the wall?'

'That's right. Why does that matter?'

'Ty, you are going to have to tell the police what happened, and all about the men you saw in Winter's house.'

'Why?'

There was nothing to do but just come out with it. 'I don't think it was drugs he was selling. I think Winter filmed you.'

'He didn't. I'd have seen it.' But his face showed a hint of fear.

'I think he had a webcam. Behind the mirror – it was one-way. I think that's what he was selling to the men in his house. Not drugs. DVDs.'

Tyler took a huge gasp of breath then, as he understood what she meant; and, when he let it out, a choking sob rose from his throat and filled the air. Kit was across the room and on her knees in front of him before she knew it. She put her arms around his huddled shoulders and held him while he cried himself out, his face buried in her shoulder. After a long while, Tyler raised his head, still snuffling, but slowing now.

'You're going to need to tell someone now, Ty, OK?'

He nodded. 'How do you know all this?'

'I've been looking into it.'

He opened his mouth to ask her more, but she was firm. 'No. I can't tell you. It's to do with work. It's all connected, I can't tell you how. But I'm sure I'm right. And there are other kids to think about here. It won't have stopped once Winter died. That route dried up maybe, but they will have found another. People like that don't stop. Ever.'

She didn't wait for his answer. She went into the kitchen and made a call. When she got through to Beth Mackay, Kit gave her a summary, leaving Len Cooper's name out of it.

'You are saying that this Micky Winter was abusing kids and

selling the films? It sounds like a long shot to me. Have you got any evidence whatsoever for any of this?'

'Tyler remembers he saw men going back and forth to the house handing over cash. They were buying something, Beth. Plus, Winter had equipment. Webcams, stuff like that. I know he was making DVDs at the centre and live-streaming stuff later, too. But the equipment he used was donated and Winter insisted it was all given back to the donor before he died. He took it away himself. Quite unusual for someone to ask for a donation back, don't you think?'

The silence told her that Beth was registering all this. 'It's unusual but it's hardly proof of a crime, is it? Who was this donor?'

'Not sure, to be honest with you. But I reckon they'd have a record at the centre. If you speak to Amy on reception, she'll know about it. See what you think when you've done that.'

'All right. I'm not promising anything. I can't see it going anywhere. But I'll send an officer up for a chat.'

'No, Beth – will you go yourself? Please?' Kit knew the whole thing was less than rock solid as yet, but she also knew that it would only take Beth Mackay seeing Len Cooper's name in that book for her to get a bee in her bonnet. And she knew Beth would then find a way.

'Well, first things first, you'd better send your laddo in to see us. I'll see what I think.'

'OK. I'm not going to bring him myself, though. It's easier for him to talk about it if I'm not there.'

'Whatever you think is best.'

Kit found the number of the probation office and made another call. Thirty minutes later, Emily Morrison arrived at Tyler's flat. She was petite and unnecessarily girly to Kit's mind, tapping up the stairs in her patent high heels and swinging a headful of auburn hair in all directions. But she was stronger than she looked. She brooked no nonsense from Tyler and soon had the arrangements made for him to speak to the police. Kit watched him leave, pale-faced and shaky, and she had to go for a walk on the promenade afterwards to get control of her swelling tears.

It was nearly the end of the summer before Kit was told that both Len and Matt Cooper had been charged. Chloe had been video-interviewed, and Steph and Nicolette's cases had been reinstated. It hadn't taken long to find out that Len Cooper had indeed attempted to bribe Steph Harman into withdrawing her case. As she had said, she hadn't accepted a penny from him. And just as she had said, it had been the sheer impossibility of winning that had got to Steph. Once she understood it, Beth sorted that out in short order. She also traced Katie Cooper to a high-dependency psychiatric unit in London, where, over time, Katie had gradually given the full story of her estrangement from the family, after years of abuse at the hands of her father.

On the day she heard the news of the charges, Kit had bypassed another dose of Georgia's simmering resentment and gone straight to Cole's office to explain how she needed a few hours off. He listened to what had happened and sent her away at once. As she made her way home, she texted Tyler.

Can u meet got news

His answer came back at once.

OK beach at 12

She hesitated about the beach, thinking it too public, but after a few seconds she realised that it was the best place they could go. The beach was their happy place, the right place to give Tyler good news. As soon as she got home, she changed into her swimming gear and shorts, locked up and set off on foot towards his flat. She knew he'd been waiting for this, but she had more to tell him than either of them had been expecting, and she couldn't wait to do it. Beth's official call that morning had ended with some off-the-record news that Kit had never dared hope for.

He was waiting for her outside, a six-pack of Stella in his hand. They walked down the high street and over the footbridge to the promenade.

'So, what is it?' There was a nervous edge to Tyler's voice. He'd been in counselling all summer with a psychologist arranged by Emily Morrison, and he was doing well, but he was still fragile and it dawned on Kit that there was no way of knowing how this conversation was going to affect him.

He'd been vindicated at last. But maybe the vindication would finally bring home the abuse, would be the final confirmation that it had happened.

'Beth called me this morning. It's good news.'

'Yeah, you said. So go on.'

'They've charged someone. His name's Len Cooper.' She paused to let him take it in. They'd reached the beach now and he put his rucksack down on the sand and fiddled about with it, unpacking a beach mat and his fags, keeping his head down. She did the same, then sat on the sand, lighting two of her own cigarettes at once and passing one to him. He sat down next to her and they both kept their eyes straight ahead towards the sea.

'Charged him for what?'

'The whole place was kitted out with cameras. Cooper and Winter did it together. I was right, but it wasn't just the therapy room, they were filming kids in the toilets and the changing rooms too.'

Tyler's breath caught in his throat. 'Sick bastards. How did they catch him?'

'No idea,' she fibbed. Beth had explained that it was the examination of Matt Cooper's laptop that had started the police on the trail. Annie had presented it to the police before they had the chance to turn her house upside down searching for it. Unsurprisingly, it had contained thousands of child-abuse images. Matt's role in Coopers' Ltd had provided the golden opportunity for Beth, enabling her to argue with her still-rattled seniors that a search of Len's business premises was justified.

She'd proceeded to oversee an exceptionally thorough sweep; her officers, not knowing what she knew about Tyler's statement and Len's donation to the youth centre, had thought the boss was going overboard on this one. Len seemed a good enough bloke to them, and they saw no reason to blame him for what his pervert son had done. Until they came across a large stash of recording equipment and DVDs hidden in a locked storage unit in a disused warehouse. The true nature of Len Cooper's connection with Micky Winter had soon become gut-churningly clear.

Tyler didn't need to know any of this yet. But there was something she had to tell him. The silence between them was tense, but Kit was struggling to phrase what she needed to say. She understood now how ashamed Tyler was to talk to her about what had happened. But she knew there was one thing that had played on his mind more than any other, since the day she had told him her theory about the one-way mirror and what Micky Winter was selling that enabled him to afford his big house on The Avenue. It was the sticking point, the thing that had prevented Tyler from being able to say that his abuse was in the past.

'There's something else,' she managed finally.

'Is it bad?' He was still ready for the system to let him down.

'No, it's not bad. Just let me tell you, please?'

He nodded, but his face remained unsure.

'It looks like there's no film of you.' She kept watching his face as she said it. 'They think it got destroyed in the fire.'

He breathed out then, long and hard. 'Good. That's really good.'

'Yeah. Danny saw to it. Without realising it, but he did.'

'I don't want to think about it anymore now. I need to get my head around it.'

She understood that he couldn't trust it yet, couldn't let himself believe there was no film of him circulating, repeating his abuse again for numerous strangers, keeping it live for unknown years to come. Beth's team had found plenty of evidence of Len Cooper and Micky Winter conspiring together, filming the abuse of children in the youth centre, and selling the films on DVD to a local paedophile ring and later to a wider audience via live streaming. Len Cooper's activities had not ended with Winter's death, but he had never been able to recreate the perfect access afforded to him by their friendship and Sandbeach youth centre.

All this had been easy to find out, but the police had found no footage that Beth could link to Tyler's rape, the date of which he'd been able to pinpoint exactly, because it had coincided with the fire at the old youth centre. 'Quite a coincidence, that fire,' Beth had said on the phone to Kit that morning, her voice dropping to a whisper. 'You'd almost think it was revenge or something.'

'Yeah, you would.' Kit had fronted it out without a pause. 'Weird, isn't it?'

Tyler was opening a can now, which he passed to her before opening one for himself. 'What happened with that bloke you told me about from work? With the two girls? Did you get him too?'

He thought he was shifting the subject. He didn't know the

connection between all the parts of it as yet. She still owed the Cooper children confidentiality. He'd find out eventually, but she couldn't be the one to tell him.

'Not sure it was me so much as his daughter, but yes, he was got.'

She thought about Lucy, brave and loving, who had overcome her father's control and done her best to protect her little sister. Kit had heard from the kids' new social worker that Lucy had taken to a communication board with delight and was using it to display some teenage attitude. It was driving Annie up the wall. Kit felt chuffed every single time she thought about that.

'Well, good. Serves him fucking well right. Why have you still got a face like a ripped dap then?'

'I know you don't want to talk about it, but I can't stop thinking about it. Danny tried to tell me, Ty, and I didn't listen. I let him down.' Her eyes filled with tears.

He drained his can before speaking. 'You are dead wrong about that. He loved you the best out of all of us. He wouldn't have told you about it even if you had wanted him to, because he was ashamed. He thought it was his job to look after me and he screwed it up. That's just the way he saw it. Now have this and shut up.'

He handed her another opened can. The sun was starting to go down. Tyler made a fire then went up to the kiosk for chips. While he was gone, she tapped out a text to Alex, arranging to call in to the café over the weekend. She sent it quickly, before she could change her mind, and just had time to read his happy reply before Tyler got back.

'What are you grinning at? You're bipolar or something, you are.'

She ignored him, and they ate their chips. When they'd finished, they ran into the warm sea and swam out until they couldn't touch the bottom.

'All right now?' he asked her when they paused, treading water and trying to get their breath back.

'Yeah, I guess.'

'That's good. It's done now, you know, the thing with me. It happened, and nothing can change it but I'm OK; I'm doing pretty well, actually. And you are going to have to learn to forget about your stupid job. You're going to be a rubbish social worker if you can't get over stuff. You'll be mental by the time you're thirty.'

'I suppose so.'

'I was just working it out – you do know you've got about forty years of this ahead of you, don't you? Wanna think about a career change?'

She laughed. 'No way. I'm good at this one.'

'So what. It's still a shit job.'

She splashed him in the face. 'Shut up. Race you?'

And they raced each other to the end of the rocks, just like they used to do when they were children.